DREAMS DO COME TRUE . . .
WITH A LITTLE HELP!

"I've been watching you for a long while now, Gigi Bernstein," the redheaded woman said. "I know all about you. And by the way, kiddo, things aren't nearly as tough as you think. I am here to help you. I'm a messenger from God."

Gigi's mind raced. This had to be an hallucination . . . although, it seemed real. Hallucinations should be vague, dream-like, but Gigi could notice every detail about this woman, like the Nikes she wore on her feet. Hallucinations didn't wear Nikes, did they?

"Let me get this straight," Gigi said sarcastically. "You're an angel and you're here to save me from eternal damnation or something, to pick up the pieces of my life and turn it around?"

"Hey, I'm an angel, not Lee Iacocca. I have my limitations." She looked at Gigi and sighed. "Okay, okay, I'll prove it to you."

The stranger took Gigi's hand. Gigi felt a tingling creep up her body in a soothing wave. She suddenly felt warm, aware, unafraid, then she gasped as she realized precisely what the feeling was. It was total, complete peace and joy.

The stranger smiled. "Get the picture?" she asked softly.

A TOUCH OF HEAVEN

SALLY CHAPMAN

PINNACLE BOOKS
WINDSOR PUBLISHING CORP.

PINNACLE BOOKS

are published by

Windsor Publishing Corp.
475 Park Avenue South
New York, NY 10016

First printing: September 1989

Printed in the United States of America

To my husband, James Osbon

CHAPTER ONE

Gigi Bernstein attempted suicide on the twelve thousand seven hundred and seventy-fifth day of her life. Future scholars and religious students would haggle for years over the details, arguing perspectives, citing obscure references and poking each other in the intellectual bellies, but finally would agree that it began like the other days—she got up, she dressed, drove to work and performed the day's toils with the usual creeping despondency that typified her some twelve thousand days. No, it wasn't until early evening that things began to truly go awry, to skid off course, like a lumbering eighteen-wheeler finally losing its brakes after a slow tortuous descent downhill.

If asked, Gigi would have agreed the day had initially seemed no different than any other. It had occurred in July, a sticky hot day, typical for Texas, the air so thick with damp heat she felt she could almost scrape it off her skin with her fingernails. She left the office at the usual time, got in her Toyota, unhooked her bra strap with a triumphant gasp of pleasure and turned the air conditioning on high, pointing the vents on her face until her black curls danced around her temples. After eluding the perils of Houston's rush hour, she steered her car into the parking lot of a white stucco building bearing the legend "Body Shop." Even the very name of the place made Gigi shudder, but she showed up anyway every Thursday at six forty-five, every single Thursday for two and a half years, because she had been taught long before that you did things you didn't like simply because you were supposed to do them, and, after all, if everybody only did what they liked, this world wouldn't be fit to live in, would it? She tried to imagine the chaos of a world filled with people doing exactly as they pleased and she conjured images of crazed sex in the streets, children gorging on ice cream, old people giddily spending all their money. It didn't sound so bad, she told herself, then laughed and shook the thought out of her mind. She grabbed her tote bag, walked inside and stealthily peeled off her clothes in a corner of the locker room where she would be concealed from the critical eyes of the other women, yet she still glanced around the door of her locker so she could steal peeks at everyone else. Gigi theorized that in all dressing rooms of all health clubs everywhere there was an uncontrollable urge among the clientele to examine other people's bodies. They all silently rejoiced in the observation of another woman's cellulite, mourned the glimpse of a firm thigh, gnashed teeth over the sight of a muscled calf. Like the predatory animals in the food chain, everyone in jazzercise knew their ranking in the all-important fitness scale. Mary was skinnier than Betsy. Sue was firmer than Mary. Gigi was thinner than the health-club shuttle bus.

As Gigi pushed her tote bag into a locker she managed a furtive glance at a long-haired brunette pulling on her tights. The girl's thighs were so thin you could have shot a cannonball through them. Probably an airhead, Gigi rationalized, believing firmly in an inverse correlation between thigh circumference and I.Q. But hark, to the left was a woman with a derriere so large the rear of her car should have read WIDE LOAD. Gigi sighed with relief that she wouldn't be the fattest in the class, then pulled on her leotard. Heading toward the aerobics room she mustered the courage to survey herself briefly in the full-length mirror. Trained from an early age to critically compare her physical self with those surreal, too-perfect females in movies and magazines, Gigi only saw her inadequacies when she looked in the mirror. She didn't really notice the light in her blue eyes, the fullness of her lips, the softness in her face that made her approachable. Staring at her reflection she saw only a plumpish, shortish woman with a prominent nose, untamable black hair and the beginnings of crow's feet around her eyes. There was something bagging around her knees. Gigi prayed that it was her tights. As she leaned over to straighten them, a hand slapped her hip sending her gracelessly on all fours.

"Hurry up, Gi. Class is about to start."

It was Sydney, looking as sleek and expensive as a racehorse. She helped Gigi back to her feet then gave her friend an affectionate pat. When Sydney was in class she wouldn't allow Gigi to arrive late, leave early or slack off on the exercises. And Sydney was always in class. Sydney grabbed Gigi's hand and led her into the exercise room.

Sitting cross-legged on the floor, Gigi watched Sydney as she did her warm-up stretches. Sydney studied her own reflection in the mirrored wall as she stretched, her expression one of total concentration.

"Come on, Gigi. Touch your toes and warm up a little," said Sydney, returning her attention to her friend.

Gigi stood up and performed a perfunctory toe touch as the music first blasted over the quadraphonic sound system. A redheaded exercise instructor name Mitzie sprinted into the room wearing a satiny lilac leotard with matching leg warmers and began twisting her torso to the beat of the throbbing music.

"Okay, ladies, let's boogie away those bulges!" Mitzie cried with inhuman enthusiasm. Sydney jumped right into the dance routine for hips and thighs, looking trim in her hot pink leotard. Gigi felt frumpy in slimming black with two toes poking out of the left foot of her tights.

Fat. It was the curse she had dealt with since she was fifteen. "Artistically shaped," Mrs. Bernstein described her daughter, comparing Gigi's ample proportions to the buxom folds of a Renoir nude. Notice, Mom, Renoir nudes are always reclining alone, Gigi wished to point out. The truth was that although Gigi was not obese, she was unfashionably chubby. She had experienced several satisfying years in high school when a little physical roundness was acceptable, even considered sexy. Now her friends viewed extra pounds of flesh like it belonged on the Elephant Man. The brand of social disapproval formerly reserved for sex with animals now fell upon those who allowed themselves the mortal sin of thick thighs and flabby upper arms. Gigi felt ashamed of her extra twenty pounds but was incapable of losing them. Like everyone else, she struggled with diets, but over the years eating became her refuge and Gigi's metabolism allowed no excesses. Eating a single Snickers made her tummy pooch, a ham and cheese sandwich could turn her thighs into saddlebags, a baked potato lodged directly on her hips. It was no accident that she had been born a Libra, the sign of the Scale.

"On the floor," Sydney instructed as the music switched to a brisk jazz and the exercise to leg lifts.

"Now flex your foot as you lift. It helps tighten the thighs," Sydney suggested. Gigi flexed her foot but her thigh hung slack.

"Something is wrong with you and I know it," Sydney said, panting as she performed the doggie kick for waist and buttocks. Gigi noticed with fascination that Sydney's thighs didn't jiggle when

11

they moved. "Are you depressed about Harold, your job, your weight or all three?"

"I'm not depressed about anything. I just need more exercise," Gigi responded with a superficial grin. What I need is for you to develop visible pantyline, Gigi thought, then disliked herself for her meanness. To avoid Sydney's eyes, she rolled over to work on the other hip.

Up and to the side. Up and to the side. Forty pairs of legs sliced the air with scissor kicks. Gigi struggled to stay synchronized with the rest of the class, but she was always up when she should have been down, in when she should have been out, inhaling when she should have been exhaling. It reminded her of the horrors of her grade-school athletic career—her body always in the wrong place at the wrong time, an unwelcome intrusion into the usual symmetry of the children's games. She had felt like an unpropitious intruder in those games, like a bug on a wedding cake, like an unexpected, offensive flat note in an otherwise perfect sonata.

Suddenly the music changed to a calypso beat. Gigi grimaced. This was the part she hated most.

"Now everybody rrrhumba!" Mitzie screeched like tires on hot pavement, and she began swiveling her chest, hips and arms, all in opposite directions. "Exercising es muy importante!"

Whatever happened to those machines with the belts that vibrated the fat off? Gigi wondered as her body chugged and throttled arhythmically to the music. Each muscle quaked, all joints rebelled, each tendon screamed for her to stop this

12

foolishness and find a more suitable hobby, like snacking. Emitting a pained gasp, Gigi collapsed on her side and turned to watch Sydney move smoothly to the music.

"Move those arms, Gigi. Firm those breasts," Sydney commanded like a drill sargeant.

With her lips contorted into a sneer, Gigi stood up and clapped her hands behind her back. She had to admit that she could feel the muscles in her chest tightening.

Sydney looked at her with a feline smile. "And don't think for a minute I've forgotten your birthday, Gigi. You're thirty-five tomorrow, right?" Sydney said loudly enough for all to hear. A few heads turned.

Gigi squeezed her eyes shut and exhaled. Thanks a lot, Syd. A thirty-fifth birthday wasn't something you wanted broadcasted. She had planned only a quiet dinner with Harold, but she had this ominous feeling that the day had something more in store for her, that she was on the verge of an unanticipated, anomalous something that waited snickering around life's corner ready to leap out and yell "Gotcha!" if she dared to rest her derriere on the whoopie cushion of fate. Gigi prayed silently that Sydney wouldn't send another birthday male strip-o-gram to her office this year. The last thing she needed was fanfare celebrating her increasingly rapid advancement into the ranks of the wrinkled. She had convinced herself that society overrated birthdays and that they weren't worth the infantile celebrations that people demanded. Gigi's last really good one had been when she turned fourteen and Howie Ragsdale had come to her party. He had led her behind the kumquat tree, put his hand up her sweater and whispered through his cake-encrusted braces that she had the greatest breasts at Pershing Junior High and that everyone in school knew it. Gigi felt woozy with pride until the middle of her sixteenth year when her thighs entered the race for plumpness and won.

The music slowed to a gently samba for the head and shoulder roll. Gigi almost liked this part.

"Roll those heads, ladies, around and around. Feel it in your chins. Feel the firming sensation," Mitzi instructed with still unceasing lung power. Gigi rolled her head around and around her shoulders, first to the left, then to the right. The sensation felt relaxing, very pleasant. She closed her eyes and tried to release the tension from her neck and shoulders.

Life had not been going well for Gigi Bernstein. She was morose. She was confused. She was unfulfilled at work and despondent at home. She had spent now thirty-five years struggling to make her life work, carefully making plans, thinking things through, putting together just the right pieces that would result in a fulfilling, fashionable life suitable for her friends' envy or a glossy two-page spread in *Self* magazine. Her life was like a souffle she had repeatedly measured, whisked and labored over but that continually fell flat into some shapeless, unappetizing concoction.

And then there was the problem of sex. It was

the one thing she felt she could be really expert at if she could only get some practice. She had been keeping a record of her acts of coitus for some time on the little calendar on the back of her checkbook. She knew it wasn't an emotionally healthy thing to do, but she was interested in the statistics. Three months of tabulations resulted in a mean distribution of two point five sexual encounters in twelve weeks. Her boyfriend Harold just didn't get turned on by her anymore, and it wasn't as if she didn't try to be seductive. She had read all the self-help sex books. She had spent a fortune at Neimans on black lacy panties and French underwired bras that lifted her breasts so high she could have eaten lunch off them, but none of them had any effect on Harold. All of her sexy lingerie remained as fresh as the day she bought them, with not a rip, not a wrinkle, not a drop of spittle. She was a P.O.W. in the sexual revolution and it looked like Harold was missing in action. And it wasn't any comfort the way oh-so-comfortably-married Sydney managed to inject sexual innuendo into everything.

"Tense your vaginal muscles during this back bend. It makes those muscles nice and tight," Sydney whispered to Gigi with a lurid wink.

With hands on the floor, Gigi gritted her teeth, clenching her vaginal muscles into a rosy little fist.

Gigi longed to marry Harold. She'd met him almost three years earlier at the law firm where

15

she worked. She had been handling a lawsuit for him, the plaintiff claiming that Harold had neglected to mention certain structural problems of a condo he had sold him, like a leaky roof and a lower floor that flooded after a heavy rainstorm. Of course the plaintiff had told the truth and of course Gigi got Harold off with paying nothing but an exorbitant legal bill that further fattened the bank account of Bausch, Bausch and Kozinsky.

Three years later Harold still sold condos with bad roofs and unanticipated indoor pools and Gigi regularly devoted herself to fixing linguini with clam sauce for him while he watched "Magnum P.I." on television. Harold was less than exciting. Harold was somewhat less than even amusing. What Harold had going for him in Gigi's eyes was that he was male and somewhat available. She saw him three nights a week and one night on the weekend. For the first time in her life Gigi was assured of a date, and for a girl who managed the punch concession at her senior prom, to be assured of a date was nothing to sneer at. Yes, she had read all the right feminist literature, made it through law school, could change the oil in the Toyota and wasn't ashamed of her own vaginal odor. But the woman's movement, with all its breakthroughs, could not eliminate the social programming that made Gigi want most of all to have a man, to have someone find her adorable, to be able to tiptoe onto a pedestal and see what life looked like from a height. She wanted warmth, she wanted understanding, she

16

wanted real communication followed by nasty sex. She wanted a relationship. What she got was Harold, who had a sex drive that waxed and waned with the moon.

"So, Daddy, one day I'll be married like you and Mommy and have my own house and little baby?" she remembered asking when she was a third-grader sitting on her father's knee.

"Of course, sugar. A big handsome prince with a good job and some business sense will sweep my little girl off her feet one day and you'll both live very, very happily ever after," he had promised her, then nuzzled her neck and tickled her until she giggled and begged him to stop.

So, Dad, where's the prince and the sweeping off the feet part? she now wondered.

I couldn't sweep you off your feet because I don't own a forklift, Harold would have told her if she dared to ask the question out loud. Which she didn't. She knew Harold fell a little short in the prince department, but then she was no Princess Di herself, was she? She was only a soon-to-be-thirty-five-year-old insecure woman desperate for a future that included more than endless nights alone in bed watching the late movie and eating barbecue potato chips with no one to care on which side of the bed the crumbs fell.

Gigi Bernstein wanted a man.

Candlelight pirouetted through the ruby prism of Gigi's filled wineglass. That evening had turned into a birthday to remember, the best since Howie

17

Ragsdale had copped that feel twenty years before. Gigi felt cozy, content and blissfully intoxicated. Across the table Harold sat, his eyes fixed upon his plate as he laboriously swirled fettucine around his fork. Incredibly cute, Gigi thought, as he sucked the strands of pasta into his mouth with a vacuum sound.

The lilting notes of an Italian opera drifted in the background and Gigi looked around the restaurant soaking up the dim, candlelit atmosphere of white tablecloths, red-coated waiters and well-dressed patrons conversing in hushed tones. Gigi's hand grazed her shoulder, smoothing the folds of the new emerald silk dress she had purchased for the occasion. Going for an Audrey Hepburn effect, she invested in a dress of simple, low-cut elegance, completing the look with swept-up hair, its thick curls wrapped into a small knot on the top of her head from which unruly tendrils sprouted in gentle rebellion.

Harold was wearing his favorite Giorgio Armani wool-and-silk-blend jacket. It was noticeably too big in the shoulders, but he had purchased it half-price at a Sakowitz year-end close-out and he thought it made him look huskily Italian. It charmed Gigi that Harold had tried to look his best for the occasion, wearing a tie and combing his hair across his skull to hide his rapidly receding hairline. To Gigi, Harold seemed as handsome as Robert Redford, as charming as David Niven, as powerful as Henry Kissinger. He had given her flowers, brought her to a romantic Italian restaurant, hadn't said one insensitive thing all evening and would probably even pick up the check. Bliss abounded. Her earlier misgivings about the evening were apparently unfounded. Gigi sat quietly and smiled dreamily at her loved one. She and Harold never talked much over dinner. He considered restaurants as places meant to satisfy one's physical needs, and any attempts by Gigi at light conversation were always responded to with primitive grunts of boredom. Usually this irritated Gigi, it feeling somewhat like sharing antelope meat with an African bushman, but tonight she was totally satisfied to sit silently and watch Harold grapple with his noodles. Tonight was special, she thought, as she reached up and touched her hands to her earlobes where new gold earrings perched delicately, a birthday present from Harold. Did the Red Sea part today as well, she wondered? Harold's attitude toward her had somehow miraculously changed. He had given her a gift, tiny gold earrings with the tiniest of sapphires. Harold's taste was so subtle. When a man gives you jewelry, Mrs. Bernstein always said, it means he's serious. What could be more intimate, more meaningful, than adornment for one's earlobes, that erogenous zone meant for nibbling, for gentle kissing, for whispered words of love? Gigi closed her eyes and savored the delicious combination of candlelight, wine and the man she adored.

"Honey?"

"What?" he garbled through a mouth of fettucine. A slender strand of pasta struggled down his chin in a futile effort to escape its inevitable demise.

"I love you," she whispered, reaching her hand across the table and entwining it with his. Gigi noted with tender amusement how uncomfortable Harold was with affection, how he squirmed slightly when she touched him, how almost painfully he smiled. It was one of the many reasons she knew he needed her, for with time, she knew she could bring out his sensitive side.

Suddenly Harold sat up stiffly, cleared his throat and clasped his hands in front of him in an unusually formal manner. A small dribble of cream sauce clung perilously to his chin. He looked a little pale; tiny beads of sweat formed on his upper lip as his eyes darted nervously around the room.

"You know, Gigi, my life has been undergoing a lot of changes since we first met." Harold spoke slowly, carefully choosing his words. "Three years ago when I met you, I was so busy trying to make big money that I never considered, well, the more personal side of my life, uh, like marriage."

Thank you, God, thought Gigi. This was it. Marriage proposal, big diamond, orange blossoms, paper napkins imprinted with both their names. Gigi rested her chin girlishly on her hand, dizzy with romance and gazed at her beloved as the words fell from his lips straight as a laser into her hungering heart.

"I mean, I don't regret the way I've prioritized things. Let's face it, I'm a guy on the fast track in this town. I had to sacrifice a few things on the way."

Would it be tasteless to wear white, Gigi wondered? Or would ecru be more appropriate for a bride of her vintage? Of course her mother would insist on white, but Gigi would stand firm. Ecru. Yes, definitely ecru, although on the whitish side.

"There's also the prospect of children, of course. I would like to have kids. I think two would be nice."

One thing you had to hand Harold—he was a late bloomer, but when he blossomed, he blossomed into the Rose Parade. First marriage, now they were having children. Would Bausch, Bausch and Kozinsky give her maternity leave? She wanted children, but she would refuse to sacrifice her career. She made a mental note to check next Sunday's classifieds for a live-in housekeeper, just to get a price range.

"So I'm sure you understand that I'm not getting any younger. Naturally, I'm still in fantastic shape, but I want to get started on a family right away," said Harold.

I'm ready to start right here under the dinner table, Gigi thought. My reproductive organs are aging even as we speak. She smiled and nodded to indicate her total and absolute agreement with Harold.

Harold took Gigi's hands into his now clammy fingers and looked deeply into her eyes.

This is it, she told herself, and closed her eyes a second to try to memorize the moment so she could describe it triumphantly to Sydney and her mother.

Harold took a deep, fortifying breath.

"I'll never forget you, Gi. I know I haven't been as good to you as maybe I should have. But I think I've learned enough to be a truly good husband to Barbie."

Years later, looking back at this incident, Gigi would still wince when she remembered the word "Barbie" cutting into her heart like a Chinese cleaver, gouging into her psyche and dicing her soul into confetti suitable for tossing upon a happy, just-married couple.

Barbie? Did he really say Barbie? Maybe it was merely Harold garbling the word "Bernstein" from too much wine. *But I think I've learned enough to be a truly good husband to Bernstein.* That had to be it. But that wasn't it.

Gigi slowly removed her hand from Harold's as her understanding of his intentions sharpened into focus. She felt a queasiness in her stomach. She put her hand to her mouth. She thought she might throw up.

"Who is Barbie?" Gigi asked. Her own self-destructiveness amazed her. She knew what the truth was. Her entire emotional infrastructure had just been annihilated, her life strategy gone from victory to debacle, yet she would request the painful details, demand an intricate description of her humiliating defeat, writhe with each piercing blow, then crawl back and beg for more.

"Who is Barbie?" she repeated, noticing the beads of sweat dripping down Harold's forehead. Harold loathed emotional confrontation. He found it embarrassing. He found it weak. He found it revealed one's innermost feelings and

Harold feared his innermost feelings might pale under close scrutiny.

"She's a dental hygienist at Dr. Baker's office. She scaled my gums two months ago. Maybe it was the laughing gas," he said, chuckling nervously, his eyes avoiding Gigi's. "But I fell for her. I would have told you sooner, but I knew you would probably take it hard."

Of course, Barbie. Gigi and Harold went to the same dentist and Gigi had had a cleaning by Barbie four months ago. Cute, perky Barbie with the blond hair, the skinny little hips and the brain that simulated the empty vastness of the great American west. Bouncy, bubbly, twenty-five-year-old Barbie.

"How could you love her more than me?" Gigi asked, inwardly incredulous of her own thirst for pain.

"Let's not do this, Gigi."

"No," she commanded in an offensive tone. "Why do you love her? What's wrong with me?"

Harold sighed with exasperation, took a deep breath and prepared to speak. Gigi could tell things were about to get dirty.

"Okay, Gigi. You asked for it, here it is. What's wrong with you? You're too fat, you're too old. You can only be a liability to me. You require too much time and too much attention. It would be dangerous to have children with you because your chromosomes are thirty-five years old. So there. Are you happy?"

Gigi backed her chair away from the table, stood up and stared at Harold for some indeterminate amount of time. To criticize her looks was abhorrent, to mention her age tasteless, but to insult her very DNA was beyond endurance. Harold shifted agitatedly in his chair, having noticed several dinner guests watching their drama. At that moment Gigi hated Harold, hated every corpuscle, every cell, every molecule in his body. What a fine line there was between hate and love, like the flip of a coin, opposite sides of the same hard, cold currency. For Gigi, it was her Waterloo. What does one do when faced with the thing one dreads most? Like a trapped animal facing inevitable destruction, her instinct was to attack, to strike blindly out at the hopelessness and inflict any damage she could before meeting her end. Harold saw an atypical wildness in her eyes. He sunk in his chair and stared at this woman before him with a sickly, tremulous expression, for deep down he feared women, like a child fears the imagined upredictability of a pitch-dark room.

"There's no need to make a scene, Gi," he whispered through gritted teeth. "I never led you on, did I? Did I ever tell you I would marry you? At least I gave you four years. You're lucky—"

At that moment Gigi swung her imitation Louis Vuitton shoulder bag and planted it directly on Harold's jaw. The impact surprised herself as much as it surprised Harold and everyone in the restaurant. Had Harold been prepared for the blow it never would have budged him, but the surprise attack coupled with the can of hairspray and newly purchased economy size bottle of Oil of Olay in her handbag sent him sprawling backward in his chair onto the floor, taking his dish of fettucine with him. It took only seconds for a team of waiters to rush to his aid and Gigi found herself suddenly surrounded by restaurant employees. As two busboys led Gigi by the arms to the door, she looked back to take a last view of the man she had loved. The manager and a waiter were picking pasta off his suit while he sat on the floor babbling incoherently, massaging his face with his hand, probably wondering how he would explain the bruise to Barbie.

Once on the sidewalk, Gigi realized self-pityingly that her swing had popped the clasp on her new French bra, and that, to add insult to injury, she had no way to get home.

CHAPTER TWO

Future scholars and religious students would bicker endlessly but ultimately would agree that Gigi Bernstein made the final decision to end her life on her thirty-fifth birthday at approximately eleven o'clock Central Standard Time. It wasn't as much a conscious decision as merely acceptance of the unceasing prostration of her life. Somewhere just outside the entrance of Di Angelo's Italian Restaurant, Gigi's lifetime depression settled into a comalike numbness that she felt would subside only for moments of extreme self-loathing. She no longer wished to be Gigi Bernstein. She wished to be a corpse.

Sitting in the fluorescent glow of the Westheimer Boulevard bus she thought about Harold, Barbie, shiny white teeth, long black coffins and birthday surprises. It's my party and I'll die if I want to, she thought morbidly. As she watched the passing traffic out the window she saw a

26

bumper sticker on a Chevy that said Expect a Miracle. She snickered. Expect to get dumped, she told herself, expect to be abused, forgotten, tossed in the junk heap. The bus dropped Gigi at the corner. The night felt warm and balmy, the kind of soft, heady evening that wrapped around you like comfortable arms. Gigi tried to memorize how it felt. She intended that evening to be her last.

Suicide seemed so dramatic. To end one's life over a man, well, it was something that only happened in Lana Turner movies. And hardly worth it, Gigi thought, when you sized up Harold in any realistic perspective. But somehow losing Harold wasn't the issue worth dying over. What hurt so badly was the toppling of the fantasy she had nurtured since childhood that life would somehow work out to be the fairy tale she had been taught to desire. That a handsome prince would emerge suddenly from nowhere and find her uniquely beautiful in all the world. That she would ultimately turn out to be very special. That someone would see her specialness and cherish it forever.

But it never happened. Not only did Prince Charming fail to turn up, she even got rejected by the frog. At thirty-five she had yet to have a relationship that lasted longer than a car loan. No one seemed to find her special at all and she certainly couldn't see it in herself. Her unendurable pain was the realization that her life would never be romantic, never magical. There were no handsome princes, no specialness, no Santa

Claus, nothing except a lonely reality. And that she couldn't face.

She walked into her empty apartment and without turning on the light sat in front of the television's glow, watched Johnny Carson and ate three Moon Pies. At least she wouldn't have to worry about her weight anymore. Dead people don't count calories. In her lap sat her beloved cat Miranda, in her right hand she held a rapidly disintegrating Moon Pie and in her left hand she held Harold's razor, which she slowly turned over and over with her fingers as Johnny and his guests exchanged gleeful quips and Ed McMahon laughed too raucously at the frailest jokes.

Gigi felt sorry about what she had done to Harold in the restaurant. Was it Harold's fault if he couldn't love her? She closed her eyes and silently wished Harold and Barbie happiness, then Johnny Carson and Gigi Bernstein bid America good-night. Gigi turned off the television, left Miranda a week's volume of cat food in her dish and went into her pink-tiled bathroom, slipping off her dress and into the Christian Dior robe she had splurged on a few weeks before. Better to die in Dior, she reasoned. She noted disdainfully that she had locked the door behind her. It seemed a futile act, since, after all, who would race in and beg her not to destroy herself? Her mother? Mrs. Bernstein would grieve for years, but "Better dead than unwed" was probably her mother's secret credo. Her friend Sydney? She would chalk it up to lack of nutrition and exercise. And Harold? As a corpse she would be so much more compatible

28

with him.

No, Gigi Bernstein was on her own. Her untimely demise would be noted by few, grieved by fewer. Once you killed yourself, no one ran around tearing their hair out wishing they had been nicer to you. They just rationalized that you were crazy. Only crazy people killed themselves.

Gigi looked at her reflection in the bathroom mirror, noticing with disgust her bedraggled hair, her eroded makeup streaked with tears. The face in the mirror had never looked the way she wanted it to. In a final act of vanity, Gigi brushed her hair and freshened her makeup applying extra blush, Passion Fruit Red lipstick and loads of Opium just in case they didn't find her body right away. She inspected the blade with macabre curiosity. Quite sharp, she decided, sharp enough to slash her dainty little wrists, the only thin thing on her body, sharp enough to drain the blood from her veins, to cut her out of life like a photograph from a magazine. She lowered the tip of the knife to her left wrist, clenched her eyes shut and made the tiniest slice in her flesh. A dot of red blood oozed from her white skin and dripped onto the tile below. She looked down and winced, then shut her eyes before she lowered the edge of the razor to make a more final slice.

"All you lost was a man. You're acting like you lost your brain," a woman's voice said from somewhere behind her. Gigi spun around, half frightened, half relieved that someone was there. She turned, expecting miraculously to find her mother or Sydney, someone psychic enough to sense her

29

tragedy and come running over to tell her everything was going to be all right.

But who she saw standing there was a stranger. Yet not quite a stranger. The woman before her leaned back casually against the door and pursed her lips, then smiled. She was petite with a heart-shaped freckled face and short curly red hair that clashed with the bright pink of the bathroom door behind her. Gigi had never seen her before, yet this woman had a quality of familiarity, like someone Gigi had known many years before, like a face she had seen on the street every day but never really known. And still she saw the face of a stranger.

"Besides, if you let blood get in the grout between the tiles you'll never get it out. For the sake of tidiness you could at least hang yourself. I mean, there must be a dozen ways to kill yourself in a bathroom without making a mess. Why, you could strangle yourself with your support hose, smother yourself with talcum powder. Spray on just a little more perfume and we could both die from asphyxiation," the woman said.

Gigi's body tensed with fear. She couldn't speak. Her mind raced about doors or windows she could have left open allowing the stranger entry. But how did the woman enter the locked bathroom door? She had always been afraid of someone breaking in, but she envisioned the attacker to be a man, someone who could rape her. Of course, with the crazies in Houston, who could guess what anyone would do?

Suddenly the stranger put a hand on Gigi's

arm. To Gigi's surprise, she didn't jump or pull away. She didn't know why. The stranger took the razor blade from Gigi's hand and dropped it in the trash can.

"On the other hand, it seems so much trouble, why not forget the whole thing. Suicide is a waste of time."

What lunacy is this? Gigi asked herself. She wanted to bolt for the door, get to a phone, but she couldn't. She was frozen in place by fear, stupid curiosity, or something she couldn't name.

"Who are you?" Gigi asked the obvious in a trembling voice. "What are you doing here?"

The stranger threw back her head, slapped her thighs and laughed. It was a nice laugh, full-bodied and sincere. She laughed until her face reddened, her eyes teared and she began to emit a rather unattractive nasal snort. After a moment she regained her composure.

"I apologize, really, but you've got to be kidding. You're getting ready to slash your wrists and you ask me what I'm doing? I think we have a little problem with priorities here, honey," she said, and pointed a delicate finger at Gigi. "The primo question is, Who are you and what are you doing?"

Gigi's mind raced with possible explanations for her current predicament. The combination of wine and emotion had sickened her mind, obviously. This was an hallucination . . . although, it seemed real. Hallucinations should be vague, dream-like states, but Gigi could notice every detail about this woman, like the small rip in her ankle length Mexican peasant dress, the well-worn yellow and blue Nikes she wore on her feet. Hallucinations didn't wear Nikes, did they, she asked herself? No, she wasn't crazy. It had to be this bizarre redhead who was the sick one. Gigi decided to play along for a while, wait until she caught the woman off guard, then run out of the bathroom, out the front door and into the street where she would scream her head off for the police.

"I'm killing myself. So what?" Gigi said in as blase a tone as possible. The stranger shook her head in disapproval.

"So what, you say? Life is a gift, a wonderful miracle bestowed by the grace of God. I hate to run the old children-starving-in-India routine on you, but don't you realize how very lucky you are to have your life? Believe me, there are lots of poor souls around who need it and would give anything to get it," she answered as she took a Band-Aid from the medicine cabinet, opened it and tried to place it on the cut on Gigi's wrist.

"Who are you?" Gigi demanded angrily, jerking her arm away, but the woman just smiled and leaned her shoulder against the wall and crossed her arms. She looked amused. She looked interested. She looked exceptionally calm, Gigi thought, for a person who had just broken and entered.

"I like this part," the woman told her. "Ah, revelation. I never tire of it. Let's see, now. Who am I? I am what you see and what you don't see, I'm life and I'm death, I'm here and I'm not here,

32

I'm light and I'm energy, I'm raindrops on roses and whiskers on kittens." The woman giggled.

"You're on drugs," Gigi said, suddenly certain this woman was a heroin addict intending to rob her and murder her for a drug fix. The stranger continued chuckling for a moment, then she straightened up into a more formal posture.

"Okay. Straight-answer time," she began. "I've been watching you for a long while now, Gigi Bernstein. I know all about you. I know about your life. And by the way, kiddo, things aren't nearly as tough as you think. The reason I've been observing you is that I have a little proposition for you. A proposition I think you'll find interesting. Very interesting. I wasn't going to hit you with it until much later, but then this little tete-a-tete with the razor came up and I had to make my move. And believe me, I don't like being pushed like this."

"What sort of proposition?" asked Gigi, wondering how she would fare if she attacked the intruder with a blow dryer and tried to knock her unconscious.

The stranger's eyes lit up with a mischievous twinkle.

"How would you like to do something really special with your life?" she queried.

"If you're a Jehovah's Witness, you can just forget it," she said.

"A Jehovah's Witness, kiddo, I'm not. I'm sort of a spirit from above. An archangel, to put it in the vernacular."

"Give me a break," Gigi said with disgust. The

stranger raised an eyebrow with annoyance.

"Look, I could burst in her with a lot of razzle dazzle, pull a few angelic numbers and have you on your knees in no time singing hallejuhah. If I wanted to. But I don't want to. It's not my style. I'm what you call subtle."

"You call breaking into my bathroom subtle?"

"A little low on gratitude, aren't we? I just saved your life."

"I didn't want it saved."

"Wrong. You were dying to have it saved, excuse the pun. In my line of business, that's the first thing you learn. Nobody really wants to die."

"And just what sort of business do you think you're in?" Gigi asked in her most legal, professional tone. The woman leaped past Gigi onto the side of the bathtub,

"Does God ring a bell?" the woman replied with a touch of sarcasm in her voice. "She's a big name around town."

Gigi lowered the toilet lid, sat down and looked at the woman perched on the side of the tub, noticing that she was leaving shoeprints on the porcelain. Life as usual had careened totally out of control. Gigi examined the stranger's face more closely for signs of advanced syphilis. It was a nice face. It radiated warmth. It was rather charismatic, actually. Gigi had heard stories of hopeless psychotics whose faces radiated warmth and charisma just before they sliced you up into croutons.

"You're on drugs. Just don't kill me. You can have all my money. Just let me get my purse. I'm a little low on cash, but I'll write you a check."

The woman rolled her eyes with exasperation, then hopped down from the tub.

"If I'm crazy, why didn't I let you kill yourself? I stopped you, for goodness sake. I'm the sane one here. You're the one with problems," she said, then hesitated a second before performing a quick deep kneebend to get down to Gigi's eye level.

"Listen to me, Gigi Bernstein. Listen to me like you've never listened to anyone before. I am a messenger from God. I am here to help you. To lift you up from what you believe is the meaningless muck of your empty existence and offer you a rather unique opportunity."

For a moment Gigi could do nothing but stare in bafflement, but she quickly collected herself. Although the intruder acted crazy, she appeared to be harmless. Gigi felt more confident.

"Let me get this straight. You're an angel and you're here to save me from eternal damnation or something, to pick up the pieces of my life and to sort of turn it around?" Gigi asked mockingly.

The redhead sighed. "Hey, I'm an angel, not Lee Iacocca. I have my limitations, but I am an angel." She stood up and flapped her arms like wings. "An a-n-g-e-l. You get it?" She could tell by Gigi's face she didn't get it. "Okay, okay, I'll prove it to you. I hate making myself a circus sideshow, but here, take my hand."

The stranger reached down and lifted Gigi's hand from her side. Gigi hesitated at first, but then succumbed, not really knowing why. The stranger held her hand lightly. Gigi felt a tingling in her fingers as the woman entwined her hand around Gigi's. It was a warm, excited tingling, unlike anything she had ever known. The sensation crept up her hand, wiggled up her arm. It filtered its way like a billion tiny electrical currents through her chest, her legs, her throat and her shoulders. In a soothing wave, the tingling filled her head, her eyes, expanded her mind, it seemed. At first Gigi was afraid, not certain of what she was feeling. It was physical sensation, but it was more than that, too. It felt as if her body and mind had expanded, had broken loose into a billion particles so that she filled the room, filled a hundred rooms, filled the city with whatever energy lay behind her thoughts and her mind. She suddenly felt warm, knowledgeable, unafraid. Then she gasped. She gasped, for she was struck with precisely what the feeling was. It was total, complete peace and joy.

Gigi looked into the stranger's eyes that now glimmered like blue moonlight. The stranger smiled.

"Get the picture?" she asked softly.

Gigi slowly nodded, her eyes wide with astonishment.

"Then listen. The reason I'm here is this. You have been chosen, Gigi Bernstein, of all the women in the world, to be the mother of the Daughter of God."

CHAPTER THREE

If an imaginative historian chose to break free from the more frequently trod historical paths, he or she would find that many of the world's earth-shaking moments have taken place in the bathroom. Surely in the solitude of the bath a multitude of essential decisions have been made that ultimately affected the world's destiny. The mind drifts to visions of Cleopatra in her milk bath, Napolean preparing his toilette, Ben Franklin bracing his chubby face with a brisk splash in the morning. Who could guess what wisdoms, what revelations, have come about in the one room where one can be assured of peace, of quiet, of ample time for reflection?

It was amidst the pastel pink of her bathroom that Gigi Bernstein grappled with the earthshaking revelation of life's new possibilities. Only she wasn't alone. Only she wasn't really with anyone else either, not in the traditional sense.

37

"I'm light and I'm energy, a dash of photons with just a pinch of gaseous matter," the archangel would tell you if you asked her who she was. And on this night near midnight, this combinatior of light, energy and gaseous matter was explaining to a Jewish American Princess that she would be the vehicle that would help change the world.

"Your mission if you choose to accept it," the angel pronounced with her continuing grin, "is to be the mother of the next Messiah. A classy position, don't you think? The pay's not so great, but the work is rewarding, and just think of the fringe benefits. And to fulfill you feminist leanings, the Messiah is going to be . . ." She paused for a dramatic effect. "A girl!" The angel crossed her arms and smiled smugly. Gigi remained sitting on the toilet lid, still numb with astonishment.

"A girl?" Gigi asked weakly.

"Sure. Why not? It's the obvious choice. God decided that this time the Messiah should truly be in Her own image, if you get my drift."

Gigi wasn't sure she did.

"God is a woman?"

"Well, in a sense," the angel explained while she picked up the Ban spray deodorant from a shelf and examined its label. "This is a difficult concept to explain to someone who had your problems with geometry, because God is a trifle more expansive than the human mind can conceive of. But to bring it down to your level, it would be fair to say that the essence of God is definitely Arpege and not English Leather.

Gigi looked on as the angel squirted some Ban into the air and sniffed its aroma.

"So why a female savior? Isn't that unusual?" Gigi asked.

"So when are saviors ordinary? They are by nature outside the norm." The angel's infatuation with Ban having worn off, she once again directed her gaze to Gigi. "Okay, straight-talk time. The first one was a wonderful guy, did a great job back then, but would be a little nonassertive for today's environment. In this day and age the job calls for someone more aggressive, someone who can really think big. That's why we thought we would go with a woman this time. They're so much more suited to the job. Sure, a man was the right choice two thousand years ago, but in today's world a woman is infinitely more marketable. And marketing is key, if you know what I mean."

"What you're saying is, that I'm going to be the mother of . . ." Gigi whispered, her eyes widening.

"Listen, Bernstein," the angel said, hands on hips. "It's an exalted position, sure, but don't think it means the cover of *Newsweek*. If you think back you'll note that the general public doesn't make a big hoopla over this stuff until after the participants are long gone."

Gigi ran her fingers through her already rumpled hair, stood up and walked to the sink. Any minute now she would be waking up, she reassured herself. Gigi looked at her pale visage in the mirror, raising her hands to her face and pulling on her cheek to see if she could feel anything. She could, so she reasoned she must be awake. The face staring back at her didn't look like the face of the Virgin Mary, she decided, and the word "virgin" stuck in her mind. "But why me?" she asked softly, speaking to the angel's reflection in the mirror. "How could you possibly choose me?"

"It was random. Consider yourself the lucky winner in the lottery of the Lord. And no offense, but you weren't my first prospect. There was a woman in Jerusalem that came up, but then that Jerusalem thing's been done to death. Then there was this interesting woman in Mexico and then the one in L. A. of all places, but they didn't work out."

"Why not?" Gigi asked.

"Ego. Most people these days can't handle this sort of thing because ego gets in the way. In your case I don't think it will be a problem."

There fell a momentary silence, a dramatic pause, a pall that settled over the bathroom. Gigi looked squeamish.

"I'm not a virgin," she announced.

"Surprise, surprise," Juanita said dryly. "You forget, I know all about you. A virgin you're not. So big deal. Times have changed, Bernstein. Who would believe that sort of thing nowadays? Nobody, at least not the people who really need to be reached. No, in this day and time it's a whole different ballgame. We have to flow with the current environment. Marketing. Don't forget that concept," she explained, and wagged her finger.

Gigi looked dubious.

"And a man?"

"A mere detail. Basically you can choose whom you like to be the father. I'm willing to give you some leeway."

"You mean I get to choose the father myself?"

"Why not? He'll play a relatively minor role, at least when we're talking big picture, and we are talking big picture. We do need him, of course, just to make the whole thing legit. The only requirement is that you feel love for him. See, it's easy."

"Men have never been easy for me."

"Good point. That's where I come in. I hate to criticize, but your taste in men is the pits, so I would like to offer my assistance in your search for just the right man. There are ways I can help you."

Gigi shot her a suspicious look.

"For instance?"

"You'll see," she answered, then smiled.

Gigi's mind spun. Things were happening too fast and too strangely. In only an hour she had gone from the precipice of death to deification. Could she really believe this was happening? Gigi felt certain that she was dealing with no ordinary person, but wouldn't God Himself, or rather Herself, come down personally to set up something as big as this? Gigi posed the question to the angel, who was beginning to look annoyed.

"Look, I know this is a tough concept, but believe me, God has providence over much, much more than what goes on here. Think of God as being at a top executive level, up to her ears in administrative work. Middle management makes all the real decisions. I'm middle management and I've decided on you."

"And what if I don't want to do this?"

"Then don't do it. No one is going to force you into anything. Me, I only make suggestions, but you were just about to slash your wrists. What have you got to lose?"

Gigi couldn't argue with that reasoning. The angel took Gigi's hand.

"Everything will be okay, but you have to trust me. You're a wonderful person. You're kind, honest, and in the way that really counts, you're quite pure. And you will bring into the world the embodiment of that love and purity in the form of a child who will touch people's lives and change the course of the world. It's important for you to know that you have the quality in life that should be treasured the most. Deep within, Gigi Bernstein, you're filled with love."

Chapter Four

On the morning after her thirty-fifth birthday, Gigi Bernstein greeted the first harkening of aurora with a pained groan coupled with the realization that once again she had over-indulged in wine, food and gut-wrenching emotion. As she opened her eyes to the daylight, the previous night's preposterous events came back to her, first with vagueness, then with crystal clarity, then with utter disbelief.

Did it really happen or was it all a dream induced by too much chardonnay, too many Moon pies and the pain of rejection? Gigi closed her eyes and remembered the razor blade in her hand, her depression over Harold, and a very weird red-haired woman who asked Gigi to be the mother of the Daughter of God.

"I'll never drink again," Gigi swore groggily. "No more booze ever." She lumbered over onto her stomach, burying her face in the pillow. It couldn't have been real, she thought, although it had certainly seemed real. But it couldn't have been real because things like that just don't happen.

Things like that just don't happen, she told herself as she lathered with Camay in the shower. Angels just don't appear to middle-aged women with emotional problems, she reasoned as she picked up the clothes she had tossed on the floor the night before. Messengers from God don't breeze into bathrooms, she assured herself as she slipped on her yellow jumpsuit, combed her hair and flossed and brushed her teeth. Gigi remembered in detail her conversation with the stranger, but she didn't remember when or exactly how the woman had left. She was there one minute and then the next she was gone, vanished, vaporized into thin air. Hallucinations were like that, Gigi reasoned, and the archangel's bizarre appearance and disappearance only confirmed the non-reality of the whole event.

Gigi sipped her morning coffee and perused the yellow pages for a psychiatrist who might be able to help her with her insecurities as well as a new and fascinating tendency toward bizarre hallucinations.

One thing she knew was very real. Harold had vamoosed. He had tossed her aside, discarded her, traded her in on a newer, racier model. The fact of it made her wince, forced her stomach to tighten into a knot. She took a deep breath and tried to think rationally. Last night she had tried to kill herself, but somehow she had survived.

Gigi raised her sleeve and saw the small cut on her wrist and she shivered at the thought of what she had almost done. She felt shaky but renewed, like someone who had survived a cataclysmic accident, like a plane crash or a hotel fire. It was time to get a grip on herself. Harold was history. Okay then, good riddance, but she had to get on with her life. Actually, for someone who had just experienced a schizophrenic episode she didn't feel that bad. Gigi took a swig of coffee and gargled it, having heard somewhere that it released more caffeine. Gazing down at the kitchen sink, she saw a platoon of ants attacking a remnant of Moon Pie from the night before. They swarmed over the countertop in an ecstatic ant frenzy, each carrying a microscopic sliver of crust and chocolate. Gigi got a can of Raid from the cabinet and took aim. She stopped. She felt generous.

"You better listen up," she warned them. "You have until three p.m. to clear out of here, or else. I have bug spray and I'm not afraid to use it." She sprayed a few warning shots in the air. A thousand pair of ant antennae perked up at the sound, then they went on about their ant business without fear, for they knew she had kept that same can of bug spray for a year and had never had the heart to use it.

Mrs. Bernstein's spike heels clicked like castanets as she maneuvered cautiously across the kitchen floor, delicately cradling a birthday cake in her hands as if it were an explosive seconds from detonation. Gigi smiled weakly, every muscle contorted into the grimace she dare not show on her face. She loved her parents but sometimes she found the compulsory visits trying. Today was worse than usual, for thoughts of the previous night kept spinning through her head with visions of the archangel, the razor blade and Harold flashing through her psyche. Fortunately there was something about being home that made her feel more secure. Here she was sitting at the kitchen table with her mother prancing around as usual, her father in the next room watching television as usual—the same smells, the same sights, the same feelings as usual. So how crazy could she be? Very crazy, she told herself, crazy enough to see, hear and feel things that didn't exist. That's the way it started, she figured. It started with a few innocent hallucinations, then in a few years she would be walking the streets having conversations with persons who weren't there, digging through garbage for soda cans and scraps of food.

"Happy birthday to yooooo . . . !" Mrs Bernstein yodeled spasmodically and Gigi could hear her father singing along in the other room while he watched the Astros. Gigi smiled at her mother, who stood before her a model of middle-class glamour and efficiency. She was a member of the Beautify Our Highways League, a charming hostess, a wonderful cook, a perfect housekeeper who wore high heels when she vacuumed, pearls when she scrubbed the toilet. Her hair, a bouffant tribute to technology, was fashionably bleached into a surrealistic blonde, a twentieth-century marvel, indestructible, eternal, coiffed and lacquered until it no longer seemed attached to her scalp but rather hovered over her head like a fluffy UFO.

Her favorite color was aqua, her favorite song "Ebb Tide," her favorite men Mel Torme and, of course, Mr. Bernstein. Gigi felt a pang of envy for her mother, for, unlike her daughter, Mrs. Bernstein was happily confident of her world and her niche within it.

". . . Happy birthday toooo yoooo!" her mother completed singing, putting an unexpected sopranic lift to the last stanza. Gigi looked at the cake, wished for non-hallucinatory sanity, then blew out the candles.

"A year older, a year better. You're a fine wine, honey, yet to reach its peak," Mrs. Bernstein said as she cut the cake into large portions and placed them on her best china. Gigi had heard the fine-wine theory from her mother every birthday since she turned thirty and she had yet to believe it. Mrs. Bernstein, after years of living, had managed to reduce her life down to a carefully selected set of aphorisms that she frequently deigned to share with family and friends.

"Art is long, life is short, so let's get on with the birthday celebration. Are we ready for our present?" Mrs. Bernstein asked gleefully after taking a box out of the kitchen cabinet and barely hiding it behind her back.

"Yes we are, Mom."

Here it comes, Gigi thought, five pairs of high-top briefs with cotton crotches and tiny little holes

47

in the fabric so her privates could drink in the air freely. Mrs. Bernstein believed that lack of air to the vagina was the cause of a multitude of female afflictions. Yes, Gigi said silently, five pairs of white panties with lacy elastic at the top, completely suitable for public viewing in case she was hit by a car and the doctors, preferably male and single, had to rip her clothes off in the emergency room, which was probably the only way she would ever get her clothes ripped off.

Gigi took the bow off the box, removed the yellow wrapping paper and paused a moment before lifting the lid and peeling back the tissue that would reveal the anticipated panties that would free her vagina as if it were Poland. She looked up at her mother and smiled at this woman who represented the one solid and predictable thing in her life. Gigi grasped the white lace nylon and lifted it for examination.

"Mother!" she cried, holding the contents with two fingers as if it were a dead rat's tail. A one-piece satin and lace bodice hung before her, an intricate construction of lingerie with a built-in bra engineered with wire. From the bottom hung garter straps, the entire outfit obviously designed to drive some unwitting male into an uncontrollable sexual frenzy.

"So, you like it?" Mrs. Bernstein asked coyly.

"I don't know. What is it?"

"It's called a Merry Widow." She seemed annoyed at her daughter's pretense of naivete. "I hope it fits," she said, cupping her own breasts with her hands and shoving them upward to demonstrate where she considered an exact fit vital. Gigi closed her eyes and moaned.

"But, Mother, what do I do with it? What could I wear it under? It's awfully stiff." Gigi kneaded the fabric to check for whalebone. Mrs. Bernstein rolled her eyes.

"You don't necessarily wear it under something," she said, dropping her voice to a naughty whisper and leaning her face close to Gigi's. "You don't want to hide it. You want someone to see it. Like Harold."

So that was it, Gigi thought. Her mother was so desperate to get her married that she was consulting Frederick's of Hollywood instead of the rabbi. Receiving sexy lingerie from your mother was the ultimate insult. Gigi noted that the garment was crotchless to allow maximum air circulation.

"I wouldn't get my hopes up about Harold, Mom," said Gigi, not wanting to hear the inevitable wails and scolding if she broke the news about Harold's engagement.

"Not to worry, hon. Another bus comes every fifteen minutes," Mrs. Bernstein said as she trotted off to replenish her ice tea.

Yeah, Mom, but the buses stop running at midnight.

A metallic wave of frigid air pelted Gigi as she swung through the elegant bronze and glass portals of Neiman Marcus. Once inside she paused by the cosmetics counter, checked her face in a mirror and reminded her reflection for the ninety-seventh time how totally sane she was, how solidly her feet were planted on the ground. Gigi peered down at her Capezio sandals just to make certain they were as planted as she thought they were, then she brushed a piece of lint off her yellow shoulder, tossed back her head and marched toward the escalator that would wisk her up to her monthly hair appointment with Lulu.

"Would you like a spray of Angel?" a voice asked behind her. Gigi spun around and saw with relief a friendly faced salesgirl holding a bottle of perfume.

"No thanks," Gigi answered with a nervous laugh. She turned and forged her way through the tastefully frenzied Saturday whirl of Neiman's patrons. Riding up the escalator she looked back and surveyed the well-heeled shoppers as they mulled over the leathers, perused the silks, the creams and emollients. They explored the gems, scrutinized the furs, conferred with the salespeople, then passed their plastic to secure their little piece of Neiman's inimitable luxury. Gigi theorized that Neiman Marcus was to Houston what the Parthenon had been to Greece, a massive monument to the culture, a statement in stone that summed all the elements that comprised it — glitz, greed and money.

Gigi hustled through the third-floor sportswear and walked into the beauty salon. A fluffy blond attendant bestowed her with a lavender gown, led her to a lavender dressing room, then to a lavender sink to have her hair washed and wrapped in a fluffy lavender towel. Afterward she made her way to the cutting area, but Lulu had yet to arrive.

"You look like hell. Last night must have been better than we expected," Sydney said. She lounged in the chair next to Lulu's, her ten toes dangling impatiently in the air as they awaited their weekly pedicure. Gigi scanned Sydney, finding her typically overdressed in a lipstick-red, rhinestoned pantsuit. In spite of all the money she lavished on clothes, Sydney usually managed to look like she had just walked out of a Las Vegas casino bar. High-heeled, ankle-strapped sandals were Sydney's wardrobe staple, making a perfect pedicure a must.

"Was this a coincidence or did you arrange it this way?" asked Gigi as she flopped down into the patent leather chair next to Sydney. Sydney interrupted her conversation with the manicurist and graced her friend with her former San Antonio beauty-queen smile.

"I planned it, of course. You told me you were getting your hair cut today and I was desperate for a pedicure and I thought, it's your birthday and wouldn't it be fun if we could both be here at the same time? And see, it's fun already. Anyway," Sydney said, turning her attention back to the bespectacled woman who was busily stuffing cotton between Sydney's pedal digits. "Arthur kept insisting that we have sex in these disgusting positions." She paused and raised her eyebrows to give her audience the chance to utilize their imaginations. "Well, I just loathe it. It makes me feel

51

like a German shepherd. So last night when he put me in one of those positions I started saying 'arf, arf' and I guess that cured him forever."

Gigi responded with the compulsory chuckle but she wasn't in the mood for Sydney's lurid chatter. Why couldn't she get last night out of her mind? She couldn't stop turning the scene over and over in her head. It absolutely couldn't have been real. No way. It was only the imaginative twisting of a mind warped by depression. She obviously made up the whole thing just to give herself an excuse not to slash her wrists, and she knew people who heard voices seriously needed psychiatric help. She remembered Joanne Woodward in *The Three Faces of Eve* and decided to check her medical insurance on Monday and make sure she was covered for psychiatry. If not, she would be in big trouble, because it would most likely take years to cure her and would cost a fortune. Maybe she could go to a women's clinic. It was definitely a female sort of problem—a madonna complex, messiah envy.

Gigi looked in the mirrored wall before her and gave her face a hard stare to see if it looked like the face of a madwoman, but it only looked to Gigi like a face that needed more lipstick. Gigi scrambled through her fake Gucci handbag for a tube of Revlon Hot Hot Red and began applying it to her lips.

"So tell me about last night," said Sydney. Gigi jumped a few inches out of her chair, smearing a streak of Hot Hot Red down her chin.

"What do you mean? What about last night?"

52

she asked nervously and wiped her reddened chin with the palm of her hand.

"Why your birthday dinner with Harold, of course. So how was it? Did he buy you anything expensive?" Sydney was now leaning over her feet, blowing on her pink polish to speed the drying process.

"Dinner was interesting," Gigi said. She immediately regretted the use of the term "interesting" thinking it would provoke Sydney into a barrage of questions, but Sydney apparently was letting it pass. Gigi reached up and touched the earrings Harold have given her. "He gave me these earrings."

Sydney leaned over to examine Gigi's ears and squinted with disapproval. "Harold's taste is so understated. So tell me what you meant when you said the evening was interesting. What happened? I want to know everything."

Gigi knew Sydney was prepared to grill her on the evening's events. She was trying to think of a suitable fib when she was saved by the dramatic entrance of Lulu, who pranced over wearing a paper birthday hat and blowing on a party noisemaker. She sang a few stanzas of "Happy Birthday," then pulled her scissors from her pocket. Colorful paper ribbons streamed from the handles.

"My present to you is a free haircut, sweetie, and if you don't mind my frankness, you can sure use it. You look like hell, which has to mean you had a great night last night."

Sydney smirked. With a flourish, Lulu pulled

the lavender towel off Gigi's head and began combing out her wet hair. To protect her pedicure, Sydney hobbled on her heels and then lodged herself behind Gigi's chair. The manicurist's cotton stuck up in fluffy white tufts between her toes.

"Get this, Lu. Gigi described her dinner last night as interesting. Something had to have happened. What was interesting certainly wasn't Harold's conversation."

"Jeezus, did he propose?" Lulu asked as she snipped at Gigi's hair. Sydney leaped forward and grabbed Gigi's hand to check for a ring. Gigi didn't want to spill the whole story, not even the part about Harold and Barbie. She noticed that although Lulu was rapidly cutting hair, she didn't seem to be paying much attention to the process.

"Harold didn't propose. We had a very nice dinner and he gave me these earrings. Nothing special happened." Gigi hated lying. Lying wasn't right, especially to old friends. It made her stomach turn into a little lump, but she couldn't tell the truth about last night. Her guilt made her irritable. "Why does everybody always want to talk about Harold all the time, anyway? First my mother, now you. Aren't there other topics we can discuss? How about politics, the environment, recipes, anything."

"Gigi's right. Discussing men is boring," said Lulu, now giving more concentration to Gigi's haircut. Gigi saw Sydney's eyes turn bitchy.

"You only say that, Lulu, because you're repressing deep heterosexual urges. You love to talk

54

about men. You want a man and you know it. Admit it."

Lulu's heart-shaped face twisted into a sneer and she took a swift, angry snip out of the front of Gigi's hair. Gigi flinched.

"That's ridiculous. I don't need men. I made a conscious choice that was right for me."

Lulu's slices into Gigi's hair were becoming more erratic and Gigi hoped this repetition of an old argument wasn't going to end up with her being bald. Lulu, petite and pretty, had been married to an accountant for eight years, but left him a few years earlier, suddenly declaring herself gay and moving in with Marlene. The friendship between Gigi, Sydney and Lulu remained strong before and after Lulu's sexual switch, but there had been an ongoing verbal skirmish between Sydney and Lulu over the validity of Lulu's sexual urges.

"Your conscious choice was to get as far away from that dull husband of yours as possible, and you didn't want to leave town so you just started telling people you were gay."

"I am gay," Lulu replied. Another sizable chunk of Gigi's hair fell to the floor. "It's your own discomfort with the political and social ramifications of your dependencies on men that make you talk this way, Sydney."

Sydney faked a laugh. "You'd like a male ramification up your you-know-what. You don't even do anything with Marlene except make bran muffins. I've been around you two and there's all the sexual energy there of a zucchini, which, by the

55

way, is what you probably use on yourself at night."

"Lulu, don't listen to her. Could we get back to my hair now? There are several large segments missing from the front here."

Lulu patted her head. "Don't worry, sweetie. I'm cutting you shorter in front to give you a little fluff around that wonderful face of yours so you can at last get Harold to propose and live out the rest of your life in marital oppression."

"At least with Harold she won't have to worry about his excessive sexual demands," said Sydney. She and Lulu snickered. Both women knew the details of Gigi's sex life with Harold. It didn't take long to tell anyone all the details. She could have fit them on a postage stamp.

Lulu had narrowed her eyes in concentration and after twenty minutes of intense creative work, Gigi sported a new haircut that was shorter, fuller and younger than the hair she had walked in with. Gigi looked at herself in the mirror when Lulu finished her blow dry. She looked good. She almost looked perky. She had always wanted to look perky, like that goddamn dental hygienist.

"I love it," said Gigi, and Sydney agreed the haircut was an improvement.

"Okay, ladies, I've got a birthday present for Gigi. Let's open it over lunch. Can you get away, Lu?" asked Sydney.

"Wouldn't miss it. You go change, Gigi, and I'll be ready by the time you are."

Lulu playfully patted Gigi's ample behind just to annoy Sydney, and Gigi walked back into the dressing room to change. As she pulled on her jumpsuit she brushed the bits of clipped hair off her neck. She hated feeling itchy. With one arm in her jumpsuit and one arm out, she contorted herself to brush the hairs from between her shoulder blades.

"Surprise, surprise!"

Gigi leaped at the sound of an almost familiar voice. Looking into the mirror on the wall she glimpsed the flame of red hair behind her. Gigi shut her eyes tightly, took a deep breath, counted to three, then opened them again. The woman still stood there. Gigi felt too stunned to speak. The angel straightened the shoulder of Gigi's jumpsuit then gave her back a slap.

"I like the cut. Trendy, very trendy."

Gigi stood stiffly for a moment, silent and disbelieving, yet the woman looked exactly as she remembered from the previous night — the same long Mexican peasant dress and those awful blue-and-yellow Nikes poking out from underneath.

"You're real," she whispered.

"You betcha," the angel responded with a grin. Gigi put her hand on her forehead to check for fever.

"Then last night was real? This whole thing is real? It's happening, or it's going to happen?" Gigi said weakly, leaning back against the lavender wall for support.

"On target again, Bernstein. Of course it will only happen if you want it to. But I think you will." The angel looked around the dressing room absentmindedly, saw a copy of *Vogue* and started flipping through the pages, studying them. Gigi watched her, still uncertain of what was real and what was imaginary.

"Hemlines are definitely dropping. Personally, I think if you've got good equipment, why not show it?" the angel said, and looked to Gigi for her opinion.

"How come you don't talk like an angel?" Gigi asked.

"So how many angels have you talked to lately?" she said curtly. "I have opinions. I don't live in a vacuum. Besides, I'm only what you perceive me to be. I'm a reflection of yourself." She smiled coquettishly.

Gigi ran her fingers through her hair, damaging her new coiffure. Could it be that she was going to be the mother of this Person? Would Gigi Bernstein, Jewish American Princess, be one day a plastic figure sitting on someone's dashboard?

"I have questions," she said. The angel put down *Vogue*.

"Okay, shoot."

"When will all this happen?"

"In time. When you're ready."

"How will I know when I'm ready?"

"You'll know."

"But how will I know?"

"You'll know, you'll know. Take it easy. You've been planning your life for thirty-five years now and haven't been too thrilled with the results. So relax for a change. Let life take its natural course."

Gigi's mouth gaped. "Its natural course? You

call my being the mother of this Supreme Being or whatever life's natural course?" Gigi asked through gritted teeth. The angel watched placidly.

"Yes," she replied.

"For Chrissakes, I'm Jewish!"

The angel emitted a terse squeak, which Gigi assumed was a signal that an angel was amused.

"Completely irrelevant," the angel said. "But if it will make you feel any better adjusted to the idea, a Messiah, or prophet if you prefer, coming to humankind will philosophically fit in nicely with all organized religions. Everybody loves a Messiah! Of course, the female angle is going to make the Pope feel silly. I can't wait to see his face."

Gigi fell into a chair. She looked up.

"Can other people see or hear you?" Gigi asked, "Because if they can, some beauticians outside are getting an earful."

"Don't worry with details. That's my job. They only hear us if I want them to hear us. And I don't. You know, you really should learn to mellow out a little, take life easier."

Gigi shook her head. "I've never been able to take life easy. I'm a worrier. I'm a neurotic shambles. Let me tell you something, uh . . . do you have a name?"

"Juanita," the angel replied.

"Let me tell you something, Juanita. You may be making a big mistake here. I've never been able to take care of myself too well, much less take on a responsibility like this. My life is a mess, it's disorganized, it's shallow, it's—"

"Let me say it for you," Juanita interrupted. "If I let you parent this child she'll be in therapy by the time she's sixteen. She'll have chocolate fetishes, father complexes. Her biggest mission in life will be to have her hair straightened. Is that about it?"

"Exactly. What you need is someone stable, someone balanced, who could be a good role model," Gigi continued in a discouraging tone. Juanita soaked up the information with no visible reaction.

"You'll do just fine," she said. Gigi grimaced.

"I won't do just fine. I still don't even believe all this stuff about angels and saviors. This sort of thing just doesn't happen. Angels just don't appear one day and turn thirty-five-year-old women into the Virgin Mary. It's an hallucination or insanity or premenstrual syndrome or something, but it's not reality."

Juanita crossed her arms and looked intently at Gigi. She was beginning to look testy and the intensity of her gaze made Gigi uncomfortable. Juanita seemed to change, as if an electric current shot through her, like a hundred-and-ten-volt plug in a two-twenty outlet. Her eyes darted, her cheeks flushed as she leaned her face intimidatingly close to Gigi's. It made Gigi wonder what an angel did when she was really pissed. She felt like bolting but Juanita had frozen her in place, locked her into position for as long as she desired. Gigi felt captured in the effervescent blue of Juanita's eyes, helpless except to wait as if hypnotized for whatever would fall from this angel's lips.

"Why not try stepping outside your insecurities for once?" Juanita said in a voice of new resonance. She swept her arms about the small dressing room like a novice Shakespearean actor. "Believe the unbelievable. Expand. Go for the gusto! Dream the impossible dream! There are miracles out there, toots. There's magic and marvels and light and wonders, electricity in the air that, if you would only open yourself up, would tingle up your spine and light up your eyes like Fourth of July sparklers. Life is a gift. It's a miraculous, fantastic, joyous gift. And, Bernstein, you haven't even taken off the wrapping yet. Believe, Gigi. Believe, just this once, that you're special, special in all the world. Because you really, truly are, whether you know it or not."

Gigi allowed the words to penetrate. Her special, she wondered? Gigi Bernstein, the unloved, the ordinary, the eternal moderate achiever, special? Special had never been in her vocabulary of self-description. But then, in the very back corner of her heart she had always had this teensy feeling that maybe she was just a little different, that maybe she was quite unique. So maybe this was it. Of course, this had to be it. Maybe she wouldn't make much of a dent in the world, but just suppose she was intended to parent a person who would? She had fantasized about having a child. This could be her big chance to make a contribution greater than an annual donation to the United Way. Things were starting to make sense. Juanita was, after all, very convincing.

"But what will this Child do, Juanita? Is she going to stop war, end starvation or save the world somehow?"

"I don't know much more about the future than you do. I get orders, I carry out orders. I can tell you this much. She will be a teacher, a very great teacher."

"And what will she teach?"

"She'll teach the world about the feminine, nurturing side of its nature. The world is essentially a feminine place, one great womb of cycles and creation, of sustenance and birth. People have forgotten that. She will remind them."

"But will people listen?"

"There are no guarantees, of course, but her influence will be strong." Juanita burst into a laugh. "What a wave she'll send through the world. She'll take a few old ideas and stand them on their ears and you and I will be around to watch it all, won't we?" Juanita slapped Gigi's knee, then looked at her hopefully. "Well, won't we?"

Gigi looked back at her. "What will the child's name be?"

Juanita's face brightened. She knew she'd made a sale.

"Whatever name you like. You can choose. Unless its something like Bambi or Muffie."

Gigi contemplated it. She considered the name Marsha, but there was an aunt on her mother's side named Marsha. Wendy would be cute, but then no, Aunt Estelle's second daughter was named Wendy.

"I've always liked the name Elizabeth. Yes, how about Elizabeth?" Gigi asked.

Juanita closed her eyes and mouthed the word silently. "Not bad," she said.

A rap on the door startled Gigi.

"Gigi? Are you still in there?" asked Lulu.

"Uh, yes. I'm here," Gigi answered, flustered.

"Look, sweetie, Sydney and I are ready whenever you are, but we need to hurry it up. I have a cut and perm at two-thirty."

"Okay, I'll be right out." Gigi kept an ear pressed to the door until Lulu walked away.

"Look, I've got to go, Juanita . . ." Gigi whispered as she turned, but Juanita had disappeared.

CHAPTER FIVE

Gigi inhaled deeply through all one hundred millimeters of her Virginia Slims Menthol. Closing her eyes, she relished the smoke that drifted through her sinus cavities and filtered gently into her lungs. Smoking was a decadence she allowed herself only once or twice a year on occasions when her anxiety level rose beyond the ozone. This was one of those times. She had also smoked five years ago when she decided to go to Europe instead of, as her mother suggested, getting her nose fixed. And when she made the decision to go to law school, instead of, as her mother also suggested, spending a year in Israel where Jewish men abounded and weren't quite as picky as they seemed to be in the U.S.

Inhale, exhale. For the past few days her mind had been swimming. She had always perceived herself as caught in limbo. She was a Jewish American Princess in heat, a cultural mutant trapped in the Twilight Zone between her soft-porn imagination and the synagogue. And Juanita's pronouncement didn't bring her any newfound serenity. On the contrary, it only confused her more. She tried but could not conjure any picture of what the future might hold for her. Leaning back in a lawn chair on her balcony she watched the sunset and the glow of her cigarette as she thought of her new responsibilities. Gigi Bernstein, mother of the Daughter of God. She hoped she would handle this better than she had handled the first thirty-five years of her life. Her biggest stumbling block, other than her own numerous personal inadequacies, would be finding a suitable father. How could she find a father for this Baby when she had trouble nailing down dates for Friday night?

Creativity would be essential. She had noticed a newspaper for Houston singles that had a personal classified section. Maybe she could advertise:

Attractive SWF seeks sensitive SWM
to be father of Messiah. Send photo.
Write to Gigi B., P.O. Box 1234

It would work except she knew she could never fall in love with a man who shopped for his dates the way he shopped for used cars. Elizabeth deserved better than that. Juanita suggested meeting men through work. The idea sounded feasible enough, but Gigi only seemed to meet men who were in the process of divorces, and they were usually neurotic, emotionally battered and fearful of women. Gigi contemplated giving the Houston singles-bar activity a try, but, then again, she wouldn't want that kind of scene described if someone ever wrote The Bible II:

"And lo, there appeared near the east bar a man draped in polyester of many colors and his clothing undone so that his chest hair floweth.

And he spake to the Mother of God, 'You come here often?'

Elizabeth definitely deserved better than that. Juanita's advice to Gigi was for her to learn to love herself. Love herself? Gigi took a contemplative drag off her cigarette, squinted her eyes and tried to imagine what it might feel like to love Gigi Bernstein, to love big hips and bushy hair, the way she floundered at parties, the way her high heels always got stuck in sidewalk grates. The way men left her. Sorry, Juanita, but feeding the multitudes with a bagel and one ounce of cream cheese would be a snap in comparison.

The sunset nestled behind Benny's Barbecue Palace, and the evening sky grew streaks of pink and purple. Gigi watched with envy as couples slid into cars and headed for whatever delights they had planned for the evening. More questions came to mind. Assuming on the outside chance that she did find a decent man to uphold his side of the arrangement, what would this Child be like? Would she receive Gigi's genealogical makeup? Would she be prone to the usual female hangups, considering her destiny? Would she crave sweets, date creeps, tend toward flabby thighs, acne and yeast infections? Would she worry about vaginal odor, would she douche, would she listen to rock music or cry at sad movies? Gigi made a note to ask Juanita about this, although Juanita always gave such vague, quippy answers.

But then, all of this questioning was premature, considering the Baby was not yet even a gleam in someone's eye.

"I'll do my best for you, little Elizabeth. I'll find you a daddy if I have to personally search every square inch of Houston's Greater Metropolitan Area."

And she was afraid she might have to do just that.

Juanita stood on the roof of the AstroDome and watched the sun's blaze edge its way behind the Houston skyline. Her dress flapped gently in the breeze. She looked down at the streets below, at the bustling traffic, the people scurrying to their destinations. She saw a world on the brink of transformation. The scene made her smile.

The coin had been tossed. It was kickoff time.

CHAPTER SIX

At seven a.m. Gigi's Toyota crept down the
concrete decline deep into the fluorescent bowels
of the Milam Building parking garage. Any driver
behind her would have noticed the array of
bumper stickers plastered on the rear of her car—
'Save The Whales', 'I Brake For Animals', 'No
Nukes.' But no one was there this early. The
garage was empty, a series of vacant stalls bearing
the stenciled names of executives who had clawed
their way into Houston's business aristocracy.

Gigi veered into a stall marked Bernstein. She
preferred to arrive at work early while the downtown traffic was less hectic and the city seemed
more tranquil. At seven-ten a.m. the one-hun-
dred-and-fifty-person legal corporation of
Bausch, Bausch and Kozinsky would not have
reached the frenzy it would attain by nine-thirty.
Gigi relished entering the empty offices, getting
that first cup of coffee, sitting back in her swivel

chair and taking a look at the *Post* to see who shot whom, which conglomerate swallowed which company, which socialite wore which dress to which marvelous extravaganza at whose fabulous home. She would then get a head start on her paperwork, look through the trade journals and outline her day's tasks. By eight-thirty the calm would be shattered, the secretaries and attorneys having filtered in, filling the expansive office with the staccato of typewriters typing and phones buzzing.

Gigi stood stiffly, briefcase in hand, as she ascended the escalator to the plaza-floor elevators that would whisk her to the well-appointed offices of B, B and K. The firm was successful due to its large corporate clients, all addicted to an endless cycle of business maneuvers that required constant legal nurturing. It was the firm's strong base in corporate law that first attracted Gigi, but since her employment there she had not exactly skyrocketed up the firm's corporate ladder. During the first few months of her employment, Bausch had frequently handed her his typing, which she would meekly accept and later sneak onto a secretary's desk. Naturally there were other women attorneys in the firm, but Gigi couldn't match their aura of professionalism and confidence. It wasn't until her fourth month on the job that a sympathetic bookkeeper explained to Bausch that Gigi was an attorney and not clerical help. Since then, after two night courses in assertiveness training and a seminar on dressing for success, she had been handed only the personal cases that inevitably cropped up for the firm's high-powered clients—the dog bites, the drunken squabbles, the speeding tickets, and of course, the divorces. Lots of divorces. Gigi spent the bulk of her time assisting Houston's most prominent executives slip in and out of their nuptial vows as easily as they did their Polo underwear. It was a job she had grown to detest. She had begged several of the junior partners for more challenging assignments and had even shown the audacity to ask Mr. Bausch himself to give her a chance at some corporate litigation, but nothing ever materialized. Too good at divorces, she had damned herself by her own efficiency.

Gigi stepped into a dimly lighted elevator. A man waited inside wearing a stiff business suit, holding an attache and a *Wall Street Journal* that lay nestled under his arm. He smiled blandly as she stepped in, then quickly returned his gaze to the lighted numbers above the elevator doors. Gigi leaned against the back of the elevator only inches from her fellow passenger. She furtively stared at him. He was handsome in the exotic, irresistible way only strangers could be handsome. He had dark hair, dark eyes, a thin even nose and, still squeaky clean from his morning shower, smelled deliciously of soap and cologne. The aroma of his aftershave filled Gigi's nostrils, and she felt a welcome, familiar warmth wash over her. Gigi had often trodden the murky waters of her psyche to understand the fascination men held for her. Did she watch too many beach party movies as a kid, play with so many plastic role models manufactured by Mattel that she emerged into adulthood only half of a potential couple—an Annette looking for a Frankie, a Barbie hungering for a Ken, a Harriet frantic for an Ozzie? There was one side of her that longed for independence, to be an aloof and self-reliant woman, but a desperation always lurked within her leaving her yearning and lusting and quivering in the knees. Men were like the toys in shop windows she had coveted as a child—shiny and colorful, laden with promise, unreal and untouchable, but if you were very, very good and truly wished hard enough. . . .

Gigi craftily dropped her purse, a lecherous smile crossing her lips. Bending to retrieve it she seized the opportunity to let her eyes roam the seductive terrain of the stranger's body, and she examined his hands, his torso, his thighs. Her lips parted as she tried to imagine him without his clothes. Yes, Mrs. Bernstein, your daughter mentally undresses men in elevators. Your daughter-the-lawyer's mind brims with images of bare bodies, sweating torsos that glisten in the mind's light, glimmer like a mirage in the heat of her soft-porn imagination. It's all in her head, Mrs. Bernstein. Why, it's a damn male locker room up there. Perhaps, Mrs. Bernstein, you should have breast-fed instead of sticking in her mouth all those phallic-shaped baby bottles filled with creamy white formula. Even using the term "formula" for the stuff implied that it held the magic answer to some problem.

Gigi closed her eyes and fantasized about the

possibilities of a man and a woman alone in a dimly lighted elevator. Gigi possessed an extensive repertoire of fantasies, but the classic elevator fornication was a favorite. In the fantasy she imagines the Muzak playing a Gershwin tune as she casually thinks about the weather, the stock market, office trivia, oblivious to the animal passion mounting in the stranger beside her. Her gaze falls innocently upon the stranger, and an obvious bulge in the man's trousers embarrasses and excites her. Unexpectedly the man turns toward her. He presses her body to the wall. She tries to protest, but he forces his mouth against hers, and her attempts to free herself are lost in the velvety heat of his breath. He deftly opens the front of her Evan Picone suit. He whimpers with yearning, for at that moment he must possess her so completely. Then his hand slides up her skirt, and she is transported somewhere between the Houston freeway and the planet Venus. His lips brush against her neck as their bodies fuse together and their soft moaning blends with Gershwin and the gentle noise of the elevator gliding up and up, never stopping.

Something flashed through Gigi's fantasy, slicing through the erotic fog like a headlight. She opened her eyes. For shame, Gigi Bernstein. Was this any way for the potential mother of the Daughter of God to be thinking, she asked herself? Shouldn't she be striving for spiritual and intellectual goals higher than that of *Playgirl* magazine? Gigi straightened her posture, wiped the lecherous expression from her face like chocolate off the face of a guilty child. Her psyche was a garbage dump, she chided herself, a refuse center for abandoned dirty thoughts, and it needed clearing out if she intended to tackle the mission Juanita had planned for her.

"Excuse me."

The doors parted on the nineteenth floor and the object of Gigi's desire exited the elevator. The doors closed and opened once more on the twenty-third floor, and Gigi stepped out and passed through the oaken portals of Bausch, Bausch and Kozinsky. She walked briskly to her office, tossed her briefcase on her desk, negotiated with the office coffee machine, then settled in her chair.

She tried to page through the latest copy of *American Trial Lawyer* but she couldn't get her mind off the Baby. The previous day in the grocery store the title of a magazine article flashed at her from the glossy cover. "Can It Work To Be A Working Mother?" the periodical quizzed as if directed specifically at her. Yet another potential catastrophe, she worried. Since marriage was not an essential piece to this puzzle, she couldn't count on a husband to pay the bills while she raised her Baby, and, unless the kid could multiply loaves and fishes, Gigi would have to work. Gigi bought the magazine and greedily consumed the article that described the various neuroses a child can develop from lack of maternal influence during those all-important formative years. Of course, this Baby would be immune to all that. Or would she? Gigi sat at her desk and conjured up a disturbing scenario:

"All right, young lady, you put on some decent clothes right this minute and go speak to the multitudes. All those people out there waiting to be saved, and all you can do is sit around and mope."

The Daughter of God bites into her chocolate Ding Dong, stubs out her marijuana cigarette, and looks at her earthly mother with contempt.

"I can't go. I'm watching *Dallas* reruns."

"But, sweetheart, you're the Messiah. You have responsibilities."

"Responsibilities? What about yours? You're never home. You're always working. What kind of nurturing and quality interpersonal guidance have you given me that fostered my self-development? Besides, I can't go out there. I think I'm getting a pimple."

Gigi sat in her chair, gripped by this nightmare until she heard a knock at the door.

"Good morning, Gigi."

Gigi looked up and saw Waldo Bernelli's abbreviated body in her doorway. Waldo, a twenty-eight-year-old Harvard-law-grad-junior-partner-rising-star, arrived at the office even earlier than Gigi to get a headstart on the day's toil.

"Hi, Waldo."

"Can I talk to you a minute?"

"Delores?"

"Among other things." Waldo sat on the edge of Gigi's desk. She put down her magazine and prepared to hear the next installment of Waldo's romantic saga. Despite his youth, Waldo Bernelli

74

was the brightest, most capable attorney in the firm. What he lacked in experience he made up for with confidence, natural ability and an unerring knowledge of the law. But when it came to Delores, Waldo was an indecisive, quivering helpless mass of human protoplasm. Since he had joined the firm two years earlier, he had confided in Gigi about his quarrels with his girlfriend. Gigi was never sure why he chose her as his confidant. She assumed he considered her a mother figure, someone who had been around the block a few times and could provide him with sage advice and counsel. At first she resented it. In fact, she had resented Waldo in general, for he had been with the firm such a short time and already worked on most of the firm's important cases while she remained stuck in her lackluster legal chores. But he came around to see her so often that gradually he grew on her. After a while she actually liked Waldo and became amused by his love troubles.

"We're fighting again. She wants money from me to go to some astrology seminar in Phoenix, and I told her that if she would just get a job, any job, she could pay for the seminar herself. How can you have a career in astrology?" Waldo tugged unhappily at his striped tie. Usually cool and collected, he became nervous when he discussed Delores. He looked slightly sweaty, like he had just jogged around the block.

"I thought she was making some money doing freelance charts."

"She was, but she never made very much and lately her handful of clients have been trickling off. Seems they didn't like the futures she was charting or something."

"Tell her you're going to stop supporting her."

"I did, but she said that Saturn was in retrograde and she couldn't handle stress right now. Anyway, she promised that as soon as the planets realign she'll start looking through the classifieds."

Gigi tried to suppress a snicker, but she couldn't.

"It's not funny, Gigi. It's really not her fault. She just hasn't found her career niche yet." Waldo smiled and started to chuckle along with Gigi. "You see, this is why I like to talk to you. The whole thing doesn't seem so serious when you're laughing about it.

"I'm sorry, Waldo. I didn't mean to laugh."

"It's okay. Besides, Delores isn't the real reason I stopped by. I have something else to discuss with you."

Waldo stood up, steadied his hands on the edge of Gigi's cluttered desk and leaned forward until their faces nearly touched. His facial expression has changed from despondency to that of cool calculation. "How would you, Gigi Bernstein, like to handle a nasty little piece of litigation over who has controlling interest in Naylor International, hmmm?" Waldo asked with the grin of a Cheshire cat.

Gigi studied him closely, eyed him suspiciously, watched him intensely for the nervous twitch or slight flickering of the iris that might indicate he was toying with her. There was something in his manner that didn't bode well.

"The Naylor International that produces oil-rig equipment? That Naylor International?" Gigi asked.

"That very one," he said. "I talked to Bausch about the case just yesterday and told him how insightful and aggressive you could be in this particular situation. He agreed and—"

"Hold it, Waldo. What do you mean by 'this particular situation'?" she questioned, her eyes suddenly narrowed into deep slits of suspicion. "What's wrong with it?"

"It involves a child."

"How?"

Waldo sat down in the green leatherette chair opposite Gigi's desk. "It's like this. The client is twelve years old. She's William Naylor's only child. Naylor died three weeks ago intestate with no binding agreement with the other company partners as to who would get what if Naylor died. Seems Naylor was slightly eccentric, especially when it came to legal documents, and he just never got around to signing certain papers. No one ever caught on. So his shares go to the kid, only the other partners don't see it that way. Our job is to defend Marcie Naylor's interest in the company, give proxy to the other partners or to her guardian but protect her right to ownership. It's going to be tricky because we've been representing Naylor International for several years, so we're walking a fine line. But you and I could handle it. You'll have to rely on my experience for the corporate side of this, but it could catapult you right out of divorce court and into the dizzying world of corporate law, Bernstein. No need to thank me, of course." Waldo leaned back in his chair and awaited a torrent of gratitude that didn't arrive.

"I know we're friends, Waldo, but you've never thrown me any bones before. Why are you pulling me in on this case? There must be a down side."

"The down side is that it's messy. The child's mother is dead, and relatives are haggling over who gets guardianship over the child and all that money. We also have to handle that part. The case involves personal litigation tangled up with corporate litigation, a sort of Gloria Vanderbilt type hassle. Bausch knows you're good with personal cases, and he also wants a female on this one. The judge is none other than the honorable Patricia Spencer, i.e., outspoken champion of female underdogs. Bausch thinks we have a better chance of cooperation if we have a female attorney on the case. Naturally, I strongly recommended you. So what do you think, Bernstein? Interested? You ought to be."

"So I'm the token female?"

"Yes, it's corny, but so what? Take your opportunities wherever you can get them. No offense, but you're not currently in a position to pick and choose your cases. You know you're good, and I know you're good. This will give Bausch the chance to know you're good. Do well on this one and you'll get others like it. Hopefully they won't be quite like this one, but they could be good solid corporate cases. Think of it, Bernstein—no more squabbles over child support, no more hassles over who hid what assets from whom. You could hit the old proverbial big time, with really huge companies with wonderfully huge problems. Sound attractive?"

Attractive Gigi thought. It sounded like the break she had prayed for. It could be the beginning of the career she always wanted, battling in the courtroom over millions of dollars instead of who got the Mercedes and the charge cards. It could mean more money, more prestige, perhaps eventually a partnership in the firm. Yes, things were beginning to fall in place. Could Juanita have had a hand in this? Maybe Juanita wanted her to be more satisfied with her work, or maybe she thought it would be good for Gigi to be around a child for a while, a sort of test drive to get the feel of it. Yes, Waldo, it was attractive. In fact it was stupendous, fantastic. Still, she had to play it cool.

"I might be interested. When could I meet with the client?" she asked in a carefully modulated voice. Waldo grinned.

"How about right now?" he said, then dashed out the door. Gigi had no time to ask questions. He was gone one minute, then returned accompanied by something blonde, dirty and four foot ten with a cigarette dangling from one lip, headphones embracing her ears and wearing a T-shirt bearing the stenciled image of Sting.

"This is Marcie Naylor," Waldo introduced cheerily. The girl looked at him with a sneer and took a drag off her cigarette.

Gigi winced. She could now guess why no one else in the office wanted the client. She grappled for something to say.

"Hello, Marcie," Gigi said in her best schoolmarm voice. Marcie did not respond, but instead remained absorbed in whatever rhythm undulated against her eardrum. Waldo removed Marcie's headphones.

"Ms. Bernstein said hello," Waldo chirped like a Boy Scout. Marcie responded by blowing smoke in his face. He faked a smile.

Gigi checked her watch. "Waldo, it's not even eight-thirty yet. What is she doing here this early?"

"Well, she's had a few problems lately," Waldo said.

"I never laid a hand on that wimp kid," said Marcie.

"Right you are, Marcie. That iguana could have gotten down his shorts any number of ways. Always remember, innocent until proven guilty." He turned to Gigi. "The school administration suggested that she have the benefit of constant supervision."

"What about her guardian?"

"It's her tennis day. Well, I'll leave you two alone, give you a chance to get to know each other. I've got a meeting," he said, and headed for the door after dumping a stack of manila folders on Gigi's desk.

"Waldo, don't leave . . ." Gigi said desperately.

"It's going to be a great case, Gi. Think of the recognition," he whispered.

80

Waldo disappeared. Marcie collapsed into the leatherette chair and sprawled one leg defiantly over the chair's arm. She looked at Gigi through steely blue eyes that showed an expression of boredom mingled with disgust.

"You don't act like you want to be here." Gigi said the obvious after an awkward silence. Marcie pulled a wad of bills from her blue jeans and held them in Gigi's face.

"Here's fifty bucks for you if you let me out of this puke hole."

Gigi shuffled some papers in an authoritative manner. Best defense is a good offense.

"You can put your money away. My job, Marcie, is to protect your financial interests in your father's company. More importantly, my job is to protect your interests in seeing that you are given a good, loving home. I need your help in accomplishing both of these." God, she sounded so stuffy, even to herself. Marcie dropped ashes on the carpet. Gigi considered for a moment what she would do to Waldo when she got hold of him. This was no ordinary twelve-year-old.

"And please put out that cigarette."

Marcie put her cigarette out on the edge of Gigi's desk.

"I can certainly see why your relatives are fighting over you," said Gigi.

"Yeah, because I'm so cute," Marcie replied.

Never one for improvisation under pressure, Gigi needed a few minutes to gather her thoughts, to strategize on how to handle the situation. She decided to try the old coffee-break routine.

"I'm going to grab a cup of coffee. Can I get you anything?" Gigi asked as she stood up. Marcie shook her head violently left and right, her straggly hair slapping her face like indignant blond whips. Gigi raced to the coffee machine, poured the dark liquid into her favorite "I Love Sea Otters" mug and guiltily added cream and three cubes of sugar. Children had never been her forte. They made her feel uncomfortable, like she was in disguise, like she was really a child only fooling people into thinking she was an adult. She feared that children recognized it immediately and would tell on her and blow her fragile cover. Perspiration had saturated the armpits of her blouse. The Naylor case could be a great opportunity, she reminded herself, well worth a few headaches, a few perspiration stains, a few insults from a child. She was, after all, an intelligent, well-educated woman who could certainly deal with a twelve-year-old. She just had to approach it right. She needed a Deborah Kerr type demeanor to deal with this kid. Yes, definitely Deborah Kerr. Calm, firm but sensitive. Gigi collected herself, grabbed her mug and walked calmly, firmly, sensitively back to her office. When she arrived, she noticed the door was closed. She grabbed the knob and turned it. It refused to move. Funny, she never realized it locked from the inside. She jiggled it, lightly at first, then with increasingly panicked vigor.

"Marcie?" she said, hoping no one else in the office would see her standing in the hall locked out of her own office.

"Screw off," the voice answered from within. Gigi's breathing quickened, her lips twisted with the mounting tension.

"Uh, Marcie, you've locked yourself in my office. I can't get in," Gigi said in as Deborah Kerr a tone as possible.

"Gee, did you go to Harvard to get that smart?" spat Marcie. What a brat, Gigi thought, as she gulped her coffee, wishing it were gin. Children probably responded to firmness. Dogs did. Okay, no more Mr. Nice Guy. "Marcie, why don't you let me in. Now. Fun's over."

"I'm not letting you in ever."

"Why not?" she asked feebly.

"Because I hate you. I hate all of you."

Gigi feared that the strain of this situation would soon start showing. She wondered if she should try begging. "Look, if you hate all of us, why did you lock yourself in? Why didn't you just leave?" Gigi asked, wincing as she heard Marcie rummaging through her desk drawers.

"Yeah, I know that was dumb, but, hey, I'm only twelve. I guess I could jump out the window. Will they fire you if they find me splat on the sidewalk? I'm your responsibility, you know. I'm a minor."

Gigi panicked for a second, then realized that the windows in modern office buildings didn't open. After taking a fortifying breath, she reasoned that she would calmly wait Marcie out, perhaps chat with her quietly through the door until she talked Marcie into unlocking it. She heard her phone ring. She heard Marcie pick up the receiver.

"She's out. She's screwing the janitor," Marcie told the caller, then slammed down the phone.

"Open this door!" Gigi whispered angrily through gritted teeth as she rattled the door violently, her image of Deborah Kerr evolving rapidly into that of Elsa Lanchester in *The Bride of Frankenstein*.

"What's going on here?"

Gigi spun around. With relief she saw Waldo. Gigi grabbed him by the arm to drag him into her turmoil.

"The little delinquent has locked herself in my office, is ransacking my drawers and speaking obscenities to my incoming phone calls," she told Waldo in a menacing voice. "This is your fault."

Jean Grover, a tall, big-boned woman who had been with the firm longer than Gigi, heard their conversation as she passed through the hallway. She stopped.

"There's a master key to all the doors," she said. "Barbara has it. Shall I get it?"

Gigi nodded. Jean came back quickly.

"Bad news. The key is in Bausch's new secretary's desk and she's out ill and we can't find her desk key. I suggest we call security. They could break the door down." Jean studied the doorknob and her smile turned fiendish. "The guards downstairs carry guns. They could shoot the lock open."

"That would scare the kid to death," Gigi said.

"Thanks, Jean, but I think a more diplomatic approach will be quite effective," Waldo said.

84

Jean shrugged and left.

Waldo placed his hand paternally on Gigi's shoulder. "Strength under pressure, Gigi," said Waldo as he gently turned the doorknob to prove to himself it was indeed locked.

"Marcie?" Waldo said quietly.

"Go fuck yourself. I can buy and sell you guys. My aunt told me so."

"This is Waldo," he added, as if that fact alone should make things better.

"Go double-fuck yourself."

Gigi smirked. Waldo still appeared calm and confident.

"Marcie, I see that you're locked in Gigi's office, and I want you to know that's okay. You can stay there as long as you like."

Gigi shot him a threatening look.

"But, Marcie, can you tell me why you've locked yourself in there?"

Silence.

"It doesn't have to be a good reason. It can be a bad reason, a silly reason, any reason." Still silence. "Is it that you're afraid of something?"

"I'm not afraid of nothing."

"Yes, you are. We're all afraid of something. You don't have to come out to tell me. I can hear you through the door."

There was an increasingly ominous silence coming from the office. Thoughts of shoving a tear-gas canister through the air conditioning vent ran through Gigi's mind.

Then they heard sniffles—juicy, fretful little inhalations of adolescent suffering that filtered through the door and into some clandestine memory cell that reminded them both for a moment what it had been like to be twelve.

"I don't want to be all alone," Marcie said in a half cry, half whisper. Gigi's face softened.

"But you're not alone. You have relatives that want you to live with them. You have friends at school," Waldo reassured her.

"My relatives are assholes. They only want Daddy's money. That's all anybody wants, including my friends. I had to pay kids ten dollars apiece to get them to come to my birthday party last year." Sniffles turned to sobs.

Gigi's gut was wrenched by that one. Insecurity was something she could understand. Waldo looked perplexed a moment, then spoke.

"I believe there is a solution to every problem. It may not be apparent at first. Things, in fact, may look really bleak, but there is always some answer somewhere."

More sniffles were heard. Waldo's credibility took a nose dive with that one, Gigi thought. Who did he think he was, Winnie The Pooh? This kid was truly depressed and with good reason. Gigi related to her. Insecurity and anxiety felt the same at twelve as they felt at thirty-five. Gigi tried harder to think of something, anything, that would make Marcie feel better, at least for the moment. She tried to think of what would make herself feel consoled if she were sad. The only thing she could think of was eating.

"Marcie, you want to go with me to eat some ice cream?" Gigi asked.

"No." The kid was stronger than she thought.

"Is there anything that will make you feel better?" Gigi tried, grasping at straws. A few more moments of silence.

"Can I press my face against the copy machine and xerox my face?"

Waldo and Gigi looked at each other.

"Sure," Gigi replied, relieved. The door opened slowly and revealed Marcie's tear-streaked face. Everyone had their weakness, Gigi thought. She took Marcie's hand, led her to the copying room and offered to turn on the enlarger, just to sweeten the deal.

CHAPTER SEVEN

It required several expensive legal minds forty-six minutes of deliberation to conclude that Marcie Naylor's emotional security as well as the dignity of Bausch, Bausch and Kozinsky might be best upheld if meetings between Marcie and her attorneys were held outside the formality of the B.B. & K. law offices. Gigi could have told them that immediately after Marcie flushed the Branson briefs down the toilet, but the formidable Mr. Bausch liked to feel decisions were his idea, to sort things out methodically. His mode of operation was to remove his Brooks Brothers jacket (to impress the New York City types), loosen his Gucci tie (to show the big-money boys he had some class) and prop his cowboy boots on the table (to let the oil-rich ranchers know he was still just a good ol' boy) and "sift through the shit," meaning the documents, evidence and personalities that comprised any legal kluge. During this initial briefing with Gigi and Waldo, Bausch insisted that every file, scrap of paper or fact regarding the Naylor case be placed on the table before him. These included juicy tidbits, like Marcie Naylor being the first sixth-grader to be suspended from McArthur Elementary for "mooning" a teacher, and that she had a thirteen-year-old boyfriend who had been arrested for various juvenile crimes. Marcie had rarely seen her father when he was alive and had been raised the past few years by a succession of illegal-alien housekeepers and gardeners, a situation that resulted in Marcie picking up some colorful Spanish phrases suitable for a Laredo locker room. Marcie had also seen a child psychiatrist for several months after she stole her father's Cadillac, perching herself on top of the Houston Yellow Pages (so she could see over the steering wheel) and driving halfway to La Grange before the highway patrol caught up with her.

There were three people requesting custody of Marcie—her aunt Angela Maynard who had temporary custody, her uncle Peter "Bubba" Naylor and a deceased uncle's widow, Loreen Naylor. Neither of the three had even spent any time with Marcie, at least not until Naylor's death and Marcie's subsequent inheritance. It was more than a mere coincidence that each of the three simultaneously developed strong nurturing instincts and an unyielding love for their rich little niece.

Bausch instructed Waldo to concentrate on the future of the Naylor International shares and Gigi was to concentrate on checking the backgrounds and suitability of the three relatives. Gigi would then make a recommendation to Judge Spencer on which relative should be Marcie's permanent guardian. The other three partners in Naylor International were vitally concerned over who became Marcie's guardian since that person could also be guardian of her financial interests. Gigi could barely suppress her disdain at receiving the non-corporate side of the workload, but Waldo assured her that the Naylor case was a necessary first step in her legal career. She had already received greater visibility with Bausch than ever before, she had to admit. With Waldo's assistance, her career was looking up. She decided to trust him since she had no other alternative.

Bausch instructed Gigi to befriend Marcie and spend some time with her outside the office. She accepted willingly for a couple of reasons. Marcie's positive feelings about the firm could possibly affect future choices for legal counsel. Fluctuating oil prices had generated an economic slump that made corporate legal battles slimmer pickings than they had been in previous times, and although Marcie was a brat, she was a very wealthy brat with a load of lucrative legal problems. Gigi considered babysitting demeaning, but she wanted to look good in front of Bausch, and she rationalized that it would be good pre-maternal training to spend time with a child. Besides, she liked Marcie. Twelve-year-olds weren't very complicated, and once Gigi got past Marcie's crusty exterior she found her bright, funny and an educational test of Gigi's patience.

She took her work with Marcie seriously, for she knew her recommendation could strongly affect Judge Spencer's final decision on Marcie's guardianship. She was determined that her recommendation be the right one, although none of the three relatives seemed like good parent material. Gigi felt sorry for Marcie, left at the mercy of attorneys, judges and relatives who cared more for her money than they did for her. The situation didn't help Marcie's personality, which already had a noticeably hostile edge.

It occurred to Gigi that Marcie needed to experience a family environment so she could see how a regular family behaved and, as a result, better express her own desires about which relative she wanted to live with. Marcie had never known a normal home life, and what better place for her to experience a warm familial glow than at the home of Wanda and Cecil Bernstein?

"Do you mind going to my mom and dad's today?" Gigi asked when she picked up Marcie at her aunt's house on a Saturday two weeks after their initial meeting. "It won't be for very long. After that we can go play video games."

Marcie pushed her sunglasses down her nose and eyed Gigi. Up until then Gigi had taken her only to boring museums, PG movies and fancy restaurants. The video-game idea sounded moderately entertaining. Marcie nodded in agreement, switched the radio to full blast, and Gigi headed for West University, an older neighborhood where her parents lived.

"So, Marcie," Mrs. Bernstein chirped maternally after the usual introductions. They were sitting at the kitchen table. "How is school?"

"It sucks," Marcie answered. Mrs. Bernstein smiled and nodded to show Marcie how hip she was. Gigi jumped in the conversation.

"Marcie is having a few problems with English, but I'm going to work with her and see if we can get her grades up."

"Oh, how nice. You know, Gigi was very good in English when she was going to school. That's one of the reasons she's a lawyer today," said Mrs. Bernstein, beaming with pride.

"English sucks," spat Marcie. Mrs. Bernstein's smile turned to ever so slight a grimace. She held up her reading glasses from their pearl neckchain so she could observe this creature more carefully. She offered to make lemonade, a sure cure for a surly child.

"Cecil!" Mrs. Bernstein yelled at the top of her lungs, even though Mr. Bernstein was only in the next room watching the Astros lose to the Reds. "Do you wanna cold drink?" Cecil made a grunting sound that his wife of thirty-six years interpreted as "Yes, darling, that would be lovely."

"Don't you think Gigi would be sexier if she dropped some poundage?" Marcie asked as she and Gigi watched Mrs. Bernstein cha cha about the kitchen.

"No, no, no. So why should she lose weight?

My Gigi looks wonderful already."

"But her tush is too big. To be sexy you have to have a tiny tush," Marcie said. Gigi cringed. She didn't like her tush being a topic of conversation.

"My daughter's tush is perfect. When she was a baby her tush was so soft I used to grab it and squeeze it, it felt so good," said Mrs. Bernstein. She held out her hands, palms up, and kneaded the air with her fingers, for a moment enraptured with the memory. She looked quite blissful. Marcie sat more firmly in her chair, afraid that Mrs. Bernstein might be overwhelmed by the urge to perform more child tush kneading.

"So, Gigi, we haven't talked since your birthday. What's new in your life?" Mrs. Bernstein asked, once more engaged in reality and pouring the lemonade into tumblers.

So what's new in my life, Mom? Not much. Harold left, I tried to kill myself and oh, by the way, Mom, I'm going to be the mother of the Daughter of God. Other than that, same old grind.

"Not much. Other than the fact that I've got a new friend here." Gigi gave Marcie a smile. Marcie tried hard not to smile back, but Gigi knew Marcie liked her.

"And how's Harold?" Mrs. Bernstein asked in an innocent voice. She cast a penetrating look at her daughter, and Gigi tensed for the onslaught.

"Harold and I broke up."

Mrs. Bernstein handed Gigi and Marcie tall glasses of lemonade.

"You'll get back together."

"No, we won't."

"So you've had fights before. Not to worry."

"He's marrying someone else."

Mrs. Bernstein clutched her throat, gasped for air and grabbed the back of a chair to steady herself.

"Cecil!" she gasped. "My asthma! Get me my asthma medicine!" Marcie jumped up quickly and raced to Mrs. Bernstein's side. Gigi remained quietly seated. She had witnessed this scene many times before.

After a few moments, Mr. Bernstein lumbered in with the sports section of the *Chronicle* folded under his arm, looking peeved at the interruption.

"The Astros are behind by two. It's the top of the eighth," he grumbled. His wife recovered just long enough to shoot him a nasty look, then resumed her asthma attack.

"My asthma medicine. I need my medicine," she wheezed.

"So when have you ever had asthma? You've never had asthma. You don't know how to spell asthma," he muttered, heading for the kitchen cabinet. He opened the cabinet door, reached for a high shelf and pulled down a Nyquil bottle filled with apricot brandy. He poured a shot into a coffee mug, handed it to his still-wheezing wife, then shuffled out. Mrs. Bernstein tossed it down with a single swallow, then took a few breaths to compose herself.

"Marcie dear, why don't you go watch TV with

Mr. Bernstein?" she requested sweetly. Marcie shrugged and left the room, figuring she could hear it all from the den anyway. When Marcie was gone, Mrs. Bernstein sternly faced her daughter.

"What happened?"

You mean how did I blow it, Gigi thought.

"We just parted ways, that's all. We were never right for each other," she explained, knowing explanations were useless.

Her mother leaned her head close to Gigi's and dropped her voice to a whisper. "Did you wear the birthday present I gave you?"

"No, Mother, I did not wear the birthday present. He just met someone else, someone thinner, younger and blonder. He's gone. Finito. There are, after all, other men in this world."

Wanda Bernstein collapsed into a chair and sighed with remorse and dashed hopes. Gigi felt sorry for her. Her mother still thought being married was the only thing that ultimately mattered. But Gigi knew there was other potential on the horizon and decided perhaps her mother should know also.

"Mom, I've got something to tell you," Gigi said, moving to the chair across from her mother. "Something wonderful."

Mrs. Bernstein looked up. To her the term "something wonderful" meant a dermatologist in River Oaks with a last name ending in b-e-r-g. In her watery, far-sighted eyes hope sprang eternal.

"Mom, I've had a vision."

Hope took a giant leap backward.

95

"Hmmm?" Mrs. Bernstein responded cautiously. Gigi interpreted the "hmmm?" as maternal support. After all, mothers always believe their daughters.

"Mom, I was visited by an angel," Gigi said in an excited whisper.

Mothers do not always believe their daughters, Gigi realized as her mother grabbed her wrist and began taking her pulse.

"And what did the nice angel say to you, baby?" asked her mother as she checked Gigi's heartbeat against her new digital watch, then examined her pupils for dilation.

"Not much," Gigi replied. She sensed she had made a tactical error.

"Look, baby," Mrs. Bernstein cooed, and patted Gigi's hand. Gigi remembered that her mother had called her "baby" a lot when she had her tonsils out at ten.

"You've been under a strain. So Harold's gone. Pffft," her mother said, as if one "pffft" and a wave of her hand could eliminate her daughter's problems. "There are, after all, lots of fish in the sea."

Gigi nodded like a good girl. At this point it was best to remain silent.

"And why don't you see that nice Dr. Goldman for a checkup?" More nods of tacit agreement. Having a thirty-five-year-old daughter who was unmarried was bad, but having a thirty-five-year-old daughter with only one oar in the water was infinitely worse.

Gigi felt enough chitchat had been exchanged

for one afternoon, so she excused Marcie and herself so they could go to the arcade. As she passed through the den Gigi kissed her father's head as he sat glued to a baseball game with Marcie by his side counting out five one-dollar bills. She had bet on the Reds.

"How are the Astros doing?" Gigi asked.

"They suck," Mr. Bernstein replied.

CHAPTER EIGHT

Neiman's Butterfly Tea Room was packed for lunch as usual with a long line of overdressed hopefuls waiting for tables. Gigi, Sydney and Lulu breezed past the crowd and grabbed a primo center table since, naturally, Lulu had connections.

The crowd bubbled and thickened around them as Lulu and Sydney immersed themselves in the usual conversations. A continued discussion about Lulu's sexual preferences and gory details about Sydney's latest nuptial erotica ricocheted about the table, but Gigi sat oblivious to the conversation, sipping a glass of white wine and staring off into space. Her mind was elsewhere. She hadn't heard from Juanita in weeks, not since their conversation in the beauty salon. Maybe Juanita had decided to use someone else for the job, but wouldn't Gigi have received some sort of notification, a rejection letter or something? If that were the case, would she be disappointed or relieved? Would she be distressed over the loss of that sense of uniqueness or delighted to shed the responsibility? She had such a mesh of feelings about it. To be singled out for such a contribution to the world was thrilling, but to lose control over one's life was frightening. To be a part, even peripherally, of such an important event was remarkable, so remarkable that she still hadn't quite tossed out the idea of it being some sort of pathological hallucination that would ultimately end with her macrameing in a state institution.

"Gigi, you haven't said one word. Where is your mind today?" Sydney demanded with a sugary southern accent. Gigi responded with a half-hearted smile.

"Where was I?" Sydney continued her story when she was certain Gigi and Lulu were both listening. "Oh, yes. Arthur kept begging me to let him come in my mouth, and well, I just hate it, it's so vulgar. So finally, after thirty minutes of whining, I let him do it. But I held it in my mouth, so afterwards, I leaned over like I was going to kiss him and I spit it back into his mouth and said, 'How do you like it?' "

Lulu shrieked with laughter. Gigi looked disgusted, sharing the feelings of several people sitting at nearby tables. The waitress arrived.

"Are you ready to order?" she asked distractedly, not bothering to hide her boredom. Gigi perused the potential lunch items on the menu. She was feeling a little depressed, and she always allowed herself something fattening when she was feeling depressed. The pasta Alfredo sounded delicious. Nothing like cream sauce and parmesan cheese dripping over pasta al dente to soothe a person's suffering. It was her idea of being good to herself, and if she wasn't good to herself, who would be? She started to express her preferences to the waitress but stopped before she could utter a sound.

"Try the spinach salad," a voice buzzed inside her head, a voice that wasn't Gigi's. Her skin went cold, then hot, her eyes widened like saucers and goosebumps sprouted all over her body. Gripping the table with white-knuckled hands, she slowly, cautiously turned her head to see if someone was there. Please let there be someone there, she prayed, but there was no one. Lulu and Sydney both ordered salads. Gigi tried to be calm. Everything was okay, she told herself. She had been under a great deal of pressure lately. It could happen to anyone. She opened her mouth to form the words "pasta Alfredo" when again a voice deep within her cerebrum whispered, "Get the spinach salad."

"Are you ready to order?" the waitress demanded as Gigi sat stupefied, perspiration forming on her upper lip.

"Gigi," the voice from nowhere whispered. "It's me. Juanita. The pasta has nine hundred and sixty-six calories. Get the spinach salad."

"Are you okay, Gi? The waitress needs to know what you want for lunch," Sydney asked her friend with a concerned look.

"I'll have the spinach salad," Gigi squeaked to

the waitress, then gulped her wine and finished off Lulu's as well.

Gigi rummaged unthinkingly through a handful of bras in the lingerie department. She grabbed a few without looking at them and headed for the dressing room, the bras wriggling from her hands like pink elastic reptiles.

"Just call me if you need any help. We have some new French underwires with lots of lift," a saleslady said as Gigi closed the dressing room door safely behind her. After lunch she had run to the lingerie department. She wasn't sure why she chose lingerie, except that it was close and she knew she could find at least brief solitude in a dressing room. Help was exactly what she needed; she just didn't know from whom. She was nervous. She was very nervous. Perspiration seeped through the underarms of her suit and her hands trembled. She just barely made it through the meal. Fortunately Sydney and Lulu were too busy discussing sex acts to notice Gigi's pallor as she wolfed down her spinach. (After receiving a message from the heavens to eat it, she figured she'd better clean her plate.) Yes, she was definitely going crazy. The certainty of it felt somehow pacifying. Houston had an excellent medical center where Gigi felt sure they would find her psychosis very interesting. She could pop a thorazine into her o.j. every morning and be just fine.

"Ciao," Juanita's voice said from behind Gigi. She tensed and whirled around to find Juanita

101

sitting on a velvet chair in the corner of the dressing room.

"Aren't you glad you don't have that heavy feeling that comes from a big lunch? I told you I could help you." Juanita picked up one of the bras Gigi held and examined it closely.

"Don't you think you're being a bit optimistic with this D-cup? I don't perform miracles."

Gigi grabbed the bra with trembling hands.

"Listen, I don't know if I can put up with this. I'm an anxious type of person, and having your voice in my brain when I don't expect it, well, I'm just not sure I can handle it," Gigi whispered tearfully, her chest beginning to break out into a rosy rash.

Juanita's brow furrowed. "Okay, I've been coming on a little too sci-fi. I can tone it down. I've had this complaint before, but believe me, you'll get used to it. You'll even learn to like me." Gigi shot her a look. "Okay, maybe you won't actually like me, but we're going to have to spend some time together if we're going to pull this Messiah thing off."

Gigi opened the dressing room door a crack, bent down and looked to see if there was anybody nearby. The coast was clear. She closed the door and turned back to Juanita.

"This is costing me my sanity. I need to talk to someone about this. I tried to tell my mother, and now she thinks I'm having a nervous breakdown," Gigi said morosely, running her fingers through her hair.

"You should have predicted that, kiddo. It's a

102

difficult concept for the average person to grasp."

"But I need someone to talk to!"

"So what am I, chopped liver?"

"But you're not even a real person. How can anyone talk to you?"

Juanita looked toward the ceiling. "Do you hear the abuse I must constantly bear?"

"Why can't you be a little more angelic?" Gigi asked with a hint of nastiness. "It would make this easier. I mean, I thought angels were supposed to be sweet and quiet, you know, with halos."

"And spacemen are supposed to look like E.T., right? Believe me, we come in all types, shapes and sizes. Sure, there are some holier-than-thous sporting white robes and singing hallejuhah. But me," she said, pointing to her chest with a cocked thumb, "I'm an individual. And don't think I don't get plenty of flack for it."

Gigi sighed, and leaned weakly against the wall. There was no sense in arguing. She was out of her league.

"So what's our next step?" Gigi asked with resignation. Juanita perked up, her body at attention, her eyes glistening.

"I thought a dose of self-improvement would be next on the agenda. That's why I made that little suggestion before lunch. You could stand to lose twenty pounds. Trust me, you'll like yourself better."

Gigi flushed with annoyance. "So that's how it is. How come everything boils down to how I look? Am I too fat, too hippy, too short, wrong nose, bad—"

Juanita interrupted. "Wrong, Bernstein. How you look really has nothing to do with it. What it boils down to is how you feel about yourself, and in your case, your weight affects that. Every time you look in the mirror you hate yourself because you think you're fat. Only you have the power to change that."

"What if I decide that I don't want to lose weight, that I don't want voices bothering me at lunch, that I don't want to go along with your game plan?"

"Anytime you want out of this all you have to do is say so. Just say ciao, and I'm bye-bye," Juanita said.

Gigi looked dubious. "All I have to do is tell you I've changed my mind and poof, you're gone?"

"Poof. I'm gone. Free will, remember?"

Gigi remembered. It was nice to know she could bail out at any time. It reduced the risk considerably. A disconcerting notion entered her mind.

"Did you have anything to do with my getting on the Naylor case?" she asked.

"What do you take me for? I don't meddle. You got that case on your own. You know, you could really be a little more sensitive to my feelings. I'm not made of stone, you know. I think. I feel. You'd think a person in my position would get a little more sensitivity from people, but no . . ."

"Okay, okay, I'm sorry. It's just that it's a great opportunity for me, and I thought maybe you helped a little, that's all."

Juanita looked appeased. "Well, it is an interesting case, isn't it? More than a case. You're dealing with a child's heart. You'll have to be sensitive to that."

"I am," Gigi replied. "Listen, Juanita, is there any purpose to this visit other than the calorie count? I have to get back to work."

"Of course. I just wanted to touch base with you, to get a status check on what your plans are for locating a father."

Gigi flushed. She had given it plenty of thought, but still had no concrete ideas.

"I don't have any plans yet."

Juanita's jaw dropped. "What? No plans? You're telling me you haven't started strategizing on this yet?"

Gigi shook her head.

"Look, kiddo, you've got to get moving on this thing. Life won't wait for you, you know. You've got to go after it yourself. You've got to grab life by the ying-yang, get aggressive, strut your stuff," Juanita said, pacing and shaking her fist in the air like a football coach in a locker room at half-time.

"And how do you suggest I grab life by the ying-yang, as you so delicately put it?"

"Strategize. Make plans."

"Like what?"

"How about starting with your current circle of friends. What are friends for, right? Start scouting around. Advertise a little. Let them know you're in the market."

"Believe me, my friends know I'm in the market."

"Then get more specific. Ask them to direct some single men your way."

It couldn't hurt, Gigi thought. Her book club meeting was next week, so she could talk to her girlfriends then. They occasionally tried to fix her up and she always turned them down because of Harold. Harold. A pain shot through her abdomen.

"I do have friends, of course . . ." Gigi began, but once again Juanita had vanished into thin air.

That angel was a pain in the ass.

"What, are you getting religious or something?" Sydney questioned as she straightened the waist of her white toreador pants. They were a trifle too tight, just the way she liked them, but they cut naggingly into her crotch and required constant adjustment. "I mean, you've always dated jerks. Men who couldn't appreciate you, who drained you dry, abused you, then left you," Sydney continued in a matter-of-fact tone. She pointed a manicured finger at Gigi. "And do you know why?"

"No."

"Because you love it, that's why. It's what makes you happy. You love being miserable, you love the drama of rejection. It satisfies some deep masochistic need in you. There's no need to be ashamed of it. It's just your idea of fun."

Gigi's high heels clicked rhythmically as she

struggled to keep up with Sydney's brisk stride and constant conversation. Gigi had noticed with dismay that being chosen as the mother of the Daughter of God had not changed her everyday life. She still awoke at six, got home at seven, snagged her pantyhose, worried about her weight, ate Moon pies in bed while she watched David Letterman, listened to Sydney's constant psychoanalysis. She felt she should be experiencing things of a more spiritual nature, but then, Juanita told her things wouldn't change much, and she had never experienced anything spiritual before.

On the third Tuesday of every month Gigi went with Sydney after work to an informally established book club they belonged to with several friends, including Lulu. Sydney's parking-lot analysis of Gigi's private life was only a warmup for the marathon of gossip, advice and exaggerated confessions that inevitably poured forth during these monthly meetings, a sort of group confessional which had become over the past two years, like menses, a monthly purge.

"So what happened to Harold?" Sydney asked.

"I just don't think Harold is the right man for me."

"He dumped you, right?"

"No," Gigi answered defensively, ashamed of the lie. "I've just decided not to see so much of him. Like I told you, I need to see other men, some nice men."

"He dumped you. Don't worry, he'll be back. He's always come back before," Sydney said, giving Gigi an encouraging pat on the shoulder.

"Harold needs you. He depends on you. He feels he has to do these things because he's obviously trying to act out some hostilities he had with his mother as a child. You see, Gigi, he sees you as his mommie, and men always return to their mommies. Dr. Goodall explained it to me last week."

Gigi didn't have the heart to tell Sydney about the new young, blond, large-breasted mommie Harold had found. Gigi wondered if the nuptials between Harold and Barbie had taken place, then cringed with the now familiar agony. If they were already married, she thought she might send them a gift just to prove to the world what a true masochist she really was. She still thought of Harold often, about how nice it was to have someone around in the evenings, someone to cook for, watch TV with, someone to sleep next to. The idea of him being married to someone else made her stomach churn. All the more reason to quickly move into her new life purpose.

She had decided to take the first step toward implementing Juanita's dictum to begin her search for a father. Step one: ask the book club if they knew any eligible men she could be fixed up with. "Fixed up." The very term implied a correction of something malfunctioning, like a broken blender or a flat tire. It aroused images of awkward introductions, strained dinner conversation, fear of sexual advances, fear of no sexual advances. Throwing herself at the book club's mercy would be embarrassing, but then again, it would be an act of martyrdom appropriate for a woman of her position. "And lo," the future accounts of her life would read, "Gigi the Martyr and Mother of the Daughter of God threw herself upon the feet of women and beggeth that single men be bestoweth upon her." She had considered testing the waters by asking Sydney if she knew any nice men, perhaps friends of Arthur's who might be interested in meeting her, but then decided she could benefit from the economies of scale if she posed the question to the group as a whole.

The club originally had met after work at the women's homes, but had recently opted to meet at Annabelle's, a mirrored bar perched on the top of the Houston Oaks Hotel. *Madame Bovary* was the month's novel, a classic title suggested by Sydney as a change in literary diet from the gossipy Hollywood biographies the women usually consumed. Gigi doubted that any of them had actually read it.

"Besides," Sydney's oration forged on, "if you meet a nice man, then you would have to be a nice girl, and you wouldn't want to do that. Nice girls don't make it in this world."

Gigi mopped beads of perspiration from her forehead as they walked through the long, hot parking lot.

"You're so callous," Gigi told her.

"Of course I'm callous. We're all callous. What woman over thirty isn't? When it comes to life expectations, Gi, you're still living in the same world you did when you were fifteen, a world of white sox, proms and nice girls and bad girls. You might as well face it. Nice girls don't make it these days. Trust me. I've been a nice girl and it got me nowhere."

"When were you a nice girl?" she asked with a laugh.

"In high school. I was a nice girl in high school. I was also a lonely girl in high school. My social life started on Friday, August 17, 1965, when I let Jimmy Riley slip his grimy hand down my sweater." Sydney smiled smugly. Gigi admired her memory for dates.

"Grow up, Bernstein," Sydney tossed over her shoulder. "Life belongs to those who taketh. Example number two. My marriage. When Arthur and I got married I sat around for two years macrameing wall hangings while Arthur screwed anything that walked. Finally I started having a few mindless affairs myself and now our marriage is working out much better. Why should men have all the fun?"

Gigi gave a heated gasp of relief when they reached the hotel. Pushing through the revolving door they relished the first metallic blast of air conditioning, rode up the elevator and stepped out into Annabelle's, pausing a moment to let their eyes adjust to the bar's darkness. Gigi spotted their friends at a corner table, the women already immersed in drinks and conversation, their hands a fluttering of gestures, red nail polish and heavy gold jewelry. You could almost see the perfume hanging like a pink fluffy cloud of vapor in the air.

"Sorry we're late. What did we miss?" said Sydney as she pulled a chair to the table and waved for the waitress.

"Nothing. We're talking about men as usual," said Maureen caustically. Maureen was going through a divorce and was still in the throes of what Lulu termed "the bitter bitch stage."

"Not men, Maureen. We're discussing husbands. Please don't get the two species confused," Lynn explained, her rouged lips sucking on the orange slice that had adorned her Mai Tai. Gigi was just managing to get settled at the table after having to untangle her spike heel from the carpeting.

"Two species?" she asked.

"Sure," said Lynn. "Men like to make love any time of day. Husbands only do it at night."

"If you're lucky, that is," replied Maureen. "My dear Richard only did it on holidays. Jewish holidays at that."

"I always wondered why you got so excited at Yom Kippur," Lulu said. The waitress carried two vodka gimlets shaken and on the rocks to Sydney and Gigi. They intended to catch up with their companions, who were a drink and a half ahead of them. Gigi looked at her friends and smiled with contentment. She, like all of them, craved the book-club meetings, especially because they rarely discussed books. Their real-life stories sparked much more interesting conversation.

"I'm not finished telling you about Richard. I was telling them about Rich when the two of you walked up," said Maureen, obviously annoyed at the interruption.

"Are we waxing redundant about good old Rich

again?" Sydney asked.

"Bor-ing," Lulu whined. Maureen shot her a look.

"He's being a prick over the property settlement. He wants to keep the house so he and that woman can move into it. Can you believe that? I'll be damned if I'll let that twit move into my house."

"You really can't call her a twit. She has more education than all of us put together," said Lulu.

Maureen glared at her. Maureen's husband had recently departed their marriage for a physics PhD five years his senior, and Maureen was having adjustment problems. Maureen reasoned that if a husband left you for a younger woman, everyone assumed he was shallow and needed someone younger to reassure his obviously weak sense of masculinity. But if a husband left you for someone older, people assumed you had to be brainless, boring or both. Maureen was into therapy, zen and pills to ease the pain of knowing that Richard left her for someone with a bigger brain and not a bigger bust.

"I actually moved walls around in the house to get some south light in the damn thing. The house used to be so dark it was paralyzing. I totally rejuvenated the house. That house is me, and I'll be damned if I'll leave it. Screw his divorce. Screw him."

"Maybe if you had, he wouldn't have left you," said Lulu.

"She tried," said Sydney, "But with Richard it went by so fast she usually missed it. She had pap smears that lasted longer than Richard."

"Richard was a very good husband," said Maureen.

"Spare us. You told me yourself two years ago that being married to Richard was like being married to your great aunt Minerva," Lulu said.

"Only with great aunt Minerva the sex would have been better," Maureen replied, then giggled along with the others.

"Maureen, you're young and you're beautiful. Richard was never good enough for you anyway. You'll find another man, this time one who'll make love to you all night," said Sydney.

"He'll be twenty-five with a behind as tight as a horse," said Lynn. "She'll be grinning so big she'll have lipstick on her ears."

"How come whenever we get together all we talk about is men and sex?" Gigi asked, tired of listening to this conversation, which was a repeat from the month before and the month before that.

"Because what we're interested in is men and sex," Sydney responded with a smile.

"Well, I'm also interested in money," Lynn interjected.

"I'm serious. Don't we have anything on our minds but how men are screwing us around?"

Lulu raised an eyebrow. "Speak for yourself. My love life is peaches and cream."

Gigi continued. "We all have college degrees here, so we're not idiots. We reached maturity during a feminist revolution. How did it escape us?" Gigi asked the group. Her comments captured their attention, and the table fell silent. Sydney leaned back in her chair and looked at Gigi.

"It didn't escape us. It's like we're living in the bowels of it," she said.

"Bowels! My God, Sydney, sometimes you're so crude it's paralyzing and I mean paralyzing," said Maureen with a groan.

"Well, see, Gigi, we've elevated the conversation from genitals to bowels," said Lulu. "We're working our way up the male anatomy. Maybe someday we'll get to the brain."

"Forget it. I've been there, it's not worth the trip. The best a man has to offer is somewhere between his knees and his solar plexis," said Sydney.

"In her case, she's talking about Arthur's wallet," teased Lynn. A chuckle went around the table.

"Could we change the subject?" Gigi asked. She could never be certain when Juanita would show up, and she didn't wish her to hear this conversation.

"What's with you today, Gi? You're in a lousy mood," said Maureen.

"There's nothing wrong with me."

"Don't believe her," Sydney interrupted. "Harold dumped her."

"He didn't dump me."

"Men are animals," Lulu said.

"Harold did not dump me. I've merely decided that he is the wrong man for me and I've decided to meet new people. New men, that is."

114

"Honey, Harold is the wrong man for anybody," Lynn said.

Gigi ignored the remark. "The point is, I need to meet some new men. I don't want to cruise singles bars and I just don't meet the right type at work. Do any of you know anyone who might have potential?" Gigi asked with her fingers crossed.

"Sweetie, whenever I find any, I try to look the other way," said Lulu.

"I don't know any men that aren't friends of Richard's and I won't tolerate your going out with a friend of Richard's," Maureen said huffily.

"I've got a great guy," Lynn said excitedly. "He's a stockbroker, a lot of fun, plays classical piano . . ."

"He's also black," Sydney interrupted. " You told me all about him a few months ago."

"So what?" Lynn said scathingly. Gigi pondered it for a second. Of course, Juanita wouldn't care, but her mother wasn't too liberal about these things and Gigi couldn't live with all the asthma attacks.

"Well, come on, everybody. Let's think about it," Marsha said sweetly. "Gigi needs to meet some new men and if we put our minds to it we can come up with some." Everybody nodded. "I'll ask Edward if he has any single friends."

"I'll ask Arthur," added Sydney.

"I'll ask around," Lynn said.

"If I come across one, I'll send him your way," Lulu volunteered.

Gigi beamed. The club had rallied behind her.

"So shouldn't we talk a little about the book?" Maureen asked. "It said in the preface it was supposed to be one of the best novels ever written."

"Okay, okay, it was a good book, a decent story. But it's hard for me to relate to those old ideas. If Emma Bovary didn't like her husband she should have dumped him," said Lynn.

"But she was struggling against conventional values. She couldn't just dump him like he was garbage," Gigi replied in defense of poor Emma. "I mean, it was all so passionate. There she was, wanting some intensity, some love in her life, but she couldn't be released from her stupid husband . . ."

"But why did she have to kill herself? That's the coward's way out. You can always find a reasonable alternative if you look hard enough, at least something better than arsenious oxide," Lynn said.

"Arsonous what? How in the hell did she kill herself, anyway?" Lulu asked, so anxious to hear the juicy details she forgot that she was revealing that she had failed to read the book.

"She took arsenious oxide," Gigi explained.

"What's that?"

"It's like chugging Drano."

Lulu grimaced, then took a gulp of her drink.

"The things men make women do," she said disgustedly, then waved the waitress for one last round.

CHAPTER NINE

For the bulk of Gigi's adult life her main criteria for choosing a man was that he be single and have an I.Q. over sixty, and often she had considered forgoing both. Now the time had come to set standards, to establish quality controls so she could efficiently sift through the male multitude for a select group of choice eligible specimens. No more self-centered, egotistical, maniacal macho types. No more cold, silent emotional mutants with ex-wife hangups and Oedipus complexes. No, this time she would be choosy. But what do you look for in the perfect male? Not superficial perfection like Paul Newman or Robert Redford. What she needed was someone perfect like a real person could be perfect. Someone you could laugh with, talk to, hold hands with, go to movies with, conceive a Messiah with. Gigi grappled with this question as she showered in the mornings, as she put on her clothes, as she drove to work, ate

117

her meals, before she fell asleep at night. When working through a problem, she was a great believer in making lists. One evening in her office after everyone had gone for the day, she came up with a list of qualities she considered essential for the father:

Kindness—He must be a good, loving person, i.e. loyal, honest, warmhearted. The Father of the Daughter of God would not lie, be unfeeling or cheat on the Mother of the Daughter of God. A love for children—Self-explanatory. A sense of humor—A dry wit and an ability to see the lighter side. A definite must. The child would very likely inherit her earthly mother's need for a good laugh once in a while. Besides, religion, while a great thing, always lacked humor. Looks—Attractive, not too attractive. A Dustin Hoffman rather than a Richard Gere. Religious beliefs—He should have some. Juanita never mentioned it as a requirement, but it should be considered. To bestow this sort of honor upon an atheist would be like giving fifty yard line Super Bowl tickets to a guy who hated football.

Gigi folded the list carefully into a perfect square and slipped it into her wallet behind her Saks credit card. She wanted to be able to go over it if she had to, although she knew it all by heart.

What she realized was this: that these qualities in a man weren't just what Elizabeth deserved. They were what she deserved as well. Didn't Gigi Bernstein deserve better than an egotistical, cold-hearted son of a bitch? Didn't she deserve somebody kind, warmhearted with a love for children and a sense of humor? If she were good enough to be the mother of this Baby she was good enough to deserve a little more than the repeated kicks in the teeth she had received from men in the past. Gigi left her office that day feeling as strong and independent as a woman in a maxi-pad commercial.

Shortly after this revelation Sydney phoned with the news flash that there was a new single male partner in Arthur's CPA firm.

"So I thought you, Bernard, Arthur and I could see the new play at the Alley Theatre and then go to dinner. You'll love Bernard. He's so East Coast intellectual," Sydney bubbled over the phone.

Gigi considered the proposition carefully. She felt excitement at coming across her first prospect, but then she didn't want to jump into anything too hastily.

"Would you describe Bernard as a very nice person?" she asked. Sydney's taste in men was often questionable.

"Oh yes, Gi. He's a sweetheart. Sent his mother roses on Valentine's Day. Pink ones."

"How about his sense of humor?"

"Wonderful. He gave Arthur the funniest card for his birthday. A scream. A total scream. You'll love him."

"What religion is he?" A brief pause on the phone line.

"Well, I'm not sure. What does it matter? It's just a date, not a bar mitzvah."

"What about children? Does he like children?"

Dead silence for a full five seconds.

"Gigi, if you're going to get freakish about this, let's call the whole thing off. I mean this is Arthur's business partner. If you start asking him if he likes children on the first date . . ."

"Don't worry, Sydney, I'm just trying to be more selective."

"It's just that you've been acting a little strange lately, Gi, like your gynecologist changed the estrogen levels in your pills or something, but I think a date with Bernard could be just the thing for you. If I can trust you not to scare him."

Gigi assured her she would use kid gloves.

Sydney gave Gigi information about the date, time, what to wear, what to think, how to act, and assured her that Bernard was a wonderful person with great relationship potential if he wasn't frightened off with questions about children and religious preferences. Gigi hung up the phone and immediately worked out to her "Jane Fonda Workout" tape and did twenty-five minutes of psychocybernetic positive visualization. She felt like an athlete getting ready for the Olympics.

Gigi was dying to tell Juanita about the Big Date but Juanita had not shown her angelic face for days. What do archangels do on their days off, Gigi wondered? Work with other poor souls, chat with God, or plug themselves in like a battery for a recharge?

Gigi managed to go to aerobics class once, get a manicure, read a book by Leo Buscaglia and buy a new dress that was sensuously attractive but not sexy. After all, the mother of the Daughter of God should not parade around in slutty clothes.

She should look sophisticated, poised, carefully groomed, right off the pages of an ad for Evan Picone. The dress Gigi chose was a simple design in rich burgundy silk. When she saw herself in the full-length mirror just before Bernard was to arrive, Gigi was quite pleased with the results. She had never looked better. She was certain she had a shot with Bernard.

Ready for her date thirty minutes early, she fidgeted with her hair, put another coat of polish on her nails, tried to watch television, finally drank a glass of wine to calm herself down. She hadn't gone out with anyone but Harold in years, which made her nervous, not to mention that she was interviewing for the father of Elizabeth. When the doorbell rang she counted to ten and took a few deep breaths. She walked to the door and opened it gracefully, with dignity and aplomb.

"Hi, I'm Bernard." The man in her doorway was tall, thin, with wavy brown hair and a moustache that sprouted timidly beneath a largish nose. He looked nice, he looked respectable in conventional gray slacks and a blue sport coat, the typical CPA uniform for an exciting night on the town. His white buckskin shoes seemed a bad sign, but he was right on time, so he received points for punctuality.

"And you must be Gigi," he said.

No, Bernie, I'm Mahatma Gandhi. Loss of points for lack of creativity on his opening line, but Gigi didn't want to be too critical. Bernard looked like potential. Gigi smiled graciously and

121

gestured for him to come in.

"Do we have time to sit and have a glass of wine before we go?" she asked daintily. Might as well scope out the territory, get to know him a little before Sydney had the chance to dominate the conversation.

"I think so. My, this is a nice place you have. What does an apartment like this cost you?"

Twenty points off for lack of class. Gigi told him what her rent was as she handed him a glass of moderately priced chablis.

"I just moved here and I haven't had the time to really look at houses to buy yet. I don't like the apartment lifestyle. Too many women chasing after someone single, and, well, successful like myself. But I like this apartment. I might check into these," he explained as he tapped the sheetrock on her wall. Gigi considered that a plausible explanation for his tasteless inquiry about her rent. After all, Bernard was a CPA. He was into dollars and cents. As he stood there sipping his wine, visually taking in her floor plan, Bernard looked sophisticated and very attractive, Gigi decided.

They sat on the sofa. Bernard chatted about his work, his life in New Jersey where he worked before moving to Houston, his family. He seemed straightforward, well-adjusted, a perfect specimen of the normal American male. Perhaps a little long-winded, but still definite paternal material. Gigi's brain tingled with the possibilities.

They met Sydney and Arthur at the Alley Theatre as the curtain rose. After they seated them-

122

selves, Gigi had Bernard on one side and Sydney on the other. Sydney continually nudged Gigi in the ribs and gave her obvious "How's it going?" looks. Gigi tried to ignore her, but with Sydney it was difficult. It was with some disappointment that Gigi noted Bernard's failure to hold her hand during the play. Sure, it was high-schoolish, but it would have been nice. Of course, Bernard was probably too shy. During the intermission, when the men went for cocktails, Sydney predictably took the opportunity for an inquisition.

"Do you think you'll sleep with him?" she asked.

"Spare me, Sydney. I just met him. I don't know if he likes me, much less if I like him."

"If I were you, I'd pounce on him. I think he's hot. Don't pass up the chance," Sydney advised as she tossed a suggestive glance at a man passing by. Gigi reddened with embarrassment.

"Sydney, not everybody is interested in jumping into bed with strangers. I'm sure we'll have a nice evening and I'll go straight home alone."

"Just be sure and give me the details if you sleep with him," Sydney said quickly as Bernard and Arthur walked up with the drinks.

The play turned out to be tedious. Gigi didn't even listen to most of the dialogue because her mind was focused on Bernard. The first act Gigi spent studying Bernard's hands, sneaking glances at his profile, wondering what it would be like to touch him, kiss him, run her fingers through his hair. She tried to imagine him naked, to find the outline of his penis underneath his trousers. She couldn't exactly locate it visually, but she knew it had be lurking in there somewhere enshrouded craftily by his Fruit-of-the-Looms. Yes, Sydney, I'd like to experience coitus with this man tonight. Feeling the familiar dampness in the cotton crotch of her Maidenform panties, Gigi shifted uneasily in her seat. Were these the kind of thoughts that should be coming from the mind of the Mother of Elizabeth? She imagined God spitting the words "You Tramp" and striking her down with toxic-shock syndrome right there in the Alley Theatre. Gigi tried to focus her thoughts on the play, on Marcie's case, on recipes for blender hollandaise, on anything but the fact that Bernard's knee was just barely touching her left thigh. By the second act she had worked out most of the major details of their future life together including a small but elegant wedding, a honeymoon in Cancun, a spacious but not extravagant home in River Oaks where they would together raise their exceptional little Daughter to fulfill her destiny:

"And what would you like for your birthday, Lizzie?"

"Oh, a big chocolate cake, a doll and how about an end to world suffering?"

Bernard and Gigi would beam at each other with parental devotion.

"And so, Precious, what do you want to be when you grow up?"

"Either a nurse or God."

It would be tough finding the kid the right toys, but she and Bernard would overcome that problem along with every other speed bump on life's dizzying highway.

When the play was over, Arthur said he was tired and gave their regrets for dinner. Gigi tried not to show her glee. She would have Bernard alone for the remainder of the evening. Surely Juanita was watching over her.

For dinner Bernard chose a Szechwan restaurant off Westheimer, a small red-walled place with unusually romantic lighting for Chinese food. They endured a few embarrassed silences in the dark booth as they attempted to talk, but on the whole, Gigi thought things were going splendidly. Bernard was loosening up, describing his clients, his ex-wife, his excellent tennis backhand, how difficult it was being single and successful in Houston. With her chin resting coquettishly on her hand, Gigi soaked up every syllable. When their food came, she noted with affection his ineptness with chopsticks as his mushi pork escaped repeatedly back onto his plate. Adorable, she thought, as Bernard went into painful detail about his divorce proceedings and precisely what items the judge awarded to his ex-wife. The red peppers in her kung pao chicken were no match for the burning in her heart.

Bernard excused himself to the men's room. Gigi's eyes followed him as he walked away and she thought proudly of her incredible luck at finding this man. She made a note to be kinder to Sydney.

"He's not right, kiddo."

Gigi leaped out of her seat as the sound stung her ear. She looked behind her. Nothing. She shivered with the knowledge of the inevitable. A light tap fell on her shoulder. Gigi turned and saw Juanita sitting in the booth next to her. She watched Juanita take a bite of her chicken, chew a second, then fan her mouth.

"Too hot," she said.

"What? What did you say?"

"I said it's hot. Really spicy. Could turn your insides into Vesuvius," she said, and gulped down some water.

"No, before that, what did you say?"

"Oh, I said he's not right. This Bernard isn't the right guy. He's nice, okay and everything, but not your type. Why waste your time?" said Juanita. Gigi stared at her.

"What could possibly be wrong with him? He's perfect. He's intelligent, pleasant, attractive." Gigi counted off his qualities on her fingers. "Wait, it's not because he's divorced, is it? That's discrimination. Besides, if you don't allow divorced men, then that eliminates most of the single males in Houston," pleaded Gigi.

"I could care less if he's divorced. I just know he's the wrong one."

"How?"

"Call it intuition."

"To hell with intuition."

"Aren't we getting snippy? Okay, straight-talk time. He's too self-absorbed. He's too crazy about himself to have anything left over for anyone else. All he's talked about all night is himself. Has he asked you one thing about you tonight?"

Gigi thought for a moment. "Yes, he asked me

how much my apartment cost."

Juanita rolled her eyes.

"Look, the deal is that he doesn't have to love me. All I have to do is love him," said Gigi.

"Don't confuse love with pride of ownership."

"But what about my needs? I do have needs, you know," Gigi replied angrily.

Juanita looked testy. "I think what we're dealing with here is a trifle more important than the state of your glands."

"There's Bernard. He's coming back. You've got to go," Gigi said.

"Actually, I was thinking of staying."

"You can't stay."

"Why not? I never get out to restaurants. I'll just have coffee and dessert. I won't talk. You'll hardly know I'm here."

"Juanita, if you'll just go I'll take you to a restaurant sometime. Really, I will."

"You say that now."

"I promise."

"Chinese?"

"I'm back," Bernard announced. Gigi froze as he slid into the other side of the booth. With her usual style, Juanita had evaporated, leaving only a trace of dampness in the air where she previously sat, a barely blue haze that only Gigi was aware of.

"Did I mention that I play the cello? And quite well, I might add," he said.

Gigi faked a smile.

Gigi squirmed uncomfortably in a low-slung, high-tech chair that made her rear sink so low her feet barely touched the floor. She felt uneasy and out of place. The room, decorated in blues and purples, gave her a creepy feeling that she was trapped inside a bruise. Perched behind a corner desk sat a burgundy-haired secretary wearing a gold necklace that said "Love Me." The plastic plants trembled as a Barry Manilow song played softly in the background. What was she doing there? she wondered. Was it a mistake, some egregious error that would make her wince with regret for years? Gigi weighed the options. On the other hand, what did she really have to lose, she asked herself, other than her dignity, her pride and her reputation if anyone ever found out?

"Establish Relationships With Professionals Like Yourself In An Enjoyable And Confidential Environment," the ad for Single World Video Dating promised. The word "Confidential" had been written in bold, black typeface so professionals like herself would know without a doubt that Single World Video Dating could keep a secret. Gigi discovered their ad in the back pages of a locally published business journal. Two weeks had passed since her luckless date with Bernard, and she had received no other offers. Even Bernard hadn't called for a second date. She wondered if he heard her talking to Juanita and thought she was a crazy person having a conversation with herself. It didn't matter, of course, since Juanita had nixed him. But there was no time for sour grapes. She had to gather prospects, widen the funnel, expand her mating possibilities. Single World Video Dating appeared an efficient, scientific approach. They boasted over five thousand clients. Surely out of the two thousand five hundred men there had to be one guy suitable for conceiving a Messiah with. It was hard, though, to overcome the feeling of degradation she associated with lowering herself to a commercial dating service. She had called Single World three times, slamming down the receiver the first two attempts when the receptionist answered. It was just too embarrassing. Then she thought about Elizabeth. She needed a father. Gigi had courageously raised the receiver, dialed the number and had hung on tightly as the bubbly receptionist welcomed her to the exciting adventure of Video Dating. Gigi asked her to describe their range of services. It was simple. For a fee, the client could arrange an appointment, drop by, fill out an extensive questionnaire about personal likes, dislikes, profession, hobbies, etc. This data was then fed into the computer where it mingled provocatively with the data of the other five thousand participants, all, Gigi assumed, in various stages of desperation. The computer matched the client with the persons it deemed suitable. The client then viewed the videotapes of the prospects and decided whom he or she wished to call for a date. It seemed reasonable enough to Gigi. The only really vulgar part was that she had to make a videotape of herself. They flashed some questions on the wall and you answered them while on-camera. Gigi did not consider herself photogenic, due to her opinion that she looked like a fat Jewish girl in photographs. She loathed to imagine what she would look like in an actual moving film.

"Hello there, Gigi. I'm so delighted to meet you," cooed a dark-haired, tan, shortish man wearing tinted glasses, tennis shorts and a La Coste pullover. "I'm Rex, your video-dating advisor."

"Uh, hi," Gigi responded in a worried voice. Rex stood before her looking garishly clean, tastelessly shiny, like freshly polished gold-flecked formica. He took her hands into his and stared meaningfully into her eyes.

"Welcome to Single World Video Dating. Filled out your questionnaire?" He smiled, exhibiting a mouthful of beautifully capped teeth. Gigi nodded affirmatively.

"Mind if I take a look at it?" he asked after he had already grabbed it and had begun to read.

"Uh hmm, uh hmm. An attorney. Very impressive," he said, flashing Gigi a practiced grin. "Let's see, it says here that you write poetry . . ."

Gigi figured they expected you to fib a little to make yourself seem more interesting.

". . . you like to play tennis, you jog . . ."

She did, after all, own a tennis racket and sometimes she walked very briskly.

". . . age thirty-two, weight one ten . . ."

Okay, so she lied. She considered it merely a marketing tactic. Rex looked at her engagingly.

"You seem like a really fun girl, Gigi. We've got a lot of great guys that will be dying to meet a gal like you."

130

Sure, Rex. Lots of guys are dying to meet me. That's why I'm here.

"Now here comes the fun part. Ready to make your very own videotape?" Rex asked, cupping her chin in his hand. Gigi nodded a yes to get him to shut up.

"If you would like to freshen up first, the ladies room is over there. See you in a sec." Rex trotted off.

Gigi retreated to the ladies room. On a shelf above the basin stood a dazzling array of personal grooming products—hairspray, mousse, tanning gel, eye shadow, powders and rouges, all the accoutrements of the desperately single. She appraised herself in the mirror. Her hair was frizzy from the humidity and her makeup had worn off. She attempted to correct the damage with the impressive variety of makeup in her own handbag. She wondered what role she should play on the videotape to make herself appealing to the widest audience. Should she be bouncy? Serious? Sexy? Sweet and innocent? A combination perhaps? Hit 'em with a little of everything?

She put down the toilet lid, sat down and pondered her reasons for exposing herself to this humiliation. She was there for Elizabeth, for the world, for herself, so she, Gigi Bernstein, could make a contribution to the globe other than the largest number of divorce settlements. She would do whatever it took, even if it meant she had to become a baby machine.

"Hey, Gigi . . ."

There was a rap on the door.

131

"You ready in there? How could a beauty like you get any better looking anyway?"

With a bag over my head, Rexy baby. Gigi took a last look in the mirror, unbuttoned her blouse a button, tousled her hair with her fingers and walked out trying to look casually exciting.

"Looking gooood!" Rex said sexily. Gigi tried not to audibly groan. He led her to a small bare room with a chair at one end and a small mounted camera at the other. On the wall behind the camera was a list of questions similar to those on the questionnaire. Operating the camera was a kid with a drug-addict pallor.

"All right, Gigi. Just sit in the chair. Take a minute to look over the questions. When I say start, just begin answering the questions, just like we were having a conversation. You know — naturally. We don't want you all tensed up, now, do we?"

Gigi gritted her teeth and examined the list. It looked simple enough. The first question asked her name, age and profession. No problem. The next question quizzed about hobbies and special interests. Okay, so far. She noticed a question about favorite movies. That was tough. She loved *Annie Hall* but declaring it her favorite movie might make someone think she was a neurotic, yuppie type. Of course, there was *Dark Victory* with Bette Davis but that would make her seem sappy, not to mention old. How about *Star Wars* . . .

"Okay, start!" Rex pointed a ringed finger at her and then to the camera. She could hear the camera whirring. She wasn't ready. She hadn't had time to go over all the questions.

"Uh . . . my name is Gigi Bernstein. I'm thirty-fi— thirty-two years old. I'm an attorney."

The drug addict had turned on a light so harsh it glared mercilessly into her eyes. She squinted to see the questions.

"Um . . . my hobbies are tennis, jogging . . ." Her mind went blank. ". . . and, uh, sky diving." Sky diving? She grimaced. She was flubbing it, but the camera whirred on.

"My favorite movie is, let's see, *Star Wars.* No, no, it's not that, it's *Sophie's Choice.*" She strained to read the last questions.

"My favorite type of man is . . . someone nice. Someone fun . . ." Gigi grappled for words less mundane. "Uh . . . someone who would be a good father," she added quickly. Rex gave her a sour look and shook his head. It was almost over. There was one word left on the sheet that she couldn't quite make out because of the light. She squinted so she could see it. She could barely make out the word "improvise." Improvise? Gigi blushed and smiled sheepishly into the camera for what seemed like infinity. Finally the camera shut off, the light went out. Gigi noticed that her blouse was wet from perspiration.

"So how did I do?" she asked Rex.

"Hey, we've got three thousand guys in our data bank," he replied, implying, she felt, that statistically she had a shot.

"So why don't we cruise into the computer room, run your data and see what the computer

133

says about your future love life?" Rex crooned, quickly regaining his composure after witnessing Gigi's disaster. Gigi followed him into another tiny room equipped with a terminal and printer. Rex informed her that her data had been fed into the computer while she was making her tape. Gigi conjured an image of her personal information lying all lumpy like oatmeal in a spoon while someone coaxed the finicky computer to open wide and take a taste.

Rex typed in a few words on the terminal. After announcing that it had accepted her data, the computer paused reflectively while it matched Gigi's information with the other data in its voluminous files. Gigi thought it was taking a very long time. Could the machine be having trouble? But she relaxed when she heard the printer begin to hum. It buzzed, printed and spit out a piece of paper bearing the name of five eligible future fathers. History was being made, Gigi mused with pride.

"And here are the lucky guys," said Rex as he presented Gigi with her output. She scanned the five names carefully.

"What are these numbers on the right?" she asked.

"Ah, those are their videotape numbers. Why don't we just cruise into the video room and take a look at these five hunks. You up for it?"

Gigi was up for it. There was a television screen with a VCR in the video room. Gigi waited there until Rex came in with the five tapes. He popped the first candidate into the machine. There was a hissing noise, a screen of snow, then the face of Bachelor Number One, Mr. Rick Lansing.

"Hey there, hi there, ho there," Rick said, oozing all over the screen. "I'm looking for a woman who knows how to love a guy and isn't afraid to show it."

Gigi raised her hand quickly to halt the tape. "No. Not him."

Rex popped Rick out of the machine and popped in Mr. Wonderful Number Two. More hissing, more snow, then the appearance of a small, sheepish-looking man, balding with glasses. Gigi noticed that on the right side of his face he had a nervous tic.

"Sorry. Not him."

Rex popped the guy out before he could even say his name. The next candidate was covered with tattoos. No dice. The next was pushing sixty. Impossible. Chromosomes too old. Gigi waited hopefully as Rex started tape number five.

A blond nicely dressed man flashed onto the screen. He reminded Gigi of a football player she had loved from afar in high school.

"Hello. My name is Byron Hodgson. I'm a stockbroker. Gee, I feel like a fool doing this . . ."

"That's my man!" Gigi said excitedly, and Rex beamed with the pride of yet another personal accomplishment.

CHAPTER TEN

"May I speak to Byron Hodgson, please?" Gigi inquired in a tiny voice, nervously twisting a lock of stray hair with her fingers.

"This is Byron," the disembodied voice answered. She found the voice a pleasant surprise. It sounded deep and melodic. It could be a voice of sensitivity, perception and compassion, Gigi thought. It could be a voice attached to a you-know-what that could father the Baby. Her nervousness heightened.

"This is Gigi Bernstein. You see, I got your phone number through Single World Video Dating, and I—"

"Just a minute," he said quickly. Muffling sounds followed. She heard the sound of a chair being dragged across the floor. A door slammed. "Okay." He was back. "I just wanted to make sure I had some privacy." He chuckled nervously. Gigi exhaled with relief. At least he would talk to her.

"Sure, well, anyway, I saw your tape and you seemed nice." Nice—what a high school term, she chided herself. "I know this is ridiculous. Really ridiculous." Gigi paused, stymied by embarrassment. She gnawed on a fingernail and left a bare spot in the crimson polish. "Maybe I shouldn't have called. I—"

"No. I'm glad you did," he interrupted. "I feel just the way you do. I mean, a dating service seems superficial from one perspective, but from another standpoint, it's all worth it if you meet somebody you like, right?"

Gigi relaxed. Byron sounded kind and sane.

"Would you like to meet after work today?" he asked suddenly, catching Gigi off guard. This was much more than she had hoped for.

"I'd love to."

"There's a bookstore called Crows on the corner of Blanche and Miller in Montrose. Could you meet me there at six?"

"I'll be there," Gigi replied as she scribbled down the name and address of the book store. They exchanged good-byes. After hanging up the phone, Gigi felt gleeful at how well the phone call had turned out. Here was a nice, attractive man who wanted to meet with her, spend a few hours of his time without knowing or caring what she looked like. He liked the way she sounded on the phone and decided she was worth his time. And he didn't want to meet her in a bar. He preferred the intellectual ambiance of a bookstore. That was either class or extreme desperation. She had her doubts about the nature of any man who resorted to computer dating, but of course, that was hugely hypocritical since she had resorted to computer dating herself. Besides, Gigi felt good vibrations about Byron.

Five hours to go until six. The afternoon predictably crept by. She dropped by the courthouse to file papers, met briefly with Waldo on the Naylor case, chatted with Angela Maynard about Marcie's latest string of truancies from school. Angela Maynard assumed that since Marcie liked Gigi she would take advice from Gigi. Gigi assured Angela that Marcie was too headstrong to take advice from anyone, but after ten minutes of Angela's pleading, Gigi agreed to speak to Marcie about improving her school attendance. After all, having an unruly child in the house all day inhibited Angela's shopping and tennis games. Gigi would have agreed to anything to get off the phone with her.

Gigi checked her Seiko. Five-thirty. Stupendous. She hurriedly packed a stack of papers into her briefcase and slid into the restroom to put on her makeup. Luckily she had on her black suit which was slimming in the hips. Her hair could look better, but then she knew from experience it could look a lot worse. She applied lipstick, blusher, a little mascara. Voila, a formerly dowdy woman had been transformed into one of moderate attractiveness suitable for public viewing. She said a prayer for Estee Lauder, then crammed her makeup back into her purse. She had only fifteen minutes to make it to Montrose.

After galloping to her car, Gigi sped out of the

parking lot and raced into the rush-hour traffic. She cut off a bus in order to make a green light, dodged oncoming vehicles, oscillated strategically from lane to lane, honked madly at slow cars. Time was of the essence. She wanted to be exactly ten minutes late. She turned onto Blanche Avenue and spotted Crow's Books. Destiny smiled and she found a parking space nearby. After turning off the ignition, she checked her hair once more in the rearview mirror, got out her comb and tamed some strays. Anxiously, she slid out of the car and headed toward the book store. On the way she rehearsed opening lines. Pausing before the glass door, she composed herself, then entered cautiously. Crow's Books was dark and quaint with framed pictures on the wall and two parakeets in a cage sitting in a corner. The sitting-room decor gave the place a uniqueness not found in bookstore chains. A pleasantly musty aroma wafted through the air. A few people milled in and out of the tables and shelves and Gigi worried if she could pick out Byron in the crowd. She checked the Sports section first, but he wasn't there. She tried Travel, then Physical Fitness, no sign of him. Maybe he had changed his mind. Very negative thinking, Gigi reprimanded herself. Perhaps he had to work a little later than he expected. She would wait ten minutes for him to show up, but no longer. Okay, fifteen minutes, but that was it. She walked over to the Fiction section, then out of the corner of her eye she spotted her love object in Cooking. His nose was buried in Jacque Pepin, his index finger traveling down a recipe. Gigi eyed him more closely. Yes, definitely him. Gigi slid furtively back into Fiction so she could ready herself. She was going to be cool. She was going to be calm. She was going to be sexually exciting in a sort of intellectual way. She counted to three and breezed back into Cooking wearing a confident smile loaded with teeth and lips.

"Hi, I'm Gigi," she said huskily as she casually leaned against a bookshelf and knocked *Pasta Perfection* to the floor.

Byron, startled, looked up. Gigi studied his expression as he bent down to retrieve the book. Was the look on his face one of pleasant surprise or of disappointment? For chrissakes, don't be a wimp, she told herself. Be strong, be confident. Hadn't Juanita told her to strut her stuff, to grab life by the ying-yang? She had never been sure of what the "ying-yang" was, but whatever it was, if she could get her fat fingers around it she was going to grab it. For her part, she was most pleasantly surprised. Byron looked even more attractive in person than he had on videotape. He smiled a smile of cutely crooked teeth as he placed the book back on the shelf.

"Hello. I'm glad you could make it," he said with admirable composure.

"Yes, well, I'm glad you could make it, too," she said awkwardly, thinking she sounded as intelligent as a Chatty Cathy doll. Her mind went blank and there was an uncomfortable silence. Fortunately Byron took up the slack.

"Do you like to cook?" he asked, motioning to the cookbooks.

"Oh yes, sort of. I don't cook very much. I'm so busy all the time." Good girl. Don't let him know that you don't cook because it's no fun cooking for one. Don't let on that your idea of a big dinner is Kraft Macaroni and Cheese, and that you eat the whole thing in one sitting.

"It's time-consuming, but I consider it a hobby. It relaxes me. I'm a stockbroker and my job can get really stressful. You should try it sometime. To come home after work and cook something from scratch is very creative. Take this book for instance." He pulled a thick book from the shelf. "It's all about risotto. Risotto is simple and yet there are literally thousands of ways you can fix it. You can get very creative with colors and textures. It's like art." He laughed. "You didn't realize you were going to get a cooking class, did you?"

Gigi smiled and wondered if it was too soon to propose.

"I got interested in cooking when I was working for a firm in Paris a few years ago. I didn't know too many people there at first, and so I took a few cooking courses in the evening to occupy myself." He pulled a volume from the shelf. "Here's an Indian cookbook that you might like. You can really use your imagination with a curry."

Gigi's imagination at that moment required no additional spicing. She was impressed, she was charmed, she was delighted. She took the two cookbooks under her arm.

"Sold," she said, meaning more than the books.

Byron laughed. "You'll have to excuse me. Cooking is my current hobby."

141

Gigi bought both cookbooks, then at Byron's suggestion, they walked down the street to a wine bar. Over white zinfandel they told each other about themselves, their jobs, their ambitions, how uncomfortable they felt at Single World Video Dating, how phony they thought Rex was. Byron seemed intelligent and sophisticated. Gigi found him very attractive. His hair was dark blond and wavy, his eyes a deep hazel and his nose a perfect piece of sculpture. He was a beautiful man who could pass on some beautiful genes to Elizabeth. Gigi hoped the kid would inherit his face and not hers.

It was ten when Byron checked his watch and said he had an early morning ahead of him. Gigi said she did also. He insisted on walking her to her car, and they walked together in a comfortable silence to the Toyota. Joyfully Gigi noted Juanita's continued absence. Before she got into her car, Byron told her he had enjoyed the evening and would like to see her Saturday night if she was free. It just so happened that she was. As she drove home Gigi kept checking the back seat, expecting Juanita to pop in and cast a few disparaging remarks about Byron. She didn't want to be taken by surprise. But there was still no sign of heavenly intervention.

Gigi glided into work the next day feeling light-hearted and festive. She hummed "Bewitched, Bothered and Bewildered" as she sipped her morning coffee.

"I'm wild again, beguiled again, a simpering, wimpering child again . . ." a voice sang outside

142

her office door. Waldo peeked in.

"You're fortunate you took up law instead of show biz," Gigi said, smiling as she looked up from the *Chronicle*.

"No argument there. You seem happy today. Glad to see it. Would love to talk but I have a meeting that's already started," he said hurriedly but with a flash of smile. He turned to leave.

"Wait, Waldo. I need to talk to you for a second. Marcie said she would stop cutting school for two months if you and I would take her to dinner at Charlie's Barbecue Palace and let her have a beer. I agreed to everything but the beer. Will you go?"

"She agreed to only two months?"

"She's a tough negotiator. She has a crush on you, you know."

"Okay, I'd love to. When?"

"How about next Wednesday?"

He grimaced. "Can't. I'm going with Delores to some planetary-alignment seminar. How about Thursday?"

"Thursday is fine."

"Great. Can we meet later this afternoon to go over some Naylor contracts? I'd like your opinion on them."

"All right. What time?"

"Three. See you then." Waldo popped out and Gigi buried her nose in yesterday's courthouse records. There was a rap on her door which she assumed was Waldo. She looked up.

"Surprise!" Mrs. Bernstein stood in Gigi's doorway swathed in hot pink ultrasuede that glowed like a neon sign. Her hair was tucked beneath a hot pink turban and a long string of fake pearls dangled from her scarved neck. With her bird-like legs shod in black patent spikes, Gigi thought her mother looked like a plump pink flamingo.

"Hi, Mom," Gigi said with restrained enthusiasm. Her mother had never visited her in her office before. It did not bode well.

"I was on my way to Sakowitz for the pantyhose sale and I thought I would just drop by and see how you were doing." Mrs. Bernstein pushed her rhinestone bifocals down her nose and took a hard, penetrating look at her daughter. "Are you feeling any better?" she quizzed.

"I didn't know I had been sick," Gigi replied, knowing very well her mother was referring to that Saturday when she tried to tell her about Juanita. Mrs. Bernstein pursed her lips in disgruntlement.

"Did you see Dr. Goldman?"

"No, Mother. I'm fine. Really."

"Seen anything . . . funny lately?"

"Not a thing."

Mrs. Bernstein relaxed and sat down in the chair opposite Gigi's desk.

"You're probably wondering why I'm here."

"It crossed my mind, Mom."

Mrs. Bernstein tilted her turbaned head and folded her hands primly in her pink ultrasuede lap.

"I though it was time we had, you know, baby, a mother-daughter chat," she said sweetly. Gigi's eyes glinted with suspicion.

"I thought we had already gone over most of

those items when I was thirteen. Is there something vital that you left out?"

"Don't be sarcastic, baby, it's not attractive. I've been thinking about you lately, and I've come to some decisions."

Gigi didn't bother to ask what those decisions were since an earthquake would not keep them from spilling off her mother's lips.

"You see, I've decided that it's perfectly okay if you never get married or never have children. Even if you decide you want to live in sin with someone, I just want you to know, it's all right with me. Well, that's what I wanted to say. I've got to get going." Mrs. Bernstein stood up and brushed imaginary dust from her dress, straightened her turban and looked at Gigi as if she, too, needed a little straightening. She noticed interrogative look on her daughter's face.

"It's just that if the pressure of not being married is hard on you, you know, making you not exactly yourself," she said with a raised eyebrow, "well then, baby, it's just not worth it. I know I've always pushed you to get married, and I read an article in *Woman's Day* last month that said that type of motherly encouragement can cause psychological problems. I don't want to cause psychological problems. It's your life. Do what you want with it. I'll always be your mother, no matter what."

Gigi sat quietly. Mrs. Bernstein peeked into the hallway to make certain it was empty, then she leaned her back against the side of the doorway like Rita Hayworth in *Blood And Sand*.

"A woman needs love, Gigi," Mrs. Bernstein told her daughter in a low, husky voice.

Gigi's eyes widened. Mrs. Bernstein's hand slid suggestively up and down her ultrasuede skirt, and she stared at her daughter, her eyes dripping with unspoken communication.

"A woman has hot coals inside her that need to be stirred occasionally, you know what I mean, baby?"

Gigi wondered if her mother had taken too many hormone supplements again. After a deliberate pause, Mrs. Bernstein leaned over the desk and pecked Gigi's cheek. She headed for the door, paused and turned to look once more at her daughter.

"You've got to go for the Roman candles while you can, otherwise you'll be left with nothing but a wet wick," she said with a flourish of her hand, then departed for other adventures.

When Saturday rolled around Byron called early in the morning to confirm their date. He asked Gigi where she wanted to go and Gigi said that she would leave it all up to him. She was feeling feminine and flexible. He would pick her up at seven.

Gigi spent the afternoon lounging around her apartment, giving herself a manicure, a pedicure, a facial, deciding what she should wear. By five o'clock, a vaporous cloud of Estee Lauder bath powder billowed into the air as Gigi anointed her most private parts in preparation for her dinner with Byron. Hair coiffed, face painted, mind settled firmly into a blissful state usually reserved for characters in Broadway musicals, Gigi felt tonight could be a turning point in her life.

The phone rang. Gigi prayed it wasn't Byron calling to cancel the date.

"Hi, Gigi. This is Sydney. Brace yourself. I just called to tell you that Bernard went back with his ex-wife."

"Really? I'm happy for him," said Gigi.

"I thought you would want to know the reason he never called you again. I didn't want you to fret over it."

"Believe me, I wasn't fretting over it. Bernard was nice, but not my type."

"My, my, aren't we getting blasé? A few months ago you would have slit your throat if you went out with someone like Bernard and he never called you again. He was quite a catch, you know," she said testily. "What's gotten into you?"

"Sydney, I had one date with the guy. I hardly knew him. Men aren't that important to me," Gigi said as she looked in her mirror and tried to decide if Byron would find her more attractive with darker eye shadow.

"Gigi, he was handsome, successful and, at the time, available."

"He was also boring and self-absorbed. I deserve better than that."

"Gi, you know you can tell me the truth. Are you on valium again?"

"Why would the fact that I'm setting a few standards for myself have to mean I'm on

147

narcotics?"

"Because you never had any standards before. I've seen you completely ga-ga over guys whose knuckles dragged the ground. I want to know what's gotten into you," Sydney demanded.

"I promise you I'm not on drugs, booze or seeing a guru. Look, I've gotta run, Sydney. We'll have drinks this week and talk. Bye."

Gigi hung up the phone and chuckled over Sydney's obvious concern about Gigi's mental state. She knew that deep in Sydney's heart the only thing she hated worse than Gigi being insecure and unhappy was Gigi not being insecure and unhappy. Sydney liked Gigi for many reasons, one of which was the fact that Gigi had always been more neurotic than she was. The possibility of Gigi becoming strong and self-satisfied left her with the uncomfortable feeling of being left behind.

By six o'clock Gigi sat stiffly on the couch, dressed to kill, waiting nervously for Byron to show up. By seven-fifteen Byron had not arrived and Gigi paced the floor and drank white wine to calm herself.

He's not going to show, she thought miserably. He's not going to show and I'll be relegated forever to the handful of social mutants who couldn't get one decent date from Single World Video Dating. She gulped her wine and headed to the kitchen for a refill, but the doorbell rang. She thanked God, sprayed Binaca in her mouth and opened the door.

"Hi," Byron said, and handed Gigi a bouquet of

flowers. "My mother called and I had trouble getting off the phone. You know how it is."

She assured him she did. A man who loves his mother. Are you listening to this, Juanita? The man is a saint.

Byron suggested an Indian restaurant so Gigi could sample a good curry before trying out the recipes in her new Indian cookbook. Gigi felt flattered that he thought of her. Harold had always been so egocentric and selfish and had rarely asked Gigi what restaurant she preferred—that is, if he took her to a restaurant at all. Yes, Byron was quite different from Harold in all the right ways. He was polite, sensitive, intelligent, urbane, good-humored and looked like Jon Voight. He was the perfect man for her and Elizabeth.

When they arrived at the restaurant, Byron lightly held her elbow as the headwaiter led them to their table. Byron pulled out her chair for her, asked her preferences on wine. He took delight in ordering dishes that she would find interesting. Gigi was charmed and hoped Juanita was watching from a chandelier.

After dinner they sipped a strange Indian liqueur and conversation focused on books.

"Have you read William Burroughs?" Byron questioned over dessert, his lips poised at the precipice of his fork. Gigi hovered across from him, downing her drink too quickly and pondering how absolutely gorgeous this man looked by candlelight.

"No, I haven't. I don't read much. No time." Good answer, she thought. Let him think your social life keeps you constantly juggling interesting work, clever friends and adoring males. God, he was good-looking. The evening was progressing well. Their before-dinner drinks had been pleasant. Dinner was spent engaged in intelligent conversation. Now after-dinner cocktails were coming off as quietly sophisticated but definitely friendly. Gigi placed her hand toward the table's center in case he wanted to hold her hand and make things even friendlier. Destiny awaited.

"Well, I think *Naked Lunch* could serve as a prophecy for the nineties. His equating need with sickness is, well, really, saying it all, isn't it?" Byron posed the question solemnly. Gigi nodded affirmatively. Need is sickness. Okay, I'll buy that. Sort of like, I've got you under my skin? Gigi crept her hand forward and slyly let the tip of one finger rest on his available hand. You could hardly consider the tip of one little finger an aggressive act, an implicit statement of "Take me, you savage, be the father of my child," now could you? Gradually one of Byron's fingers began toying with her finger as he spoke about the problems he had with his previous marriage, but words were of no consequence to Gigi Bernstein tonight. She was speaking the language of love.

Gigi excused herself to the ladies room to refresh her makeup and give herself another Binaca blast. As she looked in the mirror she noticed a pair of worn Nikes visible beneath a toilet stall door.

"Not now," she commanded of the heavens. The heavens didn't listen. Juanita burst forth from the toilet stall.

"Is that a twinkle of love I detect in your eye?" Juanita said with a silly grin. Gigi slammed her comb through her hair angrily.

"Can't a person have a little privacy?"

"Now don't get angry. I don't understand why you don't like me more. I can be so charming. I just wanted to see how things were going with the computer date," she asked as she tried on Gigi's lipstick, then puckered her lips to study the effect in the mirror. Gigi grabbed the lipstick out of her hand.

"It's going very well, or at least it was until just now. So go ahead and tell me all the things you don't like about him. Go ahead." Gigi put her comb and makeup back in her purse and snapped it shut.

"I like him. I think he's fine. A little psuedo-intellectual perhaps, but all in all, not bad," Juanita told her. "Byron could be our man," she said with a wink.

Juanita liked him. It was an omen, Gigi assured herself gleefully as she popped a Certs. Juanita took the Opium from Gigi's purse and sprayed it behind Gigi's ears.

"If I were you, I'd slow down a little. You're all over him like a fat lady on a milkshake," said Juanita.

"I think I can handle myself."

"I guess you have to have some leeway for personal style. Maybe you'd like me out there a while, just to keep the conversational ball rolling," said Juanita. She saw Gigi's expression. "On the

151

other hand, maybe not."

Juanita wiggled her fingers at Gigi as she walked out the door and headed back to Byron. She decided to make her move.

"Would you like to go to my place for a brandy?" she asked coyly. Byron looked a little nervous, but he said yes. He paid the check and they got into the car and drove through the Saturday night traffic. Byron chattered about something, but Gigi wasn't listening. She was too busy thinking and planning. She scanned Byron's profile as he drove. Willie Nelson crooned "Nightlife" on the radio. Yes, he would be an ideal father. He was kind, personable, very attractive. A helluva lot better than Harold. Maybe Byron could love her. She probably wasn't as pretty as many of the women he dated, but then, the father of the Daughter of God would be the type to go for personality.

Gigi decided it was all systems go. She kept expecting Juanita to turn up somewhere, to suddenly pop into her lap or start whispering advice in her ear. Gigi wanted to know if this was The Night. If she made love to this man, would a band of angels play trumpets and drop rose petals on the bed? It would certainly make an impression on Byron.

He pulled into the parking lot and stopped the car. Byron leaped out and ran around the car to open her door. A little provincial, but sweet, she thought. Once inside, he sat on the sofa while Gigi put a Michael Franks record on the stereo then warmed a snifter with hot tap water. After pouring a few ounces of Grand Marnier in the steaming glass she held it to her nose. Beautiful. The elixir of love.

"Aren't you having any?" Byron asked when he accepted the snifter.

"Oh no, I like to limit myself on alcohol. But you go ahead. Enjoy," she reassured him with a devilish raise of the eyebrows. Good response. Let him think you have mastered restraint, that you are in total control of your being, that you are not driven by emotional weakness and senseless habits, and please, please kiss me before I start writhing on the floor at your feet. Gigi sat down next to him and looked at him expectantly. Byron returned her gaze. He smiled, set his glass down on the coffee table, then placed his liqueur-laced lips next to hers.

Thank you, God; thank you, Juanita; thank you, Single World Video Dating. Gigi reached behind her and turned off the light as she felt two hundred and eighty thousand volts of electricity crackling up her torso. She pressed herself against him. Gigi's hormones danced a tango as his arms drew her even closer.

Thank you, Rex; thank you, Mom, for letting me be born; thank you, Mrs. Hodgson, for letting Byron be born. Her tongue traveled to his ear where it swirled playfully as her hand made haste between his thighs.

It was about that time that Byron burst into tears.

"Byron, what's wrong?" she questioned frantically, after dislodging her tongue from his ear.

153

"I . . . I . . ." he tried to speak, but could not. He looked so helpless with the tears in his eyes. Gigi felt confused and a little frightened. She wanted to help him.

"Byron, please, tell me what's wrong. Whatever it is, trust me, I'll understand."

"I'm . . . I'm gay," he said in a garbled voice.

"I don't understand."

Byron wiped his eyes with his hand and sat up straight on the couch.

"I'm homosexual. I guess I've always tried to deny it, fight it because I thought it was wrong. Trying the video dating was a last resort to prove to myself that I was a heterosexual guy. But, Gigi, being with you tonight has finally proven it to me without a doubt. I'm gay. I'm gay, Gigi. It's what I am and I think I've finally accepted it."

Gigi switched on the light and looked for Rod Serling.

"But I want to thank you, Gigi," he continued. "You've been so good, so warm and easy to be with. This has been a real breakthrough night for me. I finally know for sure what I am. And what I am is gay," Byron confessed with a relieved smile.

Gigi examined the mannequin in the window, imagined her face in place of the model's rigid features and liked the picture she conjured. She imagined herself swathed in violet silk, its soft folds brushing against her skin as she stood encircled by the arms of her lover, a lover whose face she couldn't quite visualize. His features were

154

vague, indistinguishable, but she was certain he was handsome and gazing down at her lovingly, telling her in adoring detail how desirable she looked in violet, as moist and lush as a spray of orchids. Gigi pressed one finger against the glass as if to establish some anticipated ownership of the dress behind it.

"You'd look great in that, Gigi. Purple's your color," said Lulu, as she smeared on fresh lip gloss and smacked her lips. Sydney looked on sourly, smoothing the folds of her newest, greenest, leopard-print jumpsuit.

"She'd look like a grape," Sydney spat.

Lulu bent her fingers into a claw, scratched the air and hissed at Sydney. She turned to Gigi and whispered loudly enough for Sydney to hear. "Another victim falls prey to premenstrual syndrome. We'll just ignore her, won't we? And you wouldn't look like a grape, either. Maybe a few months ago, but not now. How much weight have you lost?"

"Fifteen pounds," Gigi answered shyly, not wanting to fuel a bickering match between Lulu and Sydney. They had been sniping ever since they arrived at the mall and it was getting on Gigi's nerves. It seemed to bother her more than usual and she assumed her date with Byron had taken its toll on her psyche. Besides, she could never understand why Sydney and Lulu constantly argued, especially since they insisted on spending so much time together.

"See? Fifteen pounds," Lulu said, and waggled a finger at Sydney. "You've got to get that dress, Gigi. Let's go in." Lulu pulled on Gigi's arm, but

Gigi held back.

"I don't feel like it right now. Let's shop around a little and come back to it later," she said. The grape comment had made a direct hit. Lulu shot Sydney a scolding look, and the three women walked down the mall a few moments in silence. They cruised past the glistening shop windows, lugging their stuffed shopping bags beside them, gazing at the treasures with the dispassion that comes from having already purchased too many things.

"So what's new with you, Gigi?" Lulu asked as they paused to examine some Italian handbags. "I've heard all about the office, but you don't talk about your love life anymore. I've been dying to ask you about Harold," she said. Gigi looked at Lulu and saw Lulu's eyes fixed upon her like a cat fixed upon some moving object. Lulu wanted the gossip and she wanted it badly. Lately Gigi had been mum about her personal life. Who would understand or believe her anyway? And if she told Lulu and Sydney the real story it would probably end up as a headline in the *National Enquirer* next to a story about UFOs and two-headed babies. Gigi looked at her friends to gauge what she could tell them. Sydney looked stiff and distracted. It was strange, especially since Sydney had so enthusiastically arranged the shopping trip only one day before.

When Gigi failed to respond to Lulu's question, Lulu placed a consoling hand on her friend's shoulder.

"You know, Gigi, you can always feel free to tell

156

me anything pertaining to men. Just because you're a vegetarian doesn't mean you can't enjoy reading a recipe with beef, if you know what I mean. Sydney has filled me in about Harold, and trust me, what you need is a major change. I say we cut you short and sweep it all back from your face, like this." Lulu demonstrated by using her hands to push Gigi's hair away from her face. "What do you think, Syd? Too Joan Crawford?"

"Honest, Lulu, I don't think hair is the problem," Gigi said, untangling her friend's fingers from her tresses. "It's like this. Harold is marrying someone else."

Lulu halted, took Gigi's hand and looked at her with exaggerated remorse.

"I'm glad you finally brought it out into the open," Lulu said. "It's not healthy to keep it inside. You must be feeling desperate."

"You're acting like I just lost a leg or something. I only lost Harold. There will be other men."

"Sure there will be, you poor thing," said Lulu, cupping Gigi's face in her hands, then forcing Gigi's head onto her shoulder. "Go ahead and cry. Just let it out, let it right here in front of Lord and Taylors. No one could blame you. That filthy bastard. He probably left you for some little tramp. If she ever walks into my salon I'll shear the bitch until she looks like a Georgia peach."

Gigi appreciated Lulu's concern, but not as much as she appreciated Lulu's finally releasing her grip on Gigi's skull. The three women lined up in front of a shop window to admire some Gucci luggage, and when Gigi glanced into the glass she saw a vague figure in its reflection, the faint visage of something familiar but with a distinctly new Hollywood tackiness. Gigi turned. Juanita had on her usual dress and bedraggled Nikes, but that day she had adorned her red curls with large gardenias and she sported dark, cat-eye-shaped sunglasses that teetered on the tip of her nose. In her hand she held a Lord and Taylor shopping bag. A grin spread across her face.

"Gigi Bernstein! I thought it was you. Imagine seeing you here," she said gaily. She turned to Lulu and Sydney and extended a hand. "I'm Juanita. Gigi and I are old, old friends."

Gigi rolled her eyes. "Yes we've known each other for ages. Juanita, this is Sydney and Lulu." Gigi introduced them with a dry voice.

"Such a pleasure to meet you. What incredible kismet this it. I've got loads of shopping to do but I'd love to stop for a little lunch. Anyone in the mood for Chinese?"

Lulu started to say yes, but Gigi interrupted.

"We just ate, Juanita," she said, not certain of what the result would be if she mixed Juanita, Lulu and Sydney together. She imagined a high-school experiment in which incompatible chemicals explode into chaos.

"So you're an old friend of Gigi's. I can't believe we haven't met you before," said Lulu. Sydney didn't speak a word of hello, but remained silent with the same dull look on her face.

"Gigi just never introduces me to her friends. I can't imagine why. Why is that, Gigi?" said

158

Juanita.

All eyes turned upon Gigi. Her lips twisted into a fake smile. "I guess it's just the way you pop in and out. I never know when you're going to turn up." There was noticeable sarcasm in Gigi's voice. She looked into Juanita's shopping bag and smirked when she saw that it was empty. She wondered what Juanita was up to.

"That's me. Unpredictable as hell."

"What are you doing here, Juanita? I never thought of you as much of a shopper," Gigi said.

"Sometimes I like to browse. Today I've been through all the stores looking at baby clothes." Juanita looked at Gigi coyly. "They're so sweet, all of those little booties and bibs. Don't you agree?"

Gigi was about to tell Juanita exactly what she thought, but then her attention suddenly turned elsewhere. Sydney's body had begun to tremble. Her face turned white, then flashed pink. Her lip quivered and tears sprouted from her eyes.

"What is it?" Gigi asked, but Sydney didn't reply. Lulu started to briskly pat Sydney's cheek as if to rouse her from some petit mal seizure. Juanita looked on placidly.

"Let's sit her down," Gigi said to Lulu. "Over there." Gigi nodded toward a bench and the three women led Sydney to it and pressed her into a sitting position.

"I'm . . . I'm pregnant," Sydney muttered through her mascara-tinted tears, the utterance of her condition only increasing her trembling. Gigi and Lulu looked at each other. Juanita smiled.

"But, Sydney, that's wonderful. Being pregnant

159

is wonderful," Gigi told her, hearing the uncertainty in her own voice.

Lulu clapped her hands. "A baby! Why, it's fantastic, Sydney. We'll all love a baby!"

Sydney's tears gushed anew. Gigi sat down next to Sydney. "Does Arthur know?"

Sydney nodded.

"Is he happy?"

"Thrilled," Sydney said, her voice choked. "He's already buying baby things."

"Then what's the problem? I don't understand. You should be blissful."

"I know I should feel happy. I feel guilty about not being happy, but I'm just not sure I want it."

"Of course you want it," Lulu said. "It's your baby. You'll love it. Babies are soft and pink. They gurgle, they burp. They're cute."

"They can grow up to be convicted felons," Sydney said.

"They can grow up to be strong, honest people," Gigi threw in.

"They can grow up to despise you, to resent the way you've lived your life," said Sydney.

"But they can grow up to love you, to be a part of you," said Gigi.

"Having a baby makes you fat."

"Having a baby makes you glow."

"Having a baby—"

"Hold it, you two." Juanita held up a hand and the conversation stopped. She put down her shopping bag and sat between Sydney and Gigi. Lulu squeezed in also, so they were lined up on the bench together.

"Let's analyze this," Juanita told Sydney. "What exactly is the problem here?"

Sydney blew her nose noisily on her handkerchief. "I don't know," she said.

"You're afraid," said Juanita.

"Yes, who wouldn't be?"

"Of what?"

"Afraid of the responsibility for another person."

"But aren't you responsible for Arthur? You're married. What's so different?" asked Lulu.

"Everything. Arthur's an adult. I didn't create him. I didn't get the chance to screw him up as a child. He was already screwed up when I got him. But me with a baby? It's not natural."

"Not natural? You've got to be kidding?" said Juanita. "Why, it could be the first really natural thing you've ever experienced."

Sydney raised an eyebrow. Gigi recognized the incandescent glow Juanita got when she really started cooking on a subject. Her eyes turned hot, her face flushed, her fingers fanned and sliced the air with gestures.

"To reproduce, to re-create oneself, is the life cycle," Juanita continued. "Why, everything reproduces. Cells divide, plants make seed, suns burst into a million stars. It's the great cosmic womb and it connects women more closely to the universal pulse, because as women you can re-create with your bodies. Can't you feel it sometimes? Right around the days of your menstrual cycle your body hums, your spirit glows, your mind tunes into the cosmos."

161

"I always thought it was just cramps," said Lulu, her expression confused.

"It's the woman's birthright. The universe is feminine, it's cyclical, reproductive. To be pregnant is to plug into that cosmic femaleness and feel its power. It's a fantastic, mesmerizing thing. Can't you feel it, Sydney?"

Sydney had stopped crying and stared at Juanita with big eyes. "I don't know. Maybe I can feel it," Sydney said slowly. "I do feel sort of connected to things. Maybe I just couldn't see it before." Sydney moved her hands to her stomach. She grinned. "I don't know, Juanita. It sounds crazy, but maybe it's true."

"So go home, think about it. You'll see I'm right."

"Well, I do have to run. Arthur's going to be home soon. I have this urge to talk to him."

"I've gotta run too. Sydney, I'll drop you off. Nice meeting you, Juanita," said Lulu as the two women gathered their things. There was a new lightness in Sydney's step as she and Lulu headed for the exit.

"You know, you do have your good moments," Gigi said as soon as her friends were out of earshot.

"I like to think so. That's the first time you've ever complimented me. Thank you. A little positive feedback is quite gratifying."

"Now tell me why you're really here."

"You're so suspicious. I just like to touch base with you occasionally so we can chat, so we can share a few notions on the type of man we're

162

looking for as Elizabeth's father," Juanita said.

"We? I thought I got to choose the father, although that concept is rapidly evaporating."

"Well, of course you do, but as I mentioned, I plan to serve as a consultant on the matter. This is all very important to me."

"I will not go unaffected either. Why don't you just get to the point, Juanita? There is a point to this line of conversation I presume?"

"You're getting testy just when we were starting to get along. Okay, straight-talk time. You're angry about the thing with Bernard, aren't you? You're angry with me still?"

"Why would I be angry?" Gigi tested.

"Several possibilities. You don't think I trust you. You don't think I respect you enough to trust your judgment in finding the right father. You think I'm interfering, taking too much control in the matter when you're supposed to have free will. You think I'm pushy and overbearing. Have I hit upon anything yet?"

"You've hit on everything. Bernard was perfectly nice. He was kind, intelligent and I liked him." She didn't want to tell Juanita about his reunion with his wife.

"I'm sorry, I just didn't think he was the right guy for the job. He's not the right type. He's too stuffy and full of himself and certainly not what you would call Mr. Personality."

"Is he going to be fathering the Daughter of God or filling in for Johnny on the *Tonight Show?*"

"Remember the stipulation about the father,

Gigi? You have to feel love for him. That little rule was thrown in for a reason. I'm thinking about you, Gigi, as well as Elizabeth. I know things have been a little tough lately."

"Are you referring to my date with Byron the other night?"

"You aren't upset about that, are you? That man's reactions had nothing to do with you. And he was never really a father candidate."

"You knew Byron was gay from the beginning."

"I knew? What am I, psychic? I was as surprised as you were," Juanita said defensively. Gigi's eyes grew moist.

"All I know is that I'll never find a father for Elizabeth. Sydney gets pregnant by accident when she doesn't even want a baby and with all the planning in the world I can't even get to first base."

Juanita shrugged her shoulders. "It's a crazy world out there, but your time will come."

"I want to get plugged into the cosmic womb, Juanita."

"You are plugged in. We just haven't hit the switch yet, kiddo."

That night Gigi dreamed she was lying on a pure white satin bed floating within a velvety powder-blue sky. A band of blond, white-robed angels stood on a fluffy cloud before her, shiny gold trumpets raised as they played a brass rendition of the Beatles tune "Love Me Do." Gigi tapped her fingers to the music, then she looked up from her bed and saw something in the distance floating down toward her. As it came closer she saw that it was a large pinkish penis with gossamer wings fluttering as it floated lightly down. It came closer and closer, beckoning to her as it dipped and pirouetted buoyantly through the air. There was something ethereal about the penis, something teasing and enticing. And just as it hovered inches from her, wings beating like a hummingbird's, she stretched her fingers to reach it, but it slipped from her grasp like a thistle in a breeze.

CHAPTER ELEVEN

Men. They were like a chic disease you couldn't quite catch. Gigi longingly watched them at lunchtime as they moved through the city with their clipped hair, starched shirts and mysterious minds. There seemed to be so many of them, so why couldn't she ferret out just one, just one little Y chromosome blossomed into one not-quite-perfect male perfectly suited to Gigi Bernstein? Was it so much to ask?

After her plea to the book club a few father prospects drifted her way, with Maureen the next to bring forth a human sacrifice. His name was Phil. Maureen met him at a spiritual healing seminar, and at a peak moment when her consciousness was on a non-stop to Venus, Maureen flashed on what a perfect couple Phil and Gigi would make. It could be a relationship made in heaven, she insisted, which was precisely what Gigi had in mind, except that Phil had a few problems communicating with sentences that didn't contain the word "reality" or dealing with any concept that didn't revolve around his psychic aura. When Phil asked Gigi to transport herself to a higher level, she informed him she never transported herself anywhere she couldn't take her credit cards. It didn't require Juanita's assistance for Gigi to see Phil was a nice guy but not The One.

Lynn was the next to deliver, in the form of Barry. Now Barry had promise. A gynecologist with a taste for classical music and fine wine, Barry invited Gigi to listen to Mozart, then followed up with dinner at a quaint French restaurant. He was intelligent, charming and her mother would be so thrilled to tell her canasta club that her daughter had bagged a doctor. Gigi hoped Juanita was tuned in as Barry explained how he was divorced but wanted to remarry someday and have another child. Gigi made a mental note to give Lynn something really nice for her next birthday. After dinner they walked down a tree-lined boulevard, hand in hand. Barry told her stories about his medical school days, funny anecdotes about his parents, about his firm belief in the power and equality of women. Gigi decided to give Lynn a trip to Club Med for her birthday. Then Barry gently pulled Gigi behind a large oak tree that shielded them from view. Pressing her against the tree trunk, he kissed her gently.

"I find you very sexy," he whispered as he nibbled her neck.

167

Ditto, Gigi thought, too enraptured to speak. Barry kissed her ears, her forehead, her hair. His hands caressed her cheek and her shoulders, his tongue slipped between her lips. One hand began to drift up her skirt and Gigi wondered exactly how far the mother of the Daughter of God should go on the first date.

"Barry?" she whispered gently, but it was difficult to get his attention. His breathing grew heavier.

"Uh, Barry, honey, could we talk?" Gigi said when she heard something rip. She looked down. Barry had torn her Christian Dior control tops along with her panties almost completely off her body and was now attempting to remove his own Fruit-Of-The-Looms, albeit more carefully than he had removed hers.

"What are you doing?" Gigi asked, although fairly certain he was not giving her a free checkup.

"I want you," he mumbled hoarsely.

"How flattering, Barry, but I don't think this is the time or place." The mother of Elizabeth should not be raped behind a tree.

"I want you," he repeated, this time using his penis for punctuation. Gigi felt it jamming into her thigh. It started to hurt her leg so she grabbed it, an innocent gesture which Barry misinterpreted.

"Yes, yes, you wild bitch," Barry said in a sexual frenzy. Gigi was extremely flattered by the attention, especially after that fiasco with Byron, but still, she had her principles.

"Look, Barry, get off me, and I mean now."

"You want it. You know you want it. You're hot for it, baby, and I'm going to give it to you now."

What an arrogant schmuck, she thought. The tree bark was starting to dig uncomfortably into Gigi's behind. She pressed her knee sharply into his groin, then used her elbows to push him away. There were a few seconds of struggle, but his knees got tangled in his pants and he fell back onto the ground.

"What are you, frigid?" he shouted after her as she walked down the street with as much speed and dignity as she could muster with her panties flapping torn around her knees.

Gigi had remembered to grab her purse before leaving Barry in the dirt, so she had money for a cab home, but she didn't feel like getting into a strange cab with her clothes in shreds. It would be better to call Sydney and ask for a ride home. Gigi saw a gas station ahead, and when she got closer she found a phone booth on the corner. Hopping inside the booth quickly so no one would see her, she prayed she would have a quarter so she wouldn't have to ask the attendant for change. She dug through the bottom of her purse and came up with the precious coin. She dropped it in the slot and dialed Sydney's number. It rang six times. No answer. Who would she find at home on a Friday night? Lulu might be at home, but Gigi was in no mood for a socio-political treatise on animalistic power-mongering male behavior. Gigi looked through her pocket phone directory, then she dialed Lynn, who had gotten her into this mess in the first place and who was now receiving a water balloon in her lap for her next birthday. No answer. She considered her dilemma. She couldn't call her parents. She flipped through the directory again. The only other option she came up with was Waldo. She had agreed to work late for him a few days earlier so he would be free to take Delores to her tarot card reading. He owed Gigi one. Gigi dialed the number. A woman answered. That threw Gigi for a second, but when she asked for Waldo, the woman called out his name and he soon came to the phone.

"Hi, Waldo. This is Gigi."

"Gigi, hi!" He sounded surprised to hear from her. "What can I do for you?"

"Well, I really hate to bother you now. You have company."

"It's just Delores. We're watching a movie. Gigi, what is it?"

"Waldo, I sort of need your help." She could feel herself blushing and was glad he couldn't see her.

"What's wrong, Gigi? Where are you? I hear cars."

Gigi closed the phone-booth door.

"I'm at a pay phone at the corner of First and Branson. I need a ride home."

"How did you end up there without a car? It's pretty late."

"I had a date that didn't work out."

"Your date didn't work out so the guy left you

170

on a street corner?"

"I'll give you all the details later. Let's just say I'm in a phone booth with my pantyhose hanging off me in little pieces. Get the picture?" Gigi enjoyed making it sound dramatic.

"First and Branson. I'll be there in fifteen minutes," he said quickly, then hung up. Gigi sat down on the curb. She wished she hadn't called him. She felt embarrassed by what had happened and now Waldo would know, Delores would know, maybe the whole law office would know by Monday. But then she knew Waldo would never tell anyone if she asked him not to. He was definitely an honorable sort of person. Gigi got out her comb and lipstick and tried to fix her face before he arrived. It was a warm night, soft and balmy, with a few stars in the sky. Gigi breathed in the air and leaned back onto the grass. Now that Waldo was on his way, she felt better.

In fourteen minutes Waldo's BMW pulled up to the curb. He leaped out of the car.

"Where is the bastard. I'll kill him!" Waldo yelled, his hands in fists and his face reddened with fury. Gigi chuckled at the thought of Waldo's five-foot-eight frame tackling Barry.

Delores slid out of the car and leaned lazily against a fender, watching Waldo's ranting with concerned annoyance. It surprised Gigi how young she looked, but then she remembered that Waldo was only twenty-seven. She was prettier than the photograph on Waldo's desk. Her hair was pulled tightly into a ponytail that sprouted

171

from the top of her head, the base of the pony-tail wrapped with a thick metallic band, giving the impression it was being choked. She wore an oversized blazer and a long dark skirt that flapped around pink cowboy boots. Her black-rimmed eyes scanned Gigi up and down.

"Rough night, huh? I'm Delores," she said, pronouncing the name slowly and dramatically, as if her name itself held some voodoo.

"So where is he?" Waldo asked again, bouncing on his heels and fiercely shaking his fist.

"Oh, don't act so macho. You look silly," said Delores. Gigi thought he looked cute. Waldo ignored the remark.

"He's gone, Waldo," Gigi told him. "Don't worry. I took care of him. I just want to go home, okay?"

Waldo looked disappointed. "But, Gigi, a man like that should be beaten to a pulp. Where does he live? I'll go over there," Waldo continued through gritted teeth as he helped Gigi into the back seat of the car. Delores got in the front seat and Waldo pulled out into the traffic, gripping the steering wheel as if it were Barry's head.

"There's no need to get so mad. I'm sure Gigi can take care of herself," Delores told him, rolling down the window and sticking her head out to feel the air on her face.

"Can she? Sometimes I wonder, Gigi. I really wonder. How could you accept a date with a guy who would attack you, then leave you out on the street? Look at you. You look awful. What's all that stuff in your hair?"

Gigi reached up and felt her head. "It's tree bark. Don't lecture me."

"You should be more choosy about who you go out with."

"I took a seminar on interpersonal horizons from an astrological perspective and they said you should check out a person's charts before you get serious with him. A lot of people think astrology is sixties stuff, but it's actually a contemporary science," Delores said, her head still halfway out the window, the ponytail flapping in the wind like a windsock.

"I'll remember that," Gigi replied. The last time a man asked her what her sign was she had answered "clitoris."

Delores pulled her head back in and looked at Gigi.

"You do have a lot of stuff in your hair. It looks like ground cover," said Delores.

"It's bark. I'm sure of it."

Delores reached over the seat and started picking the bark out of Gigi's scalp, a gesture Gigi found rather friendly, one of good will, like one monkey grooming another monkey.

"Even in its current condition, I like your haircut. Who does it?" Delores asked.

"Lulu at Neiman's."

"I'll have to try her." Delores put her head back out the window, and that ended conversation for a few minutes, for which Gigi was grateful. It was Waldo who broke the silence.

"Tell me if I'm getting too personal, but why do you waste yourself on creeps like this guy tonight? I remembered meeting a boyfriend of yours that you had for a couple of years. What was his name?"

"Harold."

"Right. Harold. I met him at the office party last year. It just didn't look to me like he treated you very well. Not that I thought he took you home and beat you or anything. It was just that he didn't treat you like you were, well, valuable. People should be treated like they're valuable whether they're male or female. Do you know what I mean?"

Gigi looked at him. Yes, she knew what he meant. People should be regarded as valuable, although it was never an adjective she applied to herself. Waldo continued talking and Gigi leaned back and closed her eyes, grateful that she didn't have to talk.

"For a while I went out with a lot of girls, just to go out, you know. I guess I just wanted the companionship and the sex. But I wasn't really interested in anybody, at least not until I met Delores. You're better off staying at home than wasting your time with people who don't mean anything to you."

"But how do you meet anybody if you stay at home?" asked Gigi. Delores pulled her head inside once more and turned to Waldo, interested in his response, especially since they had met each other in a bar.

Waldo looked thoughtful. "I don't know. I think sometimes it just happens. You don't have to do anything. It just comes to you.'

"You can say that because you're twenty-seven and you're in a relationship. I've been waiting for someone to come to me for thirty-five years. If I wait much longer I'll be too old to recognize him when he gets here," Gigi said sleepily. It was getting past her usual bedtime. Delores laughed and gave Waldo a kiss.

Delores waited in the car after they arrived at Gigi's apartment. Gigi said good-bye to Delores, and Waldo walked her to her front door. After she found her keys and opened the door, she turned to him.

"Thanks for rescuing me. And I like Delores."

Waldo grinned. "Thanks. See you Monday."

"Yeah. We have a meeting at two." She started to close the door.

"Gigi, one more thing."

"Yes, Waldo?" she said in a drowsy voice.

"Promise me you won't go out with any more creeps?"

"I promise, Waldo," she whispered, then closed the door and locked it.

CHAPTER TWELVE

Gigi gnawed "Flamingo Pink" off her finger-nail as she waited in the hall for the elevator. It was typically slow around five-thirty when the throng of Milam Building workers headed home. The day had been a tough one. Sydney had called four times to share her current thoughts and feelings regarding maternity. Ever since her conversation at the mall that day, Sydney had done a reversal in her attitude on babies and was boring everyone with lengthy descriptions of fetal development and pros and cons of breastfeeding.

"See you tomorrow, Gigi."

Waldo walked up beside her and set down his overstuffed attache while he loosened his tie. He took a wrinkled handkerchief from his pocket, mopped his forehead, then stared into the cloth as if he expected to be perspiring blood.

"Waldo, it's only five forty-five. Isn't this early for you to be leaving work?" Gigi asked teasingly. Waldo gave her a serious look.

"Delores and I are fighting. Something's been funny with her lately."

"What do you mean by funny?" Gigi asked.

"Funny like this morning she took a bowl of Rice Krispies, slammed it against the wall and said she was sick of my male, power-hungry attitude. All I had done was ask her to buy granola. How does that make me power hungry?"

"Seems to me, all that makes you is granola hungry."

Waldo didn't laugh. He looked as if he wanted to go into more detail, but the elevator doors parted, beckoning them inside. The elevator brimmed with gray-suited, grim-faced professionals mentally preparing themselves to battle the traffic home. Armed with briefcases, newspapers and gym bags they stood shoulder to shoulder, staring blankly, saying nothing, as if their lives were temporarily paused, frozen in motion until they arrived at the destinations where their lives could resume once more. Gigi squeezed into the elevator next to Waldo and stood quietly, busily strategizing which side roads she would try out that evening to avoid some of the rush-hour traffic. Third floor, second floor, lobby. The elevator doors parted. Waldo waved good-bye. Gigi stepped out and faced the one sight she least expected—Harold.

Leaning passively against a potted rhododendron, he fidgeted with his keys, stared at the patterned floor. Harold looked a little plumper, a trifle paler than the last time she saw him. Her body frozen, Gigi grappled with the alternatives. Should she walk past him without saying hello? Should she stop to talk? Why would he be here? The sight of him shot a pain through her stomach, filtered a familiar weakness through her knees. She wanted to turn and run away, yet she wanted to grab him, slap his face, tell him how she loathed him.

Then he glanced up and saw her. He smiled. Now she was hooked. She had to speak to him, come up with something casual to say. Why hello, Harold, you lousy two-timing, son of a bitch. Driven anyone to suicide lately? She marched up to him bravely. Fight instead of flight.

"Hello, Harold. What's new?" She grimaced. Was it possible for her to say anything more than "What's new"? Why did Harold have this way of disrupting her emotional balance, especially now, when she was feeling at least a little stable?

"Hi, Gi. I need to talk to you."

"About what?" she replied sharply.

"About us." He took her hand into his with atypical affection. Gigi looked into his eyes and didn't see the old expression of annoyed disinterest. She searched his hand for a wedding ring and found it suspiciously bare.

"What happened to Barbie?" Gigi asked, deciding it was straight-talk time, as Juanita would have phrased it.

"That didn't work out."

Gigi studied his face for telltale traces of false-hood.

"But you were getting married."

"Yeah, well, she was too young. She wasn't sure of what she wanted. You know how it is sometimes."

Gigi did. Oh, how she did.

"She left you?"

Harold seem to bristle at the words, seemed to shake all over like a damp dog after a tumble in the mud.

"I wouldn't put it that way. It didn't work out, that's all. It was a mistake, a gigantic error. Believe me."

Believe him? Believing Harold had always been emotionally very expensive, yet now he seemed sincere, almost contrite. He looked troubled and lonely. Gigi allowed herself to relax a little. Noticing her soften, Harold made his play.

"Let's get back together, Gi. I miss you. Really, I do. I think about you all the time." He waited for her reaction but saw only the suspicion in her eyes and the stiffness in her body. "I've changed, Gigi. I want to come back. Will you let me, Gi?" he pleaded softly.

She looked up at Harold and searched his face for clues that might explain this unexpected behavior. A scene from *An Unmarried Woman* flashed through her mind. Gigi remembered the part when Jill Clayburgh's husband, after abandoning her for a younger woman, asked her if he could come back. Jill told him to kiss off. Gigi remembered stomping her feet and clapping during that part, yet now, faced with a similar situation, she felt uncertain. Should she be strong, laugh haughtily and walk away? That's what Jill Clayburgh would have done. Of course, in the movie Jill Clayburgh had Alan Bates waiting in the wings. Gigi simply stood silently and looked at Harold.

"Anyone can make a mistake," said Hitler to Eva Braun.

"Anyone can make a mistake," Nixon said to Pat.

"Anyone can make a mistake," said Harold to interrupt the uncomfortable silence.

Good point, Gigi told herself. People make mistakes. Great men and women, lousy men and women, all throughout history have made mistakes they were sorry for later. So why shouldn't Harold? After all, Harold was only human or some subset thereof. He did have a new vulnerability that at the moment she found very appealing.

"Harold, I . . ." she began, but Harold put his fingers to her lips to silence any chance of protest.

"Don't say a word," he whispered. "Just have dinner with me Wednesday night. Will you?"

She nodded.

"Perfect. Wonderful. I'll be at your place about seven." He clasped her hands once more into his.

"You don't know what this means to me, Gigi. I have so much I want to tell you. Ciao until then."

Harold turned and walked three feet before looking back over his shoulder. "And, Gi, cook something light. I'm dieting."

Seems like old times, she thought as she watched him trot jauntily out the door.

Harris County courtroom number four was a worn and musty place of yellowed walls, green tile flooring and oaken banisters ingrained with years of its patrons' woes. As steeped in tradition and as unyielding as the law itself, the room alone seemed to pass judgment on the accused. It was the walls, the oak railings, the ancient framed pictures, the dusty floors that sized up each defendant as he or she passed through the portals. It always gave Gigi a spooky feeling, especially on days when she was the first to arrive for a hearing and was alone in the courtroom. Gigi walked slowly to the front, laid her briefcase on a table, slid into a chair. She slumped forward, looked around the room to make certain she was alone, then closed her eyes, laying her face in her hands.

Harold's sudden appearance the previous evening had left Gigi in a flood of confusion. She could think of nothing else. When she arrived home the night before she couldn't eat, couldn't work, couldn't manage to flip through

New Woman magazine which might have offered some meaty article providing advice on such a matter. Instead she ran a thousand iterations through her mind of what Harold had said, what Harold had meant, should she take the risk of seeing him, had he really changed, could she trust him? How could she say no? Had she ever been able to say no?

Thoughts of Harold bounced about her cranium like pingpong balls as people filtered into the courtroom at 8:30. The Naylor hearing was first on the docket, an initial hearing involving Marcie's two greedy aunts and one greedier uncle who would attempt to slur the reputations of the others until one of the three arose as marginally fit to accept the responsibility of Marcie and her money.

Marcie would have an opportunity to speak to the judge that day, and Gigi and Waldo had prepped her for hours earlier in the week. They wanted her to be able to describe preferences and needs accurately to the judge, of course, but most of all they didn't want her to curse like a sailor in front of everyone. At the end of several preparatory sessions Marcie was answering practice questions without any noticeable obscenities and Waldo had rewarded her afterward with a couple of sips of a Lone Star beer the two of them purchased at a 7-Eleven.

"Hiya, Gi," Marcie said as she reached the front seats with her aunt Loreen, who was looking uncomfortable in her matronly gray dress with a high neck and conservative little pleats down the front. The dress looked expensive, but Loreen had most likely considered it an investment in the future. Aunt Loreen, Gigi discovered, had enjoyed a colorful career as a nude baton twirler at Mike Angelo's Beer, Pool and Dance-athon on the north side of Fort Worth. She had a brief marriage to the other Naylor brother who had died in a truck wreck three years earlier on I-35. When Loreen caught wind of the untimely demise of Marcie's father, she suddenly found religion, tossed away her baton, clothed herself and discovered a maternal instinct that could only be fulfilled at Marcie's side. It was a sweet and touching story that no one believed, including Gigi. Still, she was in the running and didn't look that bad when you considered Marcie's other alternatives.

Angela Maynard, the prima donna from River Oaks, marched regally into the room flanked by two high-priced attorneys. Angela had already done fairly well for herself due to two very lucrative divorce settlements, but with the current instability of oil and the stock market, Angela required more security than her divorces could eventually provide. Besides, she was a blood relation, she argued, always putting a deep macabre drawl on the word "b-l-o-o-d" when she referred to Marcie. Blood was thicker than water, thicker than the black crude that ran through the Naylor oil rigs, Angela swore, although no thicker than the brain of that half-witted naked baton twirler

183

or, heaven forbid, the whiskey-sodden mind of Bubba Naylor, who had also entered the pageant for guardianship.

Bubba was a jovial sort, a hard-drinking, easy-belching kind of guy who used to come frequently to his older brother for handouts. Bubba hung his head when he heard the news about his brother's death and considered it his usual rotten luck until a slick attorney from Tyler mentioned to him that little Marcie and all her attached assets were without a daddy. He assured Bubba that he probably had paternal instincts he had never dreamed of. The attorney filled his mind with pictures of limousines and beautiful blondes with breasts as big as Dallas and how he wouldn't have to pay a dime up front in legal fees if he would simply agree to give the attorney a reasonable, very reasonable cut of the action. The next thing Bubba knew, he was dressed in a Sears suit and walking willfully into a courtroom, which was one place he had spent a lot of time trying to avoid.

The three relatives spread out in the courtroom so they could sit as far away from one another as possible, although they managed to cast disgusted glances at each other as if they were inspecting the slime on the belly of a rock. Marcie insisted that she sit next to Gigi, which Aunt Angela agreed to with a begrudging sweetness that she had acquired after the urgings of her attorneys.

Marcie couldn't stop wiggling in her seat, jostling Gigi's papers, dropping her purse on the floor and scattering its contents. Gigi just smiled and tried to calm Marcie down with a few soothing words and a box of Junior Mints, but deep inside, Gigi wasn't sure she could cope with her Harold problems and Marcie's fidgeting too. Then Waldo showed. It surprised Gigi how all of the tension and hyperactivity he showed in the office disappeared in the courtroom. He seemed composed and confident. When he sat down Marcie looked at him with a schoolgirl crush in her eyes, and his presence alone temporarily transformed her into an angel.

"All rise." Judge Patricia Spencer entered the room with a dramatic sweep of her long black robes and she seated herself solemnly upon the judicial bench. The oldest female judge in the southwest, she was silver-haired, authoritative, with an excellent knowledge of the law and a well-known propensity to doze off during boring segments of testimony.

Slick attorneys, a bored judge, greedy plaintiffs and a great deal of money—the typical components of a rough day in courtroom number four, Gigi thought. She noticed Marcie stiffen, a look of fear crossing her face as the judge entered. Gigi patted her hand and tried to smile at her, but Marcie's face was fixed upon Judge Spencer.

"Bubba Naylor should be first up," Waldo said. Gigi felt something on her leg, looked down and saw Waldo drawing on her calf with a ballpoint pen. She let out a little yelp and her mouth opened in astonishment. She gave him a frosty glare, wondering what pill he could have popped to induce him to such behavior. Then she saw Marcie giggle and realized the impromptu leg art was a successful attempt at calming a frightened child. Gigi approved, but moved her chair to get out of his reach.

As Waldo predicted, Bubba walked gravely up to the judge with his attorney and made his plea for caring of poor little parentless Marcie. He began by describing the strength of his relationship with his dead brother and how on the golf course one afternoon Jack had specifically asked Bubba, with tears in his eyes, to promise that he would take care of Marcie should anything, God forbid, happen to her daddy.

"Horseshit," Marcie whispered. "Daddy didn't even play golf and he wouldn't have trusted Uncle Bubba alone with a sheep. If I end up with him I'll run away to Vegas and be a black-jack dealer, I swear. Besides, he smells." And with that she sunk down in her seat and crossed her arms with defiance. Waldo patted her arm reassuringly. Gigi doodled Harold's name across her legal pad.

After Bubba's statement there were some dis-gusted rumblings from the back of the room. Bubba was questioned routinely by the judge and then asked to sit down. Angela was next. She glided up to the judge's bench with the smooth assurance of a rattlesnake and explained to Judge

Spencer in a silky voice about the stable environment, culturally, spiritually and otherwise, that she could provide Marcie. After all, a stable home life was vitally important these days and Marcie deserved the advantages of the atmosphere Angela could provide her. Bubba Naylor, she contended, had been a heavy drinker all his life and had never once played a stitch of golf to her knowledge, and as far as Loreen was concerned, well, Loreen was privy to more men than the Oilers locker room and there were stories circulating about her that she dare not mention in a public place.

"Why, you old whoredog!" Loreen yelled from the back of the room. She wrestled herself away from her red-faced attorney and ran to the judge's bench, her blond hair flying, and proceeded to dig her long, fake magenta nails into Angela's well-moisturized arm.

"Why, I've never even been in the Oilers locker room! Ask anybody!" she implored the judge while Angela managed to free herself with the help of the bailiff and Loreen's attorney. The court reporter, looking bored, typed away. Marcie squealed gleefully, Gigi looked shocked and Waldo just sat calmly and smiled.

After everyone was settled once again in their seats, the judge brought up each of the three relatives individually, asked them routine questions, demanded routine answers, allowing no further disruptions. Judge Spencer had things in such control that she even managed a nap during

187

Loreen's exhaustive description of how wonderful she was with the children at the day-care center where she currently worked part time and how much she loved the Lord.

Waldo observed everything closely and made copious notes, which was fortunate since Gigi's mental capabilities were limited to an analysis of Harold's flaws versus attributes.

"What's wrong with you today?" Waldo asked. She had definitely decided to let Harold come over. The big question was whether she should let it go further than that. Juanita would say she was a fool. Waldo would say she was self-destructive. Sydney would say she was acting out anal-retentive tendencies. Her mother would say she was one smart cookie.

And would Harold be the father of Elizabeth? Juanita would be against it. But then, perhaps not. This could be destiny. Perhaps Harold was to be the father and it only took losing Gigi for him to realize how much he really needed her. Yes, Harold, the father of the Daughter of God. It could work. She could see the headlines: "And lo, although he leaveth her for a dental hygienist, he cameth back unto her and things were right in the heavens."

"You were sleeping and I saw you!" The words crashed through Gigi's daydream. She snapped her head up and saw Marcie before the bench shaking her finger perilously at Judge Spencer with Waldo at her side trying to calm her down.

"I saw your eyes closed for at least ten minutes. How can you make a decision as big as this if you're going to sleep through all the talking? You have to listen to these assholes to get how screwed up they really are! And are you listening? You're sleeping!"

"I wasn't sleeping, young lady. My eyes were closed so I could think," Judge Spencer responded testily, a bright blush creeping up her face.

"I know sleeping when I see it. Your lips were fluttering like you were snoring a little, like this." Marcie imitated the fluttering of Judge Spencer's lips.

"Young lady, my lips don't flutter when I'm sleeping. They flutter when I'm thinking. My lips were fluttering because I was thinking."

Gigi jumped to intervene.

"Excuse me, Judge Spencer, I apologize for Ms. Naylor's behavior, but please keep in mind the tremendous emotional pressure this child has been under," Gigi explained in a formal tone, her arm around Marcie's shoulder.

"Horseshit," Marcie muttered. "I'm about to get flushed down the toilet and this judge is catching z's."

Waldo took Marcie's elbow in hand and steered her back to her seat. A few moments of smooth talking and Gigi had Judge Spencer calmed down, but she reprimanded Gigi for Marcie's behavior. Gigi assured her it would never happen again and shot Marcie a meaningful look.

"I won't live with any of those schmucks," Marcie announced angrily as Gigi and Waldo followed her out of the courtroom. The hearing was chalked up as a disaster by all involved. Judge Spencer finally requested written summaries of each relative's family environment, economic status and personal history. Temporary custody of Marcie had been again rewarded to Angela Maynard, a repulsive alternative to Marcie, but certainly no less so than the others. She insisted on walking with Waldo and Gigi as far as the courthouse steps where she was to be whisked away in Angela's four-year-old black Cadillac.

"They're not schmucks," Gigi told her. Waldo and Marcie both shot her dubious looks.

"Okay, they're schmucks. But we have to work with what we've got, don't we?"

"What I've got is three assholes and I don't want to be within ten feet of any of them," said Marcie, cringing as Angela beckoned her into her car. Marcie raised her hands, overlapping her index fingers into a cross and holding them before Angela as if she were warding off Dracula. Angela motioned for her to get into the car. Marcie looked sadly up at Gigi. "Isn't there something you can do?"

Gigi had no reply. Waldo put his arm around Marcie's shoulder.

"Look, kid, you've got the legal team of Bernstein and Bernelli behind you," he said jovially, but Marcie didn't look convinced. She stared at them out the window of the Cadillac as it pulled away from the curb.

Standing at the base of the courthouse steps, Gigi observed the oppressive, heavy gray of the sky and noted with sullenness that it was starting to drizzle.

"What are we going to do, Waldo?" Gigi asked as Angela's car disappeared around the corner. "Not one of these people gives a damn about Marcie." She looked at Waldo for an answer. He stood there with his hands in his pockets, looking as morose as Marcie had.

"I'm afraid of one of them trying to cheat Marcie out of her money. None of them have any scruples. We'll have to lock her holdings up air tight," said Waldo pessimistically as they walked together to the parking lot. He got in his car and drove away. Gigi slid into her Toyota and started the engine.

"Ever hear the joke about God and the L.A. Dodgers?" Juanita was sitting in the passenger seat. Gigi jumped as usual, then took a deep breath and pulled the car out of the parking lot.

"Spare me the comedy today, Juanita. I'm in a lousy mood."

"So what's the problem?"

"I have to turn Marcie over to one of three equally disgusting people, none of whom love her or give a damn about anything but her money. What kind of life can she have with that going against her?"

Juanita listened as she punched in the radio

buttons one at a time.

"Well, I'll admit her prospects don't look too good right now, but life is filled with twists and turns. And speaking of twists, how is Harold?"

Gigi gripped the steering wheel more tightly. So she knew. The know-all, be-all, everyone's favorite archangel naturally had the inside skinny on the re-emergence of Harold.

"Don't start. Nothing has happened. We're just having dinner. Just a friendly dinner."

"Well, it's really none of my business, is it?"

They drove in silence except for the annoying noise of Juanita changing the radio station every two seconds.

"Juanita?"

"Hmmm?" she answered as she tuned in some mellow jazz.

"Could I conceive Elizabeth at any time or is there some special, you know, ritual that takes place?"

"Ritual? You mean like riding you through the streets naked on a wild boar or something? No, any kinkiness would be most inappropriate," answered Juanita as she turned up the volume on the radio and hummed along happily to the music. The song playing was "You Better Shop Around" by Captain and Tenille.

192

CHAPTER THIRTEEN

A thick gray cloud of smoke obscured the face of the client as he sat slumped in the green imitation-leather chair across from Gigi's desk. Greedily he sucked on a fat brown cigar, a man desperate for any small satisfaction in a world he felt had temporarily left him bereft of earthly pleasures. Gigi leaned back in her chair, squinted her eyes and tried to imagine him without his clothes, seeing in her mind's eye the flabby pale pectorals, a spongy pink belly drooping southward, bare and hairy legs like two tree stumps sticking up out of the sod.

"A man has needs, you know," he said huskily, his south Texas drawl oozing over the words like pine sap on the rough bark of a tree. He tilted upward the brim of his cowboy hat and stared at Gigi with the narrow, steely eyes of male experience. She nodded in acknowledgment. Needs.

Naturally.

"A man needs a woman he can relate to. Somebody who can make him feel good," the client continued, punctuating this flow of emotion with a subtle post-lunch belch, the existential, gastrointestinal cry of one man's suffering. He searched Gigi's face for agreement but found only meditative blankness.

"So do you think I can maybe get rid of her?" he questioned in a more childlike, pleading voice. "Cheap?"

Gigi leaned forward on her elbows, closed her eyes for a moment and examined her thoughts. She didn't want to do this, she told herself. Somehow this one nagged at her more than the others. One of the attorneys had laughingly filled her in that morning on Rucker's real situation. Married twenty-eight years to the same woman, Rucker now wanted a divorce so he could marry his new, younger girlfriend. His only grounds for divorce were male menopause. Gigi didn't want to help him, but it was her job. Rucker was a personal friend of Bausch's, and Bausch, after all, was the man who signed her checks.

The client watched this internal debate, figuring she must be really smart closing her eyes like that to think. Her eyes opened.

"Mr. Rucker," she began.

"Just call me Bart."

"Mr. Rucker, your marriage was and is an unhappy one?"

He nodded eagerly.

"You have been burdened with a wife who never understood you, criticized you, blamed you, found fault with you, spent your money in large and squandering sums?"

More nodding.

"Who emotionally emasculated you?"

His brows furrowed.

"Huh?" he replied.

"Who berated your manhood?"

"Now wait a minute here, young lady. I did my husbandly duty." His hand unconsciously slid to his crotch.

"I'm sure you did, Mr. Rucker, but still, didn't your wife make you feel like less of a man every day of your marriage by failing to support you emotionally, spiritually and intellectually, while you continued to provide her with a home and enough funds to satisfy all her needs?"

"Well, you could say that, I guess." Mr. Rucker appeared hesitant, confused, his words drifting off where they co-mingled with the cigar smoke that hung heavily in the air. Gigi eyed him through the haze with disdain.

She closed the file in front of her and the papers fluttered as if emitting one last gasp. She stood up.

"I'm sorry, but I can't help you, Mr. Rucker. My conscience won't allow it."

Rucker took the cigar out of his mouth, a large unsightly orifice which now gaped unattractively open.

"What are you talkin' about, little lady?"

"I'm talkin' about this." She handed him his file. "I can't help you. I don't want to help you. You don't need help. It's your poor wife who needs it."

Rucker sat upright in his chair, his body rigid with indignation.

"But you have to help me. I don't get this. Bill Bausch sent me in here and he told me . . ." Rucker blubbered.

"You were married twenty-eight years to, what is your wife's name?"

"Bessie," Rucker answered, looking bewildered.

Gigi moved in front of her desk and sat on its edge so she could look more directly at her ex-client.

"Twenty-eight years of marriage to Bessie. You can't just throw that away without giving it more thought, Mr. Rucker. I've heard that you only met this new girl two months ago."

"Three months ago," he said huffily.

"When Bessie married you, when she committed her life to you, I bet you didn't have a dime. I bet she married you because she really loved you, because she cared for you, because she wanted to spend her life with you."

Rucker stared at her wild-eyed. The look on her face, the tone of her voice, reminded him frighteningly of the Baptist pastor his wife made him listen to on Sundays.

"She raised your children, didn't she?"

He nodded slowly.

"She stuck by you all those years, loved you

and lived for you, and now you want to dump her like yesterday's trash. And to try to get away without compensating her properly for all those years, well, you should be ashamed, Mr. Rucker," she said with her finger wagging in his face. There was a knock at the door. Waldo stuck his head in.

"Sorry to interrupt, but, Mr. Rucker, I've got that CPA firm from New York on the phone and they're ready for the conference call. Shall I delay them?"

Rucker looked at Waldo gratefully. He stood up trembling, then bolted out the door.

"Bill Bausch will hear about this!" Gigi heard him yell as he jogged down the hall.

"What happened here?" asked Waldo, peering around the door to watch Rucker make his escape.

Gigi didn't answer, but instead chuckled, surprised at how good she felt.

"Hey a-holes!" Marcie chirped, bounding into the office. "A-hole" was, Gigi learned, a term of endearment from Marcie. At least Gigi hoped it was.

"You coming to the basketball game with us, Waldo? Starts at four-thirty," Marcie asked.

"Sorry, I've got to work late. Maybe next time." Waldo smiled, gave a wave and walked back down the hall to his office. Marcie looked crestfallen for about four seconds and then began pestering Gigi to hurry so they wouldn't miss the tip-off. Marcie's new-found interest in junior high basketball surprised Gigi until she realized it was Marcie's interest in the players that stirred her adolescent glands and not the thrill of athletic competition. Still, it was a relatively healthy interest for Marcie and Marcie was short on healthy interests. It also gave Gigi a great excuse to leave work early, and she wanted to get out of there before Rucker had the chance to complain to Bausch.

The Robert E. Lee Junior High School gym smelled of pubescent sweat and varnished wood, exactly as Gigi remembered from her own school days. Gigi watched two groups of skinny, shiny-faced boys practicing shooting baskets on the court while the cheerleaders, arrogantly pert and bouncy, practiced cheers in a corner as students filled the gymnasium. Gigi remembered it all so well, how it felt to be thirteen, pimple-faced and made wobbly in the knees by the anticipation of a world that had yet to lose its shiny newness.

The school fight song blasted over the loudspeakers and everyone stood to sing. Marcie refused to join in, feeling much too sophisticated to engage in such childish behavior, but Gigi noticed with amusement how fascinated Marcie was with the whole scene, even if she tried not to show it.

"Check out number fourteen," Marcie whispered after the game began, pointing to a tall, awkward-looking blond youth. "What a hunk."

A hunk? Hardly, Gigi decided. He looked skinny and gangly, all arms and legs. Love was different viewed from eyes controlled by a storm of hormones.

"And number twenty-six, that's Danny Gregorson. My friend Stacy made out with him at a party last week and she said when he kisses he wiggles his tongue around inside your mouth."

Gigi checked Danny out with more interest and realized with compunction that she was old enough to be his mother.

"My boyfriend Spike tried to do that to me once, but I told him it was gross. Stacy says that she and Danny are doing it, but I don't know if I believe her. She's two years older than me. Me, I guess I'm old-fashioned. I'm saving myself for high school."

Saving herself for high school? Gigi thought that must be a nineties definition for an incurable romantic.

"What do you think? Should I wait until I'm in high school to do it?"

"I think you should wait until high school to even figure out what 'it' is. You're only twelve. You should be thinking about other things. One day when you're adult enough you'll fall in love and then you'll be ready to, well, get intimate with someone."

"Did you wait until you were an adult?" Marcie questioned.

Gigi's mind wandered for a moment and flashed back on the tenth grade at Roosevelt

High School when she was hopelessly in love/lust with Eddie Bushmeyer. Eddie was a senior and a football player for the invincible Roosevelt Raiders. He was tall and broad-shouldered with white teeth and dark brooding eyes that indicated, Gigi hoped, a deep yearning for a relationship more intellectually stimulating than the shallow experiences he obviously had with his current crop of prom queens and cheerleaders. Gigi used to hang around his locker between classes just to watch him joke with his friends and flirt with the most popular girls. For a few weeks she followed him from class to class, she was so hypnotized by his aura of manliness and self-possession.

One day when she was following Eddie, thinking he had never noticed her, he turned around and stared at her for a moment, then proceeded to walk into his classroom. Gigi was dumbstruck by the fact that his gaze actually fell upon her. She wasn't sure what it meant. Perhaps it was a warning for her to stop following him. But then, maybe it was something else. Perhaps he was compelled by her magnetic force, drawn by the flow of her electrons and suddenly he realized she was alive.

Two weeks later they were at Cindi Bellow's sweet-sixteen party and Gigi, if not already intoxicated enough by the sheer presence of Eddie, had her first taste of alcohol—lemonade that had been spiked with vodka by Eddie's friends. The cloudy liquid consumed from a paper cup made Gigi feel lightheaded and confident. She dared to smile at Eddie from across the room and then, just like in her dreams, he walked over to her. They chatted awkwardly for a few moments about English and football, then Eddie grabbed her by the hand and said he wanted to show her the Bellows' back yard. Gigi was impressed by such an avid interest in landscaping. Once alone in the dark yard, Eddie had a tremendous desire to show her what was behind Mrs. Bellow's azalea bushes.

"Have you ever held a snake?" Eddie asked her. Gigi had no brothers, but she knew what rascals boys could be, always interested in snakes and bugs and grimy things. An article she read in *Seventeen* magazine instructed that the surest way to a boy's heart was to express an interest in the things he liked.

"No, but I'd like to." Gigi held out her hand and the next moment what she held was the rubbery firmness of Eddie's penis. She gasped because she had never held one before, although she immediately knew what it was. It couldn't have been anything else. She looked down and in the soft light of the moon she saw it lying in her hand.

"It's a one-eyed trouser python," Eddie explained. Gigi found it strangely rock-like. Where did he keep it during the day, she wondered? Naturally her mother had explained the basic facts of life to her, but she had never gotten down to specifics. Gigi knew it was wrong to hold Eddie's penis like that, but then, what could it hurt to just touch it? You couldn't get "preg-gars" from just holding one, she knew that much. Then Eddie asked her to stroke it. She tried awkwardly at first to carry out his wishes, then he showed her what to do. (He was such a helpful boy.) But then like a snake, it struck. Suddenly Eddie moaned and Gigi had a yucky liquid all over her hands and dress, even in her eye. She had heard masturbation could blind you, but this wasn't what she expected. By the time she figured out what had happened, Eddie was gone.

The next week at school Gigi looked for Eddie in the hallways, figuring the birthday party epi-sode was the beginning of a more meaningful relationship. But when she approached him after civics class he ignored her, and his friends snick-ered as she walked away, humiliated. She ran into the ladies room, stared at herself in the mirror and decided she was inadequate to earn Eddie's attention and that she would never be pretty enough or charming enough to win a man she wanted. Although she approached each prospec-tive relationship with optimism, deep inside she was always waiting for its premature end and via self-fulfilling prophecy, she usually got it. She didn't lose her virginity that night with Eddie, for that event happened later in college, but that evening she lost her innocence, and she spent the next twenty-five years waiting for the inevitable squirt in the eye she learned to expect from men.

Gigi looked at Marcie. Marcie wanted guidance

and advice from her, but how could Gigi give advice when men were still just as much a mystery to her now as they were twenty years earlier? What cogent knowledge had she learned from her adolescence? Always hold a loaded penis with the barrel pointing away from you? Gigi gave Marcie a cleaned-up, watered-down version of how she lost her virginity, a story so sanitized Marcie barely believed it.

"Look, Marcie, if I ever do figure anything out about men, about being a woman or about life in general, I promise to let you in on it," Gigi told her, finally frustrated by Marcie's insistent questioning.

"And if I find out anything, I'll tell you," Marcie promised solemnly, as if she were being let in on some secret pact.

Gigi smiled and wondered if either one of them would ever find out anything at all.

The following morning Gigi stared at the clock on her office wall and watched fearfully as the hand moved from nine fifty-four to nine fifty-five. She had been sitting for over half an hour watching the clock and twisting paper clips into silver S's that she pretended stood for "schmuck." She was a schmuck, she told herself. When she arrived at work that morning she found a note from Bausch on her desk saying he wanted her in his office at ten. Rucker had obviously made good his threat to complain about her. Look at the bright side. Her career couldn't go any slower, unless it came to a complete standstill. What could he do to her? She quickly ran over the possibilities. He could demote her, humiliate her, fire her. He could even get her disbarred. Then how would she support Elizabeth?

Gigi twisted a paper clip into a U for "Unemployed." She could have just gotten Rucker his lousy divorce from Bessie and have been done with it. Bessie was probably a cow who harangued the poor guy day and night, but no, she, Ms. Clarence Darrow, had to have this sudden and atypical flash of ethics. It wasn't as if she had changed anything, for she was certain Rucker's divorce got handed to someone else. Still, she had to smile when she looked back on that brief, glorious moment when she essentially told Rucker he could take his divorce and blow it out his shorts. She had shown integrity, and that was bound to be worth something, although she wasn't sure it was worth losing her job. The clock hand slipped ominously to ten. Gigi got up, put on her suit jacket and proceeded solemnly down the hall. She imagined "Battle Hymn of the Republic" playing in the background.

"Bausch wants to see me," Gigi told his secretary, Mrs. Lorenzo, who smiled politely, then stuck her head past Bausch's door to announce Gigi's arrival.

"He'll see you now," she pronounced brightly, as if seeing Bausch were a delightful event suitable for entertaining children and taming young animals. Gigi walked into his office, a room smelling of leather, polished wood and old legal volumes.

"Good morning, Gigi. Sit down," Bausch said politely, his heavy-jowled face wearing a pleasant smile. The Nazis probably wore that same smile, Gigi mused. She sat down in front of Bausch, who remained seated at his desk. There was a moment of silence and Gigi squirmed uncomfortably in her chair. The waiting was killing her. She decided to take an assertive stance.

"I know why you want to talk to me. It's about Bart Rucker. I know my approach with him was a little unusual, but I won't apologize for it. Okay, maybe I will. Not a big apology, but . . ."

Bausch held up a hand to silence her. Her discourse screeched to a halt.

"Bart explained to me what happened. He was upset, naturally, and he demanded another attorney," said Bausch. Gigi sunk a few inches in her chair and began thinking of alternative careers she could break into. She could sell makeup at Neiman's, babysit, take in laundry.

Bausch continued. "But then Bart thought it over and decided maybe divorce wasn't the answer."

Gigi looked up with hope.

"He did?"

"You may have saved a marriage, Ms. Bernstein. I suppose that's to be commended, although we did lose some legal fees."

Bausch chuckled. Gigi forced an appropriate

chuckle in return.

"The reason I wanted to see you today, Gigi, is to discuss Marcie Naylor."

Gigi sat up in her chair and leaned toward Bausch's desk, noticing an atypically warm smile on his face. She wondered what he was up to.

"What about Marcie?" she questioned cautiously.

Bausch stood up and leaned back against a credenza, affecting a casual pose that meant he was ready for a heart-to-heart conversation.

"So how are things going with little Marcie? She's a great kid. A lot of spirit in that one, don't you think?"

"Spirit" was not the word Bausch had used when Marcie set his trash can on fire a few weeks earlier. Gigi nodded, curious about where the conversation was headed.

"The big question is, of course, who will be her guardian. Do you have any firm ideas yet on that?"

Gigi took a moment to make sure she was hearing correctly. This was the first time Bausch had asked for any of Gigi's ideas about the Naylor case. In fact, it was the first time he had asked for her ideas on anything.

"Well, of course, no final decision has been made about who her final guardian will be, but we're currently—"

"What about Maynard?" he interrupted.

"Angela Maynard? I guess she's not much worse than the other two, but she seems like such a cold fish. Talking to her is like chatting with a salmon."

Bausch sat back down, folded his hands with interlocked fingers on the desk in front of him and stared earnestly at Gigi.

"Don't judge Angela too quickly. I think after you've known her a little longer you'll find she has many fine qualities."

Gigi wondered when Bausch had begun referring to the Ice Queen as "Angela." Gigi opened her mouth to express more of her opinion, but she didn't get much of a chance, for Bausch jumped in.

"You know, Gigi, I've been watching you for a while. I know you think I never notice you, but I don't miss much around here. I've seen what fine work you do. You're the kind of person I need for junior partners in this firm — hardworking, straight-headed and loyal. A team player."

Gigi's mind reeled. She was the type of person he needed for junior partners? Just a few years ago she was the type of person he thought he needed for clerical help. What had prompted this change in her status?

"I've enjoyed this little talk, Gigi. We'll have to get together again soon and discuss progress with the Naylor situation."

Bausch leaned back in his chair, giving Gigi her cue to exit.

"And don't forget to look into Angela Maynard. She's a fine woman. A fine woman," he added as Gigi walked out the door.

"What does Bausch have to gain from Angela Maynard being awarded custody of Marcie?" Gigi asked Waldo, who sat huddled over a table in the office library. Waldo kept his face stuck in his papers.

"Why do you ask?"

"Because just now he practically offered me a junior partnership in the firm if I recommend Angela for permanent custody." Waldo looked up. "Just now?"

"What a money-grubbing bastard," he mumbled, pushing his papers away from him. "Welcome to the wonderful world of law."

"What are you talking about?"

"I'm talking about the fact that Angela Maynard offered Bausch a long-term contract for Naylor International's legal business if she ends up as Marcie's guardian. When he told me about it yesterday he was laughing. I never thought he would go for it. I guess he's not laughing anymore."

"Do you think he's serious about the junior partnership?"

"Probably, but who can tell?"

Gigi collapsed into a chair next to Waldo's.

"So what do I do?"

"Easy. You do what your conscience and legal ethics tell you. Marcie is your client, not Bausch or Angela Maynard," answered Waldo.

"But the ethics aren't clear. Of course, I can't

make decisions for Marcie's future based on my promotional opportunities. On the other hand, I just told Bausch that Angela Maynard is bad, but she's not any worse than the other two. I could justify recommending her, couldn't I?"

Waldo frowned. "Don't look to me for your answer. You're handling that part of the case. It's your decision and you'll have to make it on your own."

Marcie swirled her straw in her glass before savoring a long, delicious sip. She had ordered a "suicide," a pubescent delight consisting of root beer, orange soda and 7-Up. Gigi fingered the glass of her diet Pepsi and watched Marcie's ecstasy.

"Marcie, have you thought any more about who you want to live with?"

"Sure. None of them. They're all prickheads."

Gigi sighed. "Isn't there one of them who is less of a prickhead than the others?" she asked hopefully.

Marcie blew bubbles in her drink with her straw. Gigi took a deep preparatory breath.

"What about Aunt Angela?". Gigi asked. Marcie looked at her as if she had just peed in her Pepsi.

"She's the worst."

"Look, Marcie, you've got to live with someone. You need a permanent home. Our court date is coming up and we've got to make a decision."

"Can't you do something to help me?" pleaded Marcie.

"But I'm trying to help you. What else can I do?"

"I dunno. Think of something. You're a grown-up and a lawyer. You're part of the power structure."

"Marcie, there's nothing I can do."

Marcie gave her a sidelong look. "What if I wanted to live with you?' she asked coyly.

"That's impossible. You have to live with one of your relatives."

"But I don't want to. I want to live with you."

"You can't."

"Why?"

"It just wouldn't work."

"Why not?"

"It just wouldn't. Don't harass me."

"But I thought you and I were developing sort of a relationship, you know what I mean?"

"I know exactly what you mean, and we'll always be friends and we'll always do things together. But you have to accept the fact that you have to live with one of your relatives. And if you can't make a choice between the three of them, the judge and I will make that choice for you."

Marcie cast a nasty look at her, then put her mouth back on the straw and used it to make a loud, unflattering noise.

CHAPTER FOURTEEN

Book-club member Maureen Lowden committed suicide one rainy Tuesday evening while watching the Miss Texas Pageant broadcasted live from the Houston Coliseum. The maid discovered her the following morning lying peacefully on her bed looking pale and frothy in a white Christian Dior peignoir set with the Saks tags still dangling from the sleeves, Maureen having succumbed to a toxic overdose of sleeping pills and Boodles gin. Her last act on earth was to scrawl "screw you Richard" in Estee Lauder Nutri-Rich lipstick on the divorce papers lying unsigned beside her. Revenge and self-pity had been two of Maureen's favorite pastimes and with her suicide she managed to efficiently carry out both.

The news of Maureen's death left Gigi with

the queasy remembrance of how close to suicide she herself had come. Lulu, the first to hear the news, telephoned Gigi and blurted the details in a flood of tears. Gigi found the news physically sickening. She called in ill at work and spent the day lying on her couch, crying. She knew Maureen had been depressed about her divorce, but Gigi hadn't taken it that seriously. She had reasoned it was natural for Maureen to go through a difficult adjustment period, and Maureen had always been melodramatic. Now she felt guilty for being so absorbed in her own drama that she couldn't see one of her friends suffering enough to take her own life. She pictured Maureen drinking and gossiping at one of her posh hangouts, then pictured her cold and lifeless. If she had known how depressed Maureen had been, she could have talked to her about it, tried to help her. New tears swept over her when she remembered Maureen phoning her at the office two days earlier. She had wanted to meet for a drink. Gigi had said no, that she was too busy at work to take the time. Maureen accepted her apology cheerfully and promised to call again soon. But then Maureen was always breaking promises.

Sydney called and said that the funeral would be the following day. By her voice Gigi sensed Sydney's shock, but she knew Sydney couldn't share her depth of grief, for Sydney had a way of detaching herself from things that kept her distant and safe. Gigi longed for that same safe distance, some insulation to protect her from the risk of life around her, yet at the same time she was drawn closer to it, like an animal drawn to the warmth and frightening fascination of a fire.

Lulu arrived at the funeral fashionably late looking bereaved but chic in a black linen suit. Sydney and Gigi met her outside the funeral home and the three sat together in a pew near the back, scanning the room for the other book-club members as well as any friends of Maureen they knew.

"There are more people here than were at Maureen's New Year's Eve party," whispered Sydney. "That ought to tell you something," she added soberly, although Gigi couldn't figure out what.

In the front of the room Gigi noticed a crowd of strangers that looked rural and dowdy compared to the remainder of the well-dressed grieving. Lynn slid in next to Gigi and informed her that the strangers were Maureen's family from west Texas. Maureen came from a family of poor cotton farmers, Lynn explained, which was quite a surprise to those who knew Maureen in the glitzy social circles of Houston. A small-town girl makes good story with a slight twist at the end, Gigi thought sadly.

The sermon offered few spiritual revelations.

Lulu sobbed noisily, Gigi wept and Sydney sat stoned-faced as they listened to the words about death and God and hope for the everlasting. The general theme to the sermon and prior informal discussions was that Maureen should have been shielded from the despair that consumed her, that the comfort of family and friends, if she had taken advantage of their support, could have protected her. Sydney didn't buy it. She whispered to Gigi during the sermon that it was Maureen's expectation of being protected that killed her. Guardian angels never show up, and it was those dashed hopes and delusions of abandonment that popped that pills down Maureen's throat.

"Please have me cremated when I die," Lulu said between her snifflings as the minister described what a joy Maureen had been to her parents. "And scatter my ashes over Neiman's."

"Shhh," Gigi whispered. Heads turned.

"I'm giving my body to science," Sydney said solemnly.

"Why not?" Lulu responded. "Everyone else has had it."

Sydney and Gigi shot her scathing looks. After the sermon people began filling the aisles to view the body, and Gigi and Sydney rose to follow the others, but Lulu remained seated stiffly on the bench.

"I can't bear to see her dead. No, I can't go," she whimpered, then followed because she couldn't stand to be left behind. They progressed in line to the coffin and peered down to see Maureen lying pale and posed, dressed in a navy blue Nipon. Gigi began to sob.

"She's wearing too much rouge as always," Sydney whispered after taking a look at Maureen's embalmed face.

"But the cut looks stupendous," said Lulu. "Even a goddamn mortician couldn't ruin that."

The three women walked out of the funeral home where the hearse and long line of Cadillacs stood waiting to take people to the cemetary, but the three women decided to forego the actual burial. Enough was enough.

It rained for three days straight after Maureen's funeral, an unusually heavy downpour that flooded the downtown streets and caused the rush-hour traffic to snake halfway to Beaumont. Gigi watched the raindrops as they beat against her windshield, then disappeared as the wiper performed its duty. Gigi had been stuck in a traffic jam at Main and Howard Avenue for over forty-five minutes, although she hadn't really noticed. She kept picturing Maureen laid out in her coffin wearing that eight-hundred-dollar navy blue Albert Nipon with the tiny ruffles in the bodice and wide belt. Gigi and Sydney had been shopping with Maureen when she picked it out at Lord and Taylor. It made her look skinny in the waist and big in the bust, Gigi told her, and Maureen had quickly slapped her American Express card in the saleslady's hand. Gigi loved to go shopping with Maureen because she spent her money lavishly and without concern. She had money, intelligence and good looks to burn—all the accoutrements a successful, enviable person was supposed to have in Houston, Texas. The only missing piece for Maureen had been a man. At first Gigi found it difficult to believe that the absence of a husband could cause the fracture in this perfect facade, but then again, Gigi had tried to kill herself when Harold left her, and wasn't she scrambling for a replacement even now? Every little girl needs a daddy, every Barbie needs a Ken. Society ingrained the need in you from birth, and the need grew, festered until it became larger than life, larger than the E.R.A., the N.O.W., an MBA or a law degree from the fanciest university. Walk through downtown Houston at five-thirty and all the well-educated women in their Evan Picone business suits headed for neatly arranged apartments where they inevitably sat in front of their mirrors and worried about dates just like they had in high school, just like they had in college.

Juanita spoke repeatedly of free will, but was there such a thing, Gigi pondered? It seemed free will was lost at age four when mommies gave their daughters their first Betsy Wetsy doll.

And what does a Betsy Wetsy do? It pees on you. Your very own mother whom you love and trust gives you a doll and says, "See, honey, the dollie wets just like a real baby. Isn't that wonderful?" and you make yourself believe it's wonderful. As you stare at the big wet spot on your dress, you stretch your imagination and make yourself believe that being peed on is fun, that being peed on is what you were born for. And how do you get a real baby for that purpose? You find someone to be the daddy, but until then you make yourself a receptacle for just about any male who's willing just so you can keep in practice.

Then, as you get a little older, the game gets even tougher, as tough as the torpedo tits on the Barbie doll you get when you're ten. Bouncy Barbie, the teenage beauty queen with physical proportions beyond the spectrum of the human gene pool. Painfully Gigi remembered playing the Barbie Prom Game. It was a regular kid's game with a board and dice. You would roll the dice and progress around the board, and if you won you got to go to the prom with Ken. If you lost you were doomed to go with freckle-faced, bespectacled Poindexter. Gigi had played the game a hundred times, rolling those dice with her baby-fatted little hands trying to come up just once with Ken. But no, she and Poindexter were steadies.

A car honked behind Gigi. She stepped on the

accelerator and passed through the light. Maureen had died from wanting what she couldn't have, Gigi thought. Maureen crapped out so many times at life's Prom Game she finally got tired of rolling the dice, but Gigi wasn't going to let what happened to Maureen happen to her. There would be no more longing for perfect love, for Prince Charming or dreams she could never make come true. She was going to work with what she had and be satisfied with it.

And what she had was Harold.

The Wednesday night dinner with Harold went smoothly. Gigi prepared chicken tarragon and a tossed green salad served with an expensive white wine, but she omitted dessert so Harold could watch his weight. Gigi sat across from her returned beloved as he wordlessly wolfed down his food and studied the *U.S. News and World Report*. It was so wonderful the way he kept up with current events, Gigi thought. Some men would waste their mental energy on mindless chatter, but not Harold. Several times during the meal he looked up from his magazine and smiled a smile of gratitude and contentment. He was one helluva guy, she told herself. She was lucky to have him.

"Harold, darling," she said softly as she watched him push the last few bits of chicken onto his fork with his thumb.

"Yeah?" He was a man of few words.

"I guess there's one good thing that has come from this whole situation," she said with a philosophic tone.

"What, Boo Boo?" "Boo Boo" was his new term of affection for her.

Gigi reached over and tickled his palm with her finger.

"At least you know that what you really want is to be married and have a family."

Harold looked up and closed his magazine. He looked uncomfortable. "I don't know Gigi. I'm not as sure of things as I used to be. I love you. I do know that, but don't pressure me. I don't need pressure right now." A noticeable pall settled over the room. "I think it's time for *Magnum P.I.* Ready for some TV, Boo Boo?" he asked before he bolted from the table and headed into the living room.

Okay, she wouldn't pressure him. She sat next to him on the couch and watched mindless television with him until he fell asleep beside her. After covering him with an afghan that had been knitted by her aunt Mindy, she sat in a chair and listened to him gently snore. Of course he was tired from all the emotional stress he had been through lately. Life for Harold had been complex the past few months, but life was about to get even more complicated for dear Harold, because Gigi had decided that evening that he would be the father of Elizabeth.

Gigi sucked on her ice cubes and prayed she wouldn't see anyone she knew. The hotel ballroom was tackily clothed in crepe paper, balloons and signs that read "The World's Largest Singles Party." A mirrored ball spun overhead casting spots of confetti-like light upon the crowd. Gigi watched them as they churned about, all happily holding their mixed drinks and misconceptions about the characteristics their potential dream mate should possess. They moved about the ballroom in a circular pattern as if in some mating dance, the Perpetually Single Polka, all of them eyeing each other, exchanging senseless chitchat in hopes of making a quasi-permanent connection.

"Are we having fun or what?" Juanita asked brightly, snapping her fingers to the blasting music. Gigi stuck her finger in her drink, then sucked off the gin and tonic, her eyes narrowed.

"I never should have let you push me into this. I don't call this fun."

"Then what do you call it?"

"Boring," Gigi answered. Juanita looked stunned. She took a gulp of her orange juice, then slammed down the glass.

"Boring? You call this boring? Can't you feel the electricity in this room? Why, there must be a thousand people in here dancing, laughing, talking to each other, getting to know each other better. I'm so excited I can barely keep still." Juanita flapped her arms to demonstrate the kinetic energy she was experiencing. Gigi thought she looked like an escaped zoo bird. Juanita had borrowed one of Gigi's flowered silk scarves and tied it around her hair and into a big floppy bow on top of her head. Juanita had insisted the two of them come to the party after hearing it advertised on the radio. Gigi resisted the best she could, but there she was anyway in her navy blue suit, feeling awkward and embarrassed, wearing a nametag and a "Kiss Me, I'm Single" sticker that Juanita had surreptitiously stuck on her back.

"You know, things would liven up if you would crawl off that bar stool and circulate a little. You've got to get aggressive if you're going to meet someone," said Juanita.

"I've never been the aggressive type." Gigi faked a yawn so in a few minutes she could claim fatigue and go home.

"Well, you can take a lesson from me. I'm nothing if not outgoing. Now, what do you think of that guy over there?" Juanita pointed to an uncomfortable-looking male in his midtwenties leaning against a nearby post.

"He looks too young and I hate his jacket," said Gigi.

"Is that how you judge people, by their age and clothes? Tsk, tsk. He looks nice and like he wants to talk to somebody. Go over to him,"

221

Juanita said, tugging Gigi's arm. Gigi gripped the bar for an anchor and Juanita gave up. "Okay, fine. You won't go. So I'll go."

Juanita belted down the remainder of her orange juice and marched over to him.

"Didn't we go to high school together?" she asked loudly. Viewing the scene from her barstool, Gigi covered her mouth with her hand to hide her laughter. The guy looked at Juanita with a puzzled expression, then mumbled something Gigi couldn't hear. After ten minutes of conversation, Juanita trotted back.

"He gave me his card. He wants to meet me for drinks sometime," Juanita said smugly. "I think he likes me."

Gigi chuckled. "I thought we were looking for men for me. You don't date, do you?"

"Of course I don't, but Steve liked me. I didn't have the heart to break it to him what profession I'm in."

"And what profession is that?" Gigi asked.

"The oldest profession in the world," Juanita said with a mischievous grin, then flagged down the bartender for another juice. Half an hour passed with Juanita running the "high school" line on various men before dragging them over to meet Gigi. Juanita didn't discriminate on age, size or color. She ended up with several business cards and two invitations for dinner and neither of them included Gigi. Juanita was stiff competition, for what she didn't have in looks she made up for with aggressiveness.

Sounds of "La Bamba" blasted over the loud-speakers.

"Now we're cooking! Let's dance," said Juanita. Gigi scowled at the prospect. Juanita bounced in place to the music for a moment, then, when she couldn't stand to be sedentary any longer, tore off to the center of the dance floor, encouraging a conga line to form behind her. Gigi watched, aghast at Juanita's brazenness, but within minutes there was a long line of dancers bouncing behind her, boogying through the crowd, each person's arms around the waist of the person in front of him. Many of them had kicked off their shoes. Gigi stared at the conga line enviously. It looked like fun. It looked like the kind of raucous, carefree fun she never engaged in. She wanted to join in but she felt afraid, afraid of looking foolish, of making a spectacle of herself. Her mother had always told her, "Never make a spectacle of yourself." She finished off her drink. The tail of the conga line undulated temptingly in front of her. Okay, she would do it. Gigi took off her shoes, then cautiously made her way through the crowd to take her place at the end of the line. A few more people joined in behind her. When Juanita saw Gigi, she grinned and waved.

Gigi bobbed and danced to the music, modestly at first, then with more vigor. She shuffled across the floor in her stocking feet, felt the gritty dust pressed into her soles, felt perspiration beneath her Anne Klein II blouse. She felt decadent and ribald and happier than she could remember. Suddenly the room seemed less tacky than it had before, the people more attractive. The man behind her gave her waist what seemed an innocently joyful squeeze. Gigi turned and laughed. He looked okay. The music changed to the sixties version of "Tequila" and the conga line got longer and livelier. Gigi felt the man behind her trying to squeeze more than her waist. She turned to express her disapproval and she saw Waldo leaning against a wall near the entrance. Waldo was the last person she expected to see at a singles party. Her eyes searched around him for Delores, but she was not in sight. Much to the squeezer's chagrin, Gigi broke out of the line and headed for Waldo.

"Hi, sailor," she said out of breath as she approached him. His previously forlorn expression brightened when he saw her.

"I didn't expect to see you here," he said.

"My thoughts exactly, but at least I'm single. Where's Delores?"

Waldo looked down at his feet. "We broke up."

Gigi laughed. "It won't last long. What did you fight about this time?"

"We didn't fight about anything. We really broke things off. She met someone else."

"Waldo, you're kidding. I'm sorry," said Gigi.

"Who is he?"

Waldo looked sheepish. "It's not a he, it's a she. She left me for some hairdresser she met a month ago. A Lola or somebody. I noticed for the past few weeks she was coming home with a new hairdo every couple of days, but I thought, well, that's just Delores going through some phase. It was a phase, all right, but it had nothing to do with her hair."

Gigi's eyes widened, her lips twisted into a pucker of dismay, but she quickly changed her expression to one of distant concern.

The last thing she wanted was for Waldo to remember that it was she who had recommended Lulu to Delores that night they had rescued her from Barry. Her intentions had been innocent. She had only recommended Lulu to do Delores's hair, not to do Delores.

"I'm really sorry, Waldo, but don't think it's your fault. These things happen. Besides, I'm sure it's only temporary."

Waldo smiled, grateful for the sympathy. "Don't worry about me. I'm fine. Actually, she's been gone almost a week now and I'm finding it quite peaceful. I just thought this party would be a good chance to get out and meet some people." Waldo looked at Gigi's feet. "You realize, of course, that you've lost your shoes."

"I know. I guess I better go retrieve them. I'm really sorry about Delores."

"Don't be."

"See you tomorrow."

Waldo nodded, and Gigi negotiated her way back through the crowd to locate her shoes. Her feet were getting uncomfortably sticky on the bottom. She couldn't imagine Delores and Lulu as a couple, but then she had trouble imagining Delores and Waldo as a couple as well.

When she returned, Juanita was sitting on a barstool holding Gigi's shoes in her lap.

"Meet anyone interesting?" she asked hopefully.

"No, I just saw someone from the office."

Juanita didn't hide her disappointment.

"Sorry, Juanita, but I guess I'm not really looking. You know I'm seeing Harold."

"I know, but we've been here less than an hour. Maybe if we hang around . . ."

"Sorry, Juanita. I'm ready to go home."

"Of course, I don't like to meddle in these things. If you think Harold is our man, then that's that," Juanita said, then quickly finished her drink. "Of course, he certainly wouldn't be my choice."

"But it's not your choice, is it?' Gigi said with a trace of scorn in her voice.

"I have a right to an opinion, don't I? Harold, I know, is a fabulous person. Charming, lovable, kind-hearted. And that wit of his. Just keeps you in stitches all during dinner."

Gigi glared at her but Juanita continued.

"It's just that I pictured the father as being a

226

bit more demonstrative, a trifle on the romantic side."

"I know you hate Harold."

Juanita held up a scolding finger. "Angels don't hate. I think Harold is inadequate for the job, and I think deep down inside you do too. But it's your choice. Free will, remember?"

Yes, free will, Gigi reminded herself, turning the phrase over and over in her mind like a mantra.

Harold's green Seville inched up its wheels in eager anticipation of the light transforming from red to green. Even at seven-thirty in the evening the Houston traffic remained thick, creeping its way from the central business district to the suburbs. Harold tapped the steering wheel nervously and mumbled a few curses at the sluggish driver in front of him. With rote affection, Gigi reached over to stroke his shoulder, knowing how much he despised the traffic. He steered around a car stalled at the base of a billboard that bore the legend, "For Those Who Want It All." Gigi looked at the billboard wistfully, envying the skinny blonde who smiled from the advertisement, her one-dimensional image appearing poised and confident. A dark-haired, handsome man placed a string of pearls adoringly around her neck. She was a woman loved.

"I sold a piece of property to a guy from

Chicago today and reamed him on the price. Just reamed him," Harold growled with amusement, his eyes fixed on the road in front of him.

"Really," Gigi murmured. Her mind was elsewhere. Harold pressed the horn for six seconds to express manly indignation at his delay.

"I loved it. The hard part was keeping a straight face during the closing. I mean, even the closing officer was stunned when he saw the price the guy was paying. I reamed him. Even with real estate prices down like they are, I reamed him." Harold emitted a chuckle that sounded to Gigi a little like Peter Lorre. She returned her gaze to her loved one.

"Darling, do you think it's right to take advantage of someone like that?" she questioned demurely.

"Gigi, you know nothing about it! What's right is to take every penny you can get," Harold yelled, then blasted his horn again. She hated it when he yelled, but she was determined not to get offended too early in the evening. Tonight was the night she was going to pop the question. The Question. Gigi smiled at the notion. Yes, tonight she wanted the two of them close and happy to be together, like the couples she saw in Martini and Rossi magazine ads. Men in Martini and Rossi ads never yelled at their girlfriends to eat shit. Perhaps they politely suggested that their loved one ladle Beluga caviar up a convenient orifice, but yell, never.

Harold looked at her. "Sorry, Boo Boo. I didn't mean to yell at you, but you don't know the way it is in business. You're sheltered in your little law office. You're not mad, are you?"

His Boo Boo smiled to let him know there were no hard feelings. Harold smiled back, then negotiated a hairpin turn into the parking lot of Oshman's Sporting Goods.

"Why are we going here, sweetheart?" she asked, thinking they were headed toward Rinaldo's Pizza, an establishment of romantic lighting and reasonable prices.

"Oshman's is having a storewide sale," replied Harold. He turned toward Gigi and frowned when he saw the disappointment on her face.

"We're talking a storewide sale here, Gigi," he said pleadingly. "Storewide. It won't take long. I need a new racquetball racquet."

He pulled into a parking place, turned off the ignition and jumped out of the car. Gigi followed. Okay, so Harold needed a new racquet. Nothing to get upset about. The soon-to-be-father-of-Elizabeth needed a new racquet. So who could argue?

The store was a frantic jam of customers. Gigi pushed her way through the crowd to follow Harold to the racquetball section. The frenzy heightened Gigi's excitement. The pace of life seemed to be quickening, the temperature rising. Gigi looked at the crowd around her and noticed how each person rummaged through the sports equipment, desperate to develop their bodies, to make themselves whole, never suspecting that a Messiah was on Her way. Gigi had an urge to leap on top of the ski equipment and announce to Oshman's the coming of Elizabeth. The idea amused her. Best to wait and let things take their natural course. She stood impatiently to the side and watched Harold carefully inspect each available racquet. He had started at the left end of the row and looked them over one by one, checking strings, weight and grip. Gigi sighed, knowing it would take a while. He looked cute in his casual slacks and LaCoste shirt. The wingtip shoes were a little inappropriate, but Harold dearly loved his wingtips and refused to wear any other type shoe except when playing sports. That type of eccentricity was part of Harold's charm. Not everyone saw it, but she did. And tonight she was going to tell him everything that had happened over the past months, about Juanita, Elizabeth, everything. He would be shocked, of course, but ultimately he would find it as thrilling as she did.

Gigi smiled at Harold as he took a few test swings with a racquet. Tonight would be the beginning of their life together, a beautiful life born out of a miracle. The idea was so exciting she couldn't wait until dinner to reveal the news. She had to tell him at that very moment.

"Harold, I've got to talk to you," she said,

grabbing his arm as he reached for another racquet.

"I'm busy, Gigi. Go wait in the car," Harold answered, brushing her aside and testing one more racquet for grip and weight. She would not be put off. The moment was right. She could feel it.

"Harold, I've had a religious experience," she blurted as Harold ran his teeth along the racquet strings. He looked up.

"In Oshman's?" he asked, his face glazed with incredulity.

Gigi grabbed Harold by the shoulders.

"Harold, this is going to sound crazy, but I'm desperate to tell someone and you're the obvious person to tell about it because actually you're going to be a part of it and, Harold, you're the most important person in my life. I love you," Gigi rambled breathlessly, shaking Harold by the shoulders as she spoke. He stared at her blankly. She moved her face closer to his and spoke in a deep whisper.

"An angel, Harold, an angel appeared to me several months ago. She told me I'm going to be the mother of the Daughter of God."

Gigi's face was filled with so many emotions — excitement, joy, uncertainty, fear, desire. Harold's face was momentarily filled with nothing, a blank slate Gigi watched closely for any sign of comprehension. Following a few elongated seconds of silence, he spoke slowly and clearly, without emotion.

"The weight of a racquet as well as the type and tension of the strings can be an integral factor in one's game. Choosing just the right racquet is a time-consuming process that—"

"Did you hear what I said?" Gigi questioned.

Harold jerked her like a puppet into a corner filled with ski goggles where he thought no one could hear them. He placed his hands oppressively at the base of her neck.

"Let me guess, Gigi. It's time for your period, right? Go take a Midol like a good girl so I can pick out a racquet, okay? Just don't act crazy on me." Harold patted her on the behind, then left her standing alone. Somehow, once again, control of the situation had eluded her. Leave it to Harold to reduce the coming of the Messiah to premenstrual syndrome. But why not look at the bright side? Maybe it was for the best. With Harold's delicate libido it would be imprudent to put additional pressure on him. At least she had informed him of his new responsibilities. Whether he believed her or not was his problem. She had done her duty, she had read him his rights. Now the rest was up to her. She waved to get Harold's attention, wiggled a few fingers, then went outside to wait in the car.

Like a good girl.

CHAPTER FIFTEEN

"I don't want to put any pressure on you, of course," Juanita said as she leaned back in her chair and propped her feet on Gigi's desk. "But if you're really settled on Harold as the father, I think it's time to get this show on the road."

Gigi looked up from her paperwork and noticed with distaste how lazily Juanita sprawled herself across the office furniture. A dribble of strawberry yogurt streaked across her dress, her red curls sprouted uncombed from her head like skyrockets begging for a match, the soles of her Nikes were spotted with holes. She appeared the height and breadth of irresponsibility, a woman with all the potential of a bag lady or a Mooni run amuck. Fortunately it was after 6:30 and everyone at the office had gone home so there was no one around to see her or eavesdrop on their conversation.

Harold had been a touchy subject for a few days, but Juanita had eventually given in gracefully to Gigi's wishes. Almost too gracefully, Gigi feared.

She quickly piled her papers into a neat stack and gave them an affectionate pat.

"Well, Juanita, gotta run. I've got plans with Harold tonight."

And she meant a lot more than dinner.

"We're never going out with that bitch again," Harold announced as he and Gigi prepared for bed after a less-than-festive foursome with Sydney and Arthur.

"She's my best friend, honey."

"I don't care. Sydney is a castrating bitch. And all that stuff about her pregnancy and being plugged into the cosmic whatever. It made me sick. I don't see how Arthur can stand her." Harold finished buttoning his pajamas, the ones imprinted with the little green tennis racquets that Gigi kept for him in her bottom dresser drawer, then he slid purposefully into bed. As usual, he flipped on the bedside lamp to take one last look at the *Wall Street Journal,* and Gigi smiled as he buried his nose in the paper. The moment had arrived. Standing at the foot of the queen-size bed, she slowly removed her clothing piece by piece. Her Carol Horn linen waist-length jacket somersaulted behind her. Her Anne Klein II separates hit the floor without a whimper. With her outer garments removed, Gigi placed her hands on her hips and struck a provocative pose. Only the white lace Merry Widow remained on her body, Mrs. Bernstein's birthday surprise, complete with the wire pushup bra and garter snaps that held up her nylons. It displayed her cleavage quite nicely, as Sydney had pointed out to Gigi when she modeled it for her the previous Saturday. And to complete the effect, Gigi's feet sported new Charles Jourdan heels, purplish, spiked, Joan Crawford-hurt-me pumps, footwear for the woman with lust in her heart and a fire in her loins.

She stood at the foot of the bed feeling sultry, sensual, purely decadent. Within her smoldered just a touch of Jean Harlow, a smidgen of Marilyn Monroe, the tiniest scintilla of Rita Hayworth that Gigi never realized existed. Lately when she looked in the mirror she looked almost attractive with a slimmer body and a fattened confidence that gave her an urge to take out the Merry Widow and put it to the use for which the Lord and her mother intended it. "I conceived a Messiah in my Maidenform bra," she imagined an advertisement saying. She planned to knock Harold's executive-length socks off, just as soon as she could grab his attention away from Dow Jones.

"Sweetheart, could you help me get out of

this?" she asked coyly. Harold looked up from his *Journal,* emitted a terse shriek and threw his paper on the floor.

"Good God, what is it?" he yelled, pulling the covers to his chin. It was not the reaction Gigi had been hoping for.

"It's called a Merry Widow, Harold. It's like a bra and garter belt all rolled into one," she explained, pointing out the features with her index finger. Harold looked relieved.

"Thank the Lord. I thought you were in a body cast." Harold piked up the paper once more and reimmersed himself in the editorial. The tiniest tears emerged from Gigi's eyes and she wondered if Harlow, Monroe or Hayworth ever had these problems. ("Never, ever, ever," Monroe would have said. "My lingerie always worked at MGM," Hayworth would reply. "This Harold guy's a schmuck. Lose him," Harlow would have suggested.)

"It's supposed to be very sexy, Harold. Women, very sensual women, have worn these for a hundred years. It even has a corset with whalebone."

"I believe it because it makes you look like Moby Dick. Goodnight, Boo Boo. I'm beat and tomorrow's going to be a rough day. I'm going to sleep." Harold blew her a kiss, then switched off the lamp and quickly buried his yawning face into the pillow. It took only seconds before Gigi could hear the inevitable rhythmic breathing, the fluttering of his lips. Quietly she slipped off the Merry Widow, put on her favorite blue plaid flannel nightgown and slipped into bed next to the snoring lump that constituted Harold. Pulling her knees to her chest, she took a long hard look at the object of her desire. So this was destiny? How was this any different from the past few years she had spent chasing Harold, wanting Harold, needing Harold, not having Harold?

But maybe Harold wasn't her destiny any longer. Her destiny was Elizabeth. Harold represented a mere vehicle, a brief subway ride to fate. If only he would cooperate a little more. She hated to rush him, but not only was his lack of sexual zeal delaying the conception and birth of Elizabeth, it was also causing Gigi a great deal of frustration. It was bad enough to lie in bed all alone night after night fantasizing about making love, but when you actually had a live, breathing male lying next to you it was torture. Was it wrong for the mother of Elizabeth to crave a little physical affection, an occasional romp in some not-so-clean fun? Gigi leaned over and gave Harold a light kiss on his forehead and wrapped her arms around him as she drifted off to sleep.

That night Gigi dreamed she stood in a Catholic church, perched high somewhere above the crowds. She gradually realized she was a statue on a pedestal. Hundreds of people bowed before her, muttered praised to her, kissed her feet. Suddenly the people looked up, then began backing away in revulsion. What could be wrong, Gigi wondered? She looked down at herself and discovered with horror that she wore nothing but the Merry Widow and her purple Jourdan heels.

"This is not what I had in mind," she heard her mother say to her from below, her finger wagging angrily at her daughter, and Gigi woke up in a cold sweat.

CHAPTER SIXTEEN

"After thorough consideration, I'm awarding permanent custody of Marcie Naylor to her aunt Angela Maynard," Judge Spencer announced to a quiet courtroom, her hands clasped, spectacles perched judicially down her nose.

Gigi cringed at the words, but she kept repeating to herself that her recommendation to the judge had been in Marcie's best interests. Angela Maynard represented the best choice of the three very limited possibilities available. Bubba Naylor was a half-wit. Loreen Naylor was a sleaze. All three of the relatives weren't exactly *Cosby Show* material, but at least Angela was intelligent, relatively normal and could provide the most reasonable home life for

Marcie.

Marcie didn't utter a sound when she heard it, but stared dully at Judge Spencer, accepting the pronouncement with the morose silence of a prisoner handed a life sentence. Angela smiled, lips curling just slightly, eyes narrowed like a cat's. Gigi watched her, assuming Angela silently calculated how much larger a house she could buy (in order to provide Marcie a suitable environment), how many trips to Europe she could take (Marcie would need the cultural exposure), how she could finally fork over the extravagant sum required for entrance to the River Oaks Country Club (all the better to breed you with, my dear). She would do her best not only to spend Marcie's money but to transform her from an irascible but lovable child into an overgroomed, designer-swathed deb queen. It made Gigi shiver. It made Waldo sigh. It made Loreen and Bubba want to puke their lunches since it put the lid on quite a few plans of their own.

"Bitch," Loreen tossed over her shoulder like a shovel full of manure as she stomped out of the courtroom. Bubba just shook his head grievedly as he saw the big-breasted blonde, the red Cadillac, the imported beer and his fast-talking attorney fade from his life forever. Neither one said a word of good-bye to Marcie. Marcie sat alone on the oaken bench looking solemn and stony-eyed as Angela Maynard and

240

her attorney stood in the corner and talked dollars and cents. Gigi tried desperately to think of something optimistic to say.

"Well, it looks like the tough part is over. Now you can settle down to school and your friends and not have to worry about where your home will be tomorrow," Gigi said too brightly as the courthouse cleared. Marcie looked up at her with scorn.

"No one will be fighting over who gets me anymore, that's for sure. And I guess I'm out of your hair now." Marcie slipped on her black mirrored sunglasses and turned to leave. Gigi stopped her.

"Wait a minute. We're still going to be friends, aren't we?"

"What, are you afraid I won't pay my bill?" Marcie said.

The words stung, but Gigi tried not to show it. "I don't deserve that. I thought we were friends."

Marcie glared at her hatefully.

"Some friend. You tricked me. You cheated me. Aunt Angela told me you made the judge give me to her so your stupid law firm could be our lawyers forever. All you wanted was money just like everybody else, and I hate you!"

Gigi saw the tears in Marcie's eyes as she haughtily swung her hot pink handbag over her shoulder. "Well, I'm off to my loving Auntie

241

Angela." She turned on her heels and galloped toward the door.

"It had nothing to do with money, Marcie. I did what I thought was best for you. There was nothing else I could do," Gigi called after her, but Marcie didn't stop to listen.

"Marcie, you can't just run out of here without discussing this further!" Gigi yelled, and slammed a fist down on the bench in frustration.

"So take it to my lawyer!" she heard Marcie shout back from the hallway. Gigi stood there and stared at the door. A hand on her shoulder made her jump. She turned and saw Waldo, who had returned from the judge's chambers.

"I'll give her a call tomorrow. She'll be okay," he told her soothingly, but Gigi didn't believe him.

"She thinks I sold out to Angela, but it's not true. I had to recommend Angela. You understand, don't you?"

Gigi studied Waldo's face but she couldn't read his expression.

"Look, we have to be at the Lansing meeting in thirty minutes and I've got some prep to do. We better get going," he said after a pause.

"You think I was wrong, don't you? You think Bausch bribed me to recommend Angela and I went for it. But what was I supposed to do, hand her over to that slob Bubba, or worse,

242

the nude baton twirler?"

"I never said you were wrong, Gigi."

"You don't have to. I can see it now in your face. But what else could I have done?"

Waldo sighed unhappily. "Not too much. You could have stalled them perhaps until we came up with a better idea, but then, there weren't any better ideas. You did what you had to do. You did what I would have done."

"So why do I feel so terrible? I feel like I failed."

"If you did, we failed together. I'm in this just as much as you. Come on, let's go. It's not doing us any good to rehash it now."

They drove in Gigi's car back to the office. Although she tried to make pleasant conversation, Waldo remained silent. It disturbed Gigi because usually Waldo was so talkative. She considered asking him what was wrong, but she decided it would be better to leave him alone. Road construction added ten minutes to their trip, and by the time they made it to the Lansing meeting, it had already begun. The meeting was in the conference room, a room that Gigi had never been in before, at least not when she had been invited. Three men and one woman sat around an oblong table. The client, James Cameron Lansing, sat on the left next to Bausch. He stared out the glass wall at the Houston skyline and nervously drummed his fingers. He didn't look like a happy man, but then Gigi didn't think any of them looked like they were having too good of a time. Bausch frowned as she and Waldo stepped in and closed the door quietly behind them. The last time someone had frowned at Gigi that way had been in the third grade and Gigi had ended up standing in the corner. Bausch loathed tardiness.

"Angela Maynard got Marcie," Waldo suddenly blurted in Bausch's direction.

Bausch's expression didn't change. "Really. I want you to meet Mr. Lansing."

Mr. Lansing nodded, but Waldo didn't seem to notice.

"I don't feel too good about it. I think we misjudged —" Waldo said, but Bausch interrupted.

"Now now, Waldo. Take a seat," Bausch said through a taut smile. Gigi and Waldo sat. Gigi felt concerned about Waldo. He was acting strangely.

"We'll catch you up to where we are," Bausch said to them, and the words made Gigi want to chuckle. Before the Naylor case she never would have been included in a meeting like this one, concerning a small but lucrative corporate merger. Bausch had asked her to participate on the case and at first she had been excited. Now she would have preferred to be elsewhere.

Bausch rambled off the Lansing details and

Gigi took notes. She looked at Waldo a few times. He doodled distractedly on the back of his papers.

"Waldo, let's hear from you now," Bausch said. Waldo jerked up in his seat. He looked at Bausch.

"What?" Waldo's eyes looked a little glazed.

"Your presentation. The preliminaries on the contract. You're ready?"

Waldo fumbled with the papers in front of him. "Yes, of course," he answered weakly, not sounding like the Harvard grad legal eagle Bausch had described to Lansing only hours before. Lansing shot Bausch a look. As Waldo stood up, a paper flew mischievously out of his stack, and lifted by the draft from the air conditioning vent, fluttered for a moment in midair above the table. All eyes in the room transfixed on the floating object during its few seconds of flight, as if it were a piece of paper temporarily and joyously reprieved from the usual sedentary world of paperness and for one glorious moment experienced the lightness of being for which they all yearned. The paper performed one last giddy somersault before Bausch snatched it out of the air and thrust it back at Waldo. Waldo took the paper and stared at it, wingless and wrinkled, then slipped it back in with the others. He flipped the switch that brought a screen humming down from the ceiling, then turned on a transparency projector that sat on one side of the table. A two-by-three-foot reflection of a contract appeared on the screen. Mr. Lansing smiled with satisfaction. Bausch settled more comfortably in his seat. Gigi and her co-workers poised pens above paper to take notes. Waldo tripped on the projector's power cord and caught himself on the side of the table, sending a cup of coffee streaming across the top.

"Good God!" Bausch cried out as he leaped from his chair to avoid the caffeine river. An ambitious law clerk pointed to the screen.

"That's not the right contract. That one's for Bruner and Merrill."

Gigi looked at the screen. It wasn't Lansing's contract. Gigi had never known Waldo to make such a stupid mistake.

"What is that on your tie?" Lansing asked loudly, his tone of voice curious yet offended. Waldo looked down at his tie which had flipped over during his stumbling, revealing a figure imprinted on the underside. Everyone took a look, casually at first, then with more interest, for the underside of the tie depicted a partially clothed woman. Her hair was long and dark, her skin a walnut tan, her breasts bare, disproportionately large, looming like tawny moons over a grass skirt that swayed in an imaginary breeze.

"That woman is naked," Bausch informed everyone, as if perhaps the little tart had slipped off her blouse when Waldo wasn't looking. A few people chuckled. Lansing wasn't one of them. Waldo quickly flipped his tie back to its correct position so that once again all that could be seen were conservative stripes.

"Okay, she's nakęd. So what?" Waldo said, daring a challenge. Gigi closed her eyes and cringed.

"I don't think it's appropriate in a business setting," said Bausch.

"And I don't think it's anybody's business what I have on the backside of my tie."

Bausch reddened, then glared at Waldo like a mean dog. "It is my business."

"Great. You wanna check out my jockey shorts, just to make sure they're not covered with something inappropriate? Who knows what's down there. Hell, let's take a look, shall we?" Waldo asked, beginning to unbuckle his belt.

Bausch turned to Lansing. "I want to apologize for his behavior. This is unforgivable. He's been under a great deal of stress —"

"Don't apologize for me," Waldo interrupted. "I like my tie. I love my tie."

"Waldo, I think you should leave and cool off a little," said Bausch, now with real concern.

"No problem. I'm going. I'll go get some

paints and I'll paint a little bra on her and I'll be back. Wait for me," Waldo said, then stomped out the door.

The room fell quiet. After a few uncomfortable seconds Gigi broke the silence.

"I think I'll go talk to him," she said, quickly making her exit before Bausch could protest. She looked down the hall, saw Waldo re-buckling his belt. He looked at her and smiled.

"That was almost fun, wasn't it?" he said calmly. Gigi hustled toward him.

"They could fire you over this."

Waldo shrugged. "They won't fire me. They need me. I'm too good. Besides, I'm the only Law-Reviewed Harvard graduate Bausch has got. Bausch thinks it impresses clients."

"Well, you certainly impressed Lansing. Waldo, what got into you? You acted crazy."

"I don't know, but it felt good. Bausch is an asshole and I'm tired of sucking up to him. Besides, Marcie gave me this tie. You didn't know that, did you? She asked me not to tell you because she thought you wouldn't approve of the decoration. I wore it today to please her, but I guess it didn't do much good, did it?"

"You've been under stress, Waldo, with Delores leaving you and everything."

"I don't care about Delores leaving. Her being gone has lifted a big weight off me. I feel great. Have you ever noticed how you and I are always around when we need each other? Don't you think that's nice?"

"What I think is that you should go back into that meeting and apologize, Waldo."

"No way. Besides, it would be better to let Bausch cool off. I'll talk to him tomorrow. I'll claim temporary insanity due to stress and he'll give me a vacation. God knows I need one. Hey, you want to go to Hawaii? Think of it, Gigi—sun, sand, the ocean."

"And hula girls?" she said.

"My favorite. I'll buy you a grass skirt and a lei."

"I don't think so."

"What you need is time to think it over. Let's get out of here. I know a sleazy little bar around the corner where we can get a drink." Waldo grabbed her hand and pulled her down the hall.

"I'll pass, Waldo. It's only two o'clock and I still have work to do, but you go."

"You'll be sorry you missed it. If you change your mind, I'll be there a while. Hope to see you later," he said.

Gigi watched him as he walked jauntily past the receptionist and out the door. She considered going back to the meeting, but the prospect was less than appealing. If she didn't go back, Bausch would assume she was counseling Waldo, whom he assumed was having a nervous breakdown. But she knew what constituted Waldo's problem, or at least part of it. Like her, he was upset about Marcie. Waldo's way of dealing with it was to erupt in a meeting. Gigi's way of dealing with it was to erupt inside. Men were lucky, she thought. They were better at blowing up, externalizing things and getting it out and over with. Gigi had read somewhere that people who internalized anger were the ones who got cancer. Ever since reading it, whenever she felt some negative emotion she imagined her cells mutating, little normal healthy cells dividing and turning into unrecognizable, uncell-like monsters.

Gigi went to her office and packed her briefcase. She could still catch Waldo. After taking the elevator, she jogged through the building lobby and down the street to the corner location of the Cub Room Bar. She pushed through the wooden door and found herself in a dim, smoky room decorated with blinking neon beer signs and Christmas tinsel and lights. Old men huddled over drinks, two men played chess in a corner, a waitress leaned lazily against a counter. Gigi scanned the room but there was no Waldo. In his state of mind he could have decided to skip the drink and fly to Zanzibar. She walked up to the bar, flung down her briefcase and slid onto a barstool.

"I'll have a martini, dry with a twist," she

told the bartender. All her life she had wanted to order a martini but never had. She was not a good drinker, but she could take the bus home if she had to. The bartender brought her the crystal liquid that shimmered in the pink glow of a neon sign. She tasted it and found its bitterness repugnant and pleasing. There was a sense of comfort in the bar, a dimly lit womb-like quality that made her feel separate from the world outside. Taking tiny sips of her martini, Gigi's thoughts rolled through her mind like the colored bubbles of oil that undulated in a glass container advertising a malt liquor.

"I'll have a Schlitz," a voice said a few feet away. Gigi turned and saw Juanita three stools down.

"We don't have Schlitz, lady," the bartender told her. Juanita was undaunted.

"How about a coke with a cherry?" Juanita looked at Gigi. "Come here often?" Juanita moved to the stool next to Gigi's. "May I join you?"

"Consider us joined."

"You've never seemed like the bar type to me. Bad day?" Juanita asked.

"Angela Maynard got custody of Marcie."

"Didn't you anticipate that? You recommended it."

"But I didn't expect to feel so horrible about it. What do you do when you don't have any options?"

"You drop back and punt," Juanita said. The bartender brought Juanita's coke. She bit the cherry off the stem, rolling it around inside her cheeks before biting into it.

"Cheer up, Bernstein. Things are looking up for you and we've got a dozen things to discuss. There are a few little items about Elizabeth that I need to—"

"No, Juanita. I don't want to discuss Elizabeth. Not now."

"What's going on with you, Gigi? You sound funny."

"I don't know what's going on with me."

"You do know. Tell me and don't spare the details."

"It's just that ever since Maureen died, and now everything with Marcie, well, it's made me examine myself a little, and I don't like what I see."

"Don't be so hard on yourself. Everyone has flaws. Everybody has disappointments, big ones. But you can't sit around and cry in your beer, especially not you. You have a big future."

Gigi twisted on her stool to face Juanita. "That's what I want to talk to you about."

"I don't like the tone of your voice."

"Juanita, I'm not sure I want to be Elizabeth's mother."

Juanita jumped, startled, then pushed her

coke away and put one arm around Gigi's shoulder. "Okay, let's be calm. It's perfectly natural for you to feel a little uncertain. Think of it as opening-night jitters."

"It's more than that. I've changed, Juanita. I'm not sure how, but I'm not the same person I was when you met me."

"Of course you're not. That was the point, wasn't it? I don't mean to be critical, but you were a mess when I found you. You were depressed, insecure, with the stability of plutonium. But together we've taken your mess of a life and we're shaping it into something wonderful, something stupendous."

Gigi smiled. "You're the best thing that ever happened to me. I know that."

Juanita smiled back and blushed a little. "Ditto for me, Bernstein. Sometimes this doesn't even seem like work. So why don't we just keep things going along like they are."

"Because I'm not sure I want them to."

"Okay, so you're not sure. But don't jump into any hasty decisions. I can help you. That's my business, but you have to tell me what's wrong."

"It's not that anything's wrong. In fact, something's finally right. All my life I've waited for a miracle, for someone to come along and save me. I thought I needed it because I thought I was weak. But I don't feel weak anymore and now I need control of my life back. I want to create my own happiness, be responsible for my successes and and my failures. I don't want to be saved anymore. I'm not sure I want any miracles."

"But don't you see, there were never any miracles anyway. There was always only you," Juanita said softly. Her eyes searched Gigi's as she waited for a reply, but there was none. Gigi got up without speaking and, before walking out the door, left a twenty on the bar, for she knew angels never carried any money.

CHAPTER SEVENTEEN

Concerning the seduction of Harold, Gigi had at last hung up her garter belt with calm and resignation, like a good soldier having turned conscientious objector. A new serenity had seeped its way into her heart, a subtle peacefulness that allowed her to place sex with Harold back into the recesses of her mind. She had been too concerned with Marcie lately to think much about anything else, and besides, she had this intuitive feeling that her life was steering its own course and that the best option was to sit back and enjoy the ride. Gone were the negligees, the black pushup bras, the articles from *Cosmopolitan,* the nocturnal longings. She just didn't care much anymore. She walked into her kitchen that Thursday morning wearing a battered chenille robe and an unstifled yawn as she scratched her hip comfortably and wondered if she had any coffee.

And Harold sat at the breakfast table hidden behind the *Wall Street Journal*. He had been staying over on a regular basis, and the platonic nature of their relationship had ceased to perplex Gigi. She said good morning, Harold answered with his usual grunt, and a smile crossed Gigi's face. All was well with the world. Life was in order. Almost. The nagging doubt was Marcie. The thought of Marcie's final words at the courthouse still hung over her like a dark cloud. Gigi had tried to call her several times, but Marcie refused to talk. Gigi had to have faith that everything would work out for Marcie, because there was nothing more she could do. It was a legal case, although an interesting one, but still a legal case, and she had done her best. She resolved to take Waldo's advice, give Marcie some time to adjust and then renew their friendship on a completely non-professional basis. Gigi leaned against the kitchen counter and stared groggily into space. She yawned, scratched her crotch and considered the intricacies of life as she peeled her morning banana and stuck it lazily into her mouth.

Harold watched her. Peering out furtively from the side of an editorial on capital gains taxation, he watched her intently, measured her visually, studied the tangled black of her hair, her eyes filled with sleep, her mouth stretched into a latent yawn, the curl of her fingers as they scratched her pelvis. His eyes roamed her like she were uncharted territory, as if he were truly seeing her for the very first time.

Gigi felt suddenly uneasy, instinctively alerted to the laser pierce of Harold's vision. She lowered her eyes and saw Harold fixed upon her like a cat fixed upon some irresistibly shiny object. There was something in his eyes she had never seen before, something dark and furtive, electric hot, something white and smoldering. She could almost see the wisps of smoke curling up from his balding head. Then her eyes widened.

What she saw there was lust.

Harold put down his paper. Gigi put down her banana. Harold rose from the table. Gigi braced herself as if for an anticipated jolt.

"Harold, honey . . ." she squeaked with trepidation, but Harold heard nothing except the newly found rhythmic pulsing in his brain and scrotum. He lifted her off her feet into his arms, his eyes never leaving hers, and carried her toward the bedroom.

Gigi's mind raced with the possibilities. This was it. The world must wait no longer, for the savior (saviorette?) was about to be conceived. Somehow she expected a little fanfare, some music, a drum roll or maybe a chorale of angelic voices. A few hallelujahs perhaps? But all she heard was the morning traffic outside and the unfamiliar sound of Harold's heavy breathing.

She wished she had showered, although Harold didn't seem to care as he buried his face in the various nooks and crannies of her body. This was a momentous occasion. Now prone on the rumpled bed, Gigi lay still as Harold fumbled with her bathrobe, as he struggled with his trousers. This is it, Gigi thought. This is finally it. Take me, Harold, and fulfill destiny. Gigi watched, breathless, as Harold removed his clothing and poised himself to make his initial world-transforming thrust.

And then the phone rang.

CHAPTER EIGHTEEN

Gigi would never know for sure what cosmic force propelled her to answer that ringing phone. She didn't wait a second to weigh the alternatives. There was an urgency to the ring, a desperation to the vibrato that forced her to rescue the receiver. It begged, it whined, it pleaded for her attention. Gigi's fingers stretched to grasp it, but fell inches short, for Harold's body still writhed on top of her. For the first time in his life struck blind and deaf by lust, Harold didn't perceive what was happening, but misinterpreted Gigi's struggle beneath him as a sign of her passion.

The bedroom resounded with the tormented vibration of the phone's fifth ring. Gigi drew upon sufficient adrenaline to push Harold off her and grab the receiver.

"Hello?" she said, garbling the words, still breathless from her labor.

"Gigi, it's Waldo."

Gigi heard the anxiety in his voice.

"Something's wrong," she said.

"You haven't read the paper? It's all over the business section."

"What is it?" Gigi asked, not noticing that Harold had regained his alertness and now lay naked on the bed, staring at her with yearning and open-mouthed disbelief at her lack of interest.

"Gigi, Naylor International is down the tubes, filing for bankruptcy," Waldo spit out in a rush of words. "Naylor had doctored financial statements in order to raise capital. Some bankers got suspicious when the drop in oil prices didn't seem to affect the company, so they've been secretly investigating for weeks. The other partners were either in on the scam from the beginning or discovered it after Naylor died and kept their mouths shut until they could clear out. Two of them have disappeared. One got scared and spilled the story to the bankers yesterday. It's an incredible mess, and the reporters are all over it, but, Gigi, that's not the worst part."

There was an ominous silence. Marcie, she thought, Marcie was bankrupt as well.

"Where's Marcie?" she asked.

"Gone. I called Angela Maynard this morning

as soon as I found out. She told me that Marcie ran out of the house last night and still hasn't come back. Gigi, I'm worried about her. I know it's not really our business anymore, but I want to find her. You know that shrewish aunt could care less about Marcie now that she's a financial liability instead of a meal ticket. Angela hadn't even called the police. If we don't look for Marcie, who will?"

Still holding the receiver to her ear, Gigi twisted to look at Harold, who now lounged on his side, partially covered with a tangled sheet. He peered at her lasciviously, crooking his index finger to beckon her back into his arms. She thought only for a second.

"Waldo, be in front of the Milam Building. I'll pick you up in thirty minutes," Gigi said hurriedly. She hung up the phone, leaped out of bed and scrambled through her closet for clothes. Harold remained on the bed looking sadly frozen. His jaw hung with astonishment and unsatiated ardor.

"You're leaving?" he queried weakly. Gigi didn't turn to look at him as she pulled a cotton dress over her head, then quickly pulled on pantyhose and shoes.

"Sorry. Gotta run."

"But, Boo Boo, my love, we had something going here, you know. The old colored lights were flashing."

Gigi turned just briefly to look at Harold

before she dashed out.

"But, honey . . ." he whimpered as Gigi raced out of the bedroom, unintentionally slamming the front door behind her.

Even in autumn the morning air was summery warm. Gigi started the Toyota and turned on the air conditioner. During the bumper-to-bumper traffic entering the freeway, she managed to comb her hair, put on some lipstick and straighten her hose. She reached downtown and spotted Waldo in front of the Milam Building.

From the end of the block, Gigi could see him standing near the street, his hands stuffed deep in his pockets, his baby face looking feverish. When he saw Gigi's car his countenance brightened. She pulled to the curb and he jumped into the seat beside her.

"Waldo!"

They heard the cry of his name only a few yards away. Their heads turned in unison and they saw Bausch trotting up to the car. He leaned down and stared in the car window, and Waldo had no choice but to roll it down.

"Glad I caught you," he said, panting from the unanticipated morning trot. "Where are the two of you off to?"

"We're going to look for Marcie Naylor," Waldo explained quickly, trying to get rid of Bausch so they could leave.

Bausch snorted. "You haven't heard, then. Naylor International is bankrupt. They haven't got a dime. Why, they probably won't even be able to pay their legal bills, so forget the Naylor case. We have bigger things to work on. Gigi, I need you back at the office right away. Bernard Jenson's son is in jail and I need you to get him out."

Gigi leaned over Waldo's lap so she could speak directly into Bausch's face.

"Bernard Johnson's son can stay in jail until he rots. I'm sorry, but we're in a big hurry," Gigi said calmly, then shifted her car into first and pulled away from the curb with a screech of tires.

Waldo shot Gigi a stricken look.

"Now you really could get fired for that. In fact you probably will."

Gigi brushed the air with her hand. "I never liked that job anyway. In fact, I hated that job."

She pressed the accelerator and zoomed through a yellow light. After glancing at Waldo she noticed he was still staring at her.

"Waldo, forget about it for now. We need to concentrate on Marcie, and we don't have time to drive around aimlessly. Where should we look for her? Any ideas?"

"I don't really know where to start. Right now I don't know much of anything," he mumbled. It surprised Gigi to see the worry in his face.

"It's okay. Really, Waldo, things will be all right," she said soothingly, feeling suddenly strong and capable. "Let's see Angela Maynard.

She's bound to know something that will help us. There must be a dozen places to look," Gigi said. Waldo smiled hopefully.

After reaching the tree-lined uppercrustedness of River Oaks, Gigi turned down Miller Lane and pulled the car in front of the home of Angela Maynard. It was a smaller house than the average in that wealthy area, but it still exuded that manicured look of money from the sculptured hedges to the uniformed Mexican maid who answered the door. She led them into the den where Angela lay weeping, draped across a salmon-colored sofa. A kaleidoscope of pill bottles and a white French telephone lay on a table beside her. Distraught and pale, Angela looked shaken, her usual perfect chignon coif falling in disarray about her face. Gigi and Waldo exchanged a pitying look. Angela appeared so upset, perhaps she cared about Marcie after all.

"Angela?" Waldo said softly. Angela looked up bleary-eyed.

"It's you," she replied bitterly.

"We've come to help find Marcie," explained Gigi, hoping the news would offer the poor woman comfort. Angela struggled to raise herself on her elbows.

"Oh really? Well, if you find that little brat you can keep her. She stormed out of the house last night when we got that dreadful news about the company." Angela fell back against the pillows and began weeping more earnestly. "I can hardly afford to take care of a child, especially a juvenile delinquent like that one. Just the bail alone will be a fortune." Angela blew her nose noisily into a linen handkerchief. "All that money. Gone. Pfft. Like that," she said wistfully, staring off into space.

Waldo sneered and tugged at Gigi's arm, motioning to leave. As they walked toward the door they could hear Angela mumbling "pfft, like that" repeatedly to herself, a helpless query into the fickleness of the fates.

"Pssst!" they heard behind them as they stepped outside onto the porch. They turned and saw the maid's head sticking out the front door.

"I tell you where to go for Marcie," she whispered. Gigi and Waldo stepped closer to hear her.

"That woman," she said, pointing back inside the house. "She really bitch. Marcie is a good girl. You want Marcie, you go to drive-in tonight. She be there with friends."

"Which drive-in?" Gigi asked. The maid looked perplexed.

"No se. I heard talk. It's a dog movie. Mean dog." She heard sounds inside. "I must go," she said hurriedly. Her head disappeared and the door closed.

"A mean dog movie at the drive-in? How many can there be?" Waldo asked.

"Let's get a paper," said Gigi. At the moment the door opened, a hand reached out and dropped a crumbled newspaper section at their feet, then the door shut once more. Gigi picked it up. It was the movie section of the *Chronicle*.

"Thanks," she said in the door's direction. She scanned the movie ads. "There it is, *Bloodsucking Canines* at the Lone Star Drive-in. But it doesn't begin until eight."

"So what do we do until then?"

"There are still lots of places she could be. I know she hangs out at the Hot Rocks record store on Fremont, at the Avalon Drugstore sometimes or any of the video arcades around here."

"Where to first?"

"Hot Rocks should be close. Let's try there." Pulling out into the traffic, Gigi noted that Waldo seemed perfectly at ease letting Gigi take command of the situation. He sat in the car staring out the window, tapping his fingers idly on his leg. He looked worried. He said nothing. Gigi scanned his profile and thought for the first time that he was actually handsome in an impish sort of way. Dumb Delores, she told herself and wondered what attractions Lulu had that Waldo didn't.

Hot Rocks Records was empty, and afterward they tried the arcade at the Galleria, which proved equally fruitless. After the arcade Waldo called Angela Maynard just to check if Marcie had returned, but Angela gave an abrupt "No," then hung up. Next they tried the school, then the police, but there had been no sign of Marcie. At noon they stopped at the Avalon Drug Store, ate hamburgers at the counter, wanting to be there a while in case Marcie showed up for lunch. It was no use. By two o'clock they began trying every video-game arcade in the vicinity of Marcie's school. Waldo would read the address from the Yellow Pages he had stolen from a phone booth, Gigi would run in, take a look around, then give the manager a description of Marcie. Two of them remembered Marcie because she was such a good customer, but neither of them had seen her that day. The rest shook their heads and stared at Gigi blankly.

At five-thirty Waldo called the office to check messages. Most of the messages were from Bausch, who wanted to see both of them immediately, but Waldo didn't call him. At seven-thirty they headed for the Lone Star Drive-in and paid the admission to see *Bloodsucking Canines,* the current attraction. The maid had seemed certain Marcie would be there.

Gigi suggested they check out the snack bar first. Her heels sinking into the gravel, she leaned on Waldo as they headed through the maze of parked cars toward a low white building in the rear of the drive-in. Stereos blasted, pubescent girls giggled and pseudo-macho sixteen-year-old boys shouted to each other from cars and trucks. With shrieks and squeals, chocolate-smeared children played on the sagging merry-go-round outside the snack bar as their parents looked on lazily and gobbled their popcorn and Eskimo Pies. Yeech, Gigi thought, surveying the scene. Why had the drive-in movie seemed so exotic when she had been in high school? Either the drive-in had changed or she had. She remembered it as a temple of erotic promise, filled with velvety darkness and the mesmerizing glow of the movie screen. It had been the site of forbidden love in the back seats of Chevys with seventeen-year-old high school quarterbacks who seemed a cross between James Dean and Apollo. Unfortunately Gigi rarely even made it to the front seat of a Chevy, much less the back seat, and when she did it was inevitably with a pimple-faced, bespectacled type who won science fairs and asked Gigi out only because his mother and Gigi's mother had arranged it against his will.

"Would you like a Coke or anything?" Waldo asked when they entered the bright fluorescence of the snack bar. Gigi nodded and they fell into line behind thirty loud teenagers who all appeared to be chain-smokers. None of them were Marcie. But it was still early, Gigi told herself. If she made frequent trips to the snack bar during the movie she was bound to see her, knowing Marcie's propensity toward Cokes and hot dogs.

"God, I love junk food," Waldo said.

Gigi noticed with disgust the popcorn, hot dog, pizza, two Cokes, a Snickers and two Reese's Peanut Butter Cups he had piled on his tray. How could a man his size pack away so much food? she wondered. She grabbed a Fudgesicle and guiltily put it on the tray. When in Rome, she reasoned.

After a quick check of the ladies room to make sure Marcie wasn't inside, the two maneuvered their way back to the Toyota. It took Waldo ten minutes to assemble his food around him so he could reach it easily and by that time the movie had begun. Gigi hooked the speaker to the window and turned up the volume loud enough to drown out the sound of Waldo's munching. First they watched the previews of coming attractions, which included two blood-and-gore movies and a film seemingly about young boys at camp trying to peak into the girls' shower. Stupid, thought Gigi, but she noticed how fascinated the Harvard law grad seemed to be with these brainless movies. The last time Gigi was at a drive-in they still had cartoons of soft drinks and candy boxes with little legs that danced across the screen before the movie began. How had things changed so much without her knowing it?

The feature attraction began and Gigi stole some of Waldo's popcorn and settled in. They planned to take turns every twenty minutes checking out the snack bar for Marcie. During the first twenty-minute lag Gigi watched the beginning of the movie depicting a large Doberman becoming rabid. Dramatic music intimated impending doom for the cast of characters that included scantily dressed aerobic instructors on a picnic. Blood spilled in the first ten minutes. Sinking lower in her seat, Gigi checked her watch every thirty seconds to see if it was time for a snack-bar check. She despised gory movies.

"I'll go first," she said to Waldo when sixteen minutes had passed. Waldo answered with a grunt, never ungluing his eyes from the screen.

As Gigi passed through the parked cars she found that many couples were already embroiled in heated passion in the front seats. No one had ever made a pass at Gigi at a drive-in. It was one of the great traditions of growing up in America she had missed. Popular psychological theory held that people's personalities, strengths and weaknesses were already formed by age three, but Gigi disagreed. For her it was the years in high school that created the imagined inadequacies, the unfulfilled desires she had spent the remainder of her life trying to compensate for. Maybe that was why Marcie seemed so important to her now. After all, Gigi had grown up a Jewish American Princess with doting parents, yet her ego was as fragile as a marshmallow. What would happen to Marcie with her parentless situation? There was no sign of Marcie in the ladies restroom or the snackbar, but Gigi picked up a Milky Way so the trip wouldn't be a total waste.

As she made her way back to the Toyota she surveyed the progress of several situations of automobile amour. One progressive couple had already moved to the back seat. Gigi got into her car, guilty about the chocolate on her breath, but Waldo didn't notice. He was mesmerized by the rabid Doberman ripping a man into dog chow. After the next twenty minutes passed, Gigi volunteered to make the second snack bar run, and after that, the third. By that time almost all the movie patrons under twenty had made it to their back seats and Gigi wolfed down two Butterfingers and a hot dog.

"Did you see her?" Waldo asked when Gigi returned from the third trip. The Doberman was trying to smash in the windows of a Volkswagen so he could make spareribs out of the bouncy blonde inside. Gigi shook her head. Waldo slumped in his seat.

"So what do we do now?" he asked.

"We check out all the cars," Gigi replied. Waldo shot her a questioning glance.

"What do you mean?" he asked slowly.

"I mean you take half of the drive-in, I take the other half and we look in all the cars for Marcie."

Waldo's eyes widened with horror.

271

"You can't mean what you're saying," he said. "People will think we're perverts if we look into all the cars." He dropped his voice an octave. "You know what people do at drive-ins."

"That's what makes it so simple. Marcie is with her girlfriends. She'll be in the only car with the passengers sitting upright. Now, do you want the cars to the right of the snack bar or to the left?"

Waldo shrugged his shoulders. "Left."

"Great. I'll meet you back here." Gigi got out of the car and walked long enough to make sure Waldo got out also, then she began walking past the first row of cars nearest the screen. From that vantage point the blood spilled by the killer Doberman was nauseatingly larger than life, and Gigi averted her eyes as she scanned the cars, seeing no one who looked like Marcie. She tried the second row, the third and fourth, peering into the cars. When she looked too closely into one car, a black-haired youth rolled down his window and made several unsavory remarks. Gigi apologized red-faced when she noticed his date was mostly unclothed.

Only two more rows to go, Gigi said to herself, looking back toward the snack bar. The hopes of finding Marcie became bleaker with every car she passed. Marcie could be halfway to Los Angeles by now, Gigi thought, and she shuddered at the ideas of all the things that could happen to a twelve-year-old child alone in the city.

Gigi passed by the last car on the last row. She had seen six kids smoking dope, eleven drinking booze straight from the bottle and had picked up several interesting sex tips, but no Marcie. A wave of depression crept its way over her, then she brightened. Surely Waldo had found her.

Gigi picked the gravel out of her shoe and found her way back to the car. She opened the door and got inside. Waldo was alone.

They exchanged a look. It was a look of disappointment, a look of guilt, a look of fatigue. It was then that Gigi began to cry. She wasn't sure why she started crying. It was one of those messy, heaving cries that swelled up out of nowhere, bubbled up from some ground spring of despondency, probing far beyond the moment's tragedy into past failures and imagined pains of the future. She sobbed because she had failed Marcie, failed Maureen, failed Juanita, and then, of course, failed herself. She cried because nothing in life ever seemed to work the way she wanted it to. The tears rolled, streaking her face with remorse and mascara, while Waldo looked on with astonishment.

"Jeezuz, what's the matter?" he said. Gigi couldn't catch her breath to answer, nor did she have an answer to give him.

"Gigi, talk to me. Please talk to me," Waldo pleaded softly. She would not comply, but pressed her head against the car window, trying to hide her tear-streaked face. Waldo looked on frantically. Looking around for a tissue, he finally grabbed a napkin soiled with popcorn butter and tried to wipe the tears from her face. Gigi pushed his hand away.

"Gigi, if you don't stop . . ." he sputtered as he continued to dab at her face with the napkin. "I can't stand to see you cry. When I see someone I love cry, I start crying too. I'm weird that way. It's very embarrassing for me." He stopped for a moment. He looked at Gigi for a reaction, but found none. She only stared outside the window. Waldo sat silently for a moment as if weighing his alternatives, then gently he lifted her face with his fingers and turned it toward him.

"Gigi, I don't know for sure what's bothering you. You don't have to spill your guts to me, but I'm going to spill my guts to you. I might as well since things have already gotten emotional, and if I don't do it now I may never get another opportunity." He took a long, deep breath. "I love you, Gigi. I've wanted to tell you for weeks. I love you. I want to be with you, all the time, always. And I want to start now."

Gigi couldn't believe what he was saying. She heard the words, but it seemed impossible that he could be speaking them. It crossed her mind that perhaps he had overdosed on sugar and was on the hallucinatory throes of a glucose high.

274

"No. You love Delores," she told him, as if the word "Delores" could snap him back to reality.

"Delores? I never loved Delores. I was lonely and she needed me and we latched on to each other. That's not love. I couldn't understand why it didn't matter to me when she left. Then it hit me. It was because I didn't care for her. I couldn't care for her. It was you I wanted." Waldo grinned and began to kiss her fingers, one by one.

Gigi pulled her hand away. "I don't understand this, Waldo. You couldn't possibly mean what you're saying. I'm seven years older than you."

"So what? It just means more coordination between the years of our sexual peaks."

"But it would never work out. You in love with me? How could you think that you're in love with me? We'll just forget this happened and—"

"How could I think I'm in love with you?" said Waldo. "Gigi, there's everything here to love. I love the way you are at work. I love the way you are when you're not at work. You're funny and you're kind, intelligent, sensitive. And you're lovely to look at. Have you ever looked deeply into your eyes? It's a wonderful thing to do. You should try it sometime." He leaned over and kissed her gently. "I love you. That's all there is to it, and I think you love me too. If you don't, you'll learn. You can practice every day. You see, it's just something you'll just have to accept, a concept you'll have to get comfortable with, because I won't give up on it. I love you. Maybe it isn't the kind of love where when we first met bells rang and we ripped our clothes off. It's better than that. It sneaked up on us. It grew out of our being together. It seems more real to me than anything I've felt before."

Gigi stared at him. His hair was rumpled, his eyes damp, glasses fogged and his nose slightly reddened. And she never witnessed such warmth and strength in a human being before.

"Just please kiss me, Waldo," she whispered.

And he put his arms around her, planted a hundred gentle kisses on her hair, her cheeks, her forehead. Then he pressed his lips against hers, and amidst the passion she noticed with affection that he tasted like Reeses Peanut Butter Cups.

Waldo pulled back and looked adoringly at her.

"I love you too, Waldo," Gigi told him, her face still teary.

"Good, because I want to marry you, Gigi. Right away," he said joyfully. "Let's go get our blood tests tomorrow." He threw his arms around her and hugged her close to him.

It's happening, she thought. I'm going to marry Waldo and he'll be the father of Elizabeth. She felt such joy, not only for herself but for Elizabeth, for Juanita, for everybody. Tears of happiness trickled down her cheeks.

"Yes, let's get the blood tests tomorrow. I want to marry you. I want to live with you, grow old with you, have children with you—"

"Gigi, wait," he interrupted, his face suddenly more serious. "I have to tell you something. You probably don't know this because I've always kept it quiet, but I've been married before, when I was in law school."

Gigi shrugged her shoulders. "That doesn't matter to me."

"But there's something else," he said solemnly. "You see, I learned during my marriage that I can't have children. I mean, I'm okay in every other department, of course, but you can't conceive with me. I love children and I want them. I want them very much. I just always figured my wife and I would adopt." Waldo looked down squeamishly. "Does all this change anything?"

Gigi's heart stopped when she heard it. The happy images of Waldo and Elizabeth and their future together blurred out of focus. She felt as if she were teetering on the edge of something, balanced precariously on the top of a wall with Waldo on one side and Elizabeth on the other. Gigi's eyes fixed on Waldo's face filled with need and love for her. She had never had that before. It was what she had wanted for so many years and all she had to do now was reach out and grab it, but to do it she would have to exclude Elizabeth from her life. Gigi wondered what would happen if she resigned from her exalted position. Would thunderbolts drop from the sky, would a black hole in space gulp down the stars as retribution for Gigi's trespass? But God was love, wasn't she? God would understand. She was a woman. Juanita could easily find someone else to be the mother of Elizabeth. Juanita had said herself that Gigi was just a lucky winner in the lottery of the Lord. Waldo was different. He needed her and only her and she loved and needed him.

"It doesn't matter, Waldo. I love you. We'll work it out. We'll adopt children, lots of them," she blurted out happily, then threw herself on top of him to kiss him.

They walked hand in hand up the sidewalk toward Gigi's apartment. They had hardly exchanged a word for the past hour, but they didn't have to. It was funny, Gigi thought, but it was as if this was where all along she had truly belonged. She grasped his hand more tightly. She looked toward her apartment door to see if she had remembered to leave the porch light on.

Then, out of the pitch darkness, something large leaped out of the bushes and hurled itself in front of the romantic couple. Gigi screamed and clutched Waldo for safety.

"Harold!' she cried when she was able to see the intruder's face. "Harold, what are you doing?"

Harold blocked the walkway, jaw set, fists on hips, exuding the countenance of a man scorned. "What are you doing? The way you ran out this morning. And who is this guy?"

"Hi, I'm Waldo Bernelli." Waldo smiled politely and stretched out a hand that Harold refused to acknowledge. Harold grabbed Gigi's arm and pulled her away from Waldo, who was now looking anxious.

"Gigi, we've got to talk. We've got to make plans," Harold told her as she tried to free herself from his grip. She had forgotten about Harold. Gigi looked perplexed. Waldo looked worried. Harold looked stunned when something belted him in the knees and sent him sprawling on the ground.

"Waldo, quick! Hold him down!" Marcie yelled as she tried to sit on Harold's legs. Gigi dropped to her knees and hugged Marcie, the weight of her body only shoving Harold more firmly into the ground.

"Where have you been?" Gigi asked.

Marcie scowled. "I've been here since four o'clock waiting for you. Where have you been, anyway? Here I am in big trouble and you and Waldo are out doing kissie-facies. I saw you holding hands."

"Uh, could you get off me, please?" Harold requested. Gigi lifted Marcie to her feet. Covered with leaves and indignation, Harold stood up and brushed himself off in as dignified a manner as possible. Marcie gave him a demonic look.

"You're lucky I came along when I did. I saw this jerk jump you. Shouldn't someone call the police on this guy?"

"No, this is my friend Harold. Marcie, Harold. Harold, Marcie," Gigi introduced.

"Nice to meet you. Now, Gigi, where were we? I don't like you going out with other guys like this," Harold said in a whimpering tone.

Waldo broke in. "Now wait a minute. Gigi can decide for herself who she wants to be with."

"And she has always wanted to be with me," Harold replied. He took Gigi's hands in his and looked into her eyes. "Haven't you, Boo Boo? It's like an old movie. We've had our ups and downs, our misunderstandings, but there's going to be a happy ending."

"Oh, somebody gag me," said Juanita walking up the sidewalk, her arms crossed. "I think it's a little late for B-movie lines."

"Stay out of this," warned Gigi.

"Who is this?" asked Harold.

"Uh, it's my cousin," Gigi answered.

"Hi, my name is Waldo, this is Marcie and Harold," Waldo said and shook Juanita's hand.

"You have a cousin named Juanita?" Harold asked.

Juanita stepped between them. "Look, I don't want to butt in, but . . ."

"I can handle this myself," said Gigi.

"Gigi, I think we should talk," said Waldo.

Harold gritted his teeth and, in a fit of machismo, grabbed Gigi by the shoulders and faced her.

"I love you and I want to marry you. I don't know who this other guy is, but get rid of him. He can't mean anything to you. What you and I have together is special. I mean, we've been together for years," he said in a forceful voice.

Waldo bounded in and removed Harold's hands from Gigi.

"I've known her for years too, and I haven't abused her and taken her for granted," Waldo said, then turned to Gigi. "More than anything, Gigi, I just want you to be happy, and if you tell me you love Harold, then I'll understand and I'll leave you alone. But if you don't love Harold, well, I've already told you how I feel about you. I love you and I want to share my life with you, if you'll let me."

"Listen to Waldo," Juanita chimed in.

"Don't listen to him," spat Harold.

"Well, hell, let's take a vote," said Marcie. "All those for Waldo, let's hear a big round of applause," she said, holding her hand above Waldo's head. Juanita clapped.

"Stop it!" Gigi cried, backing away from them all. "I don't need anyone's help here. I can make my own decisions."

There was a dramatic pause, all eyes riveted on Gigi. She turned to Harold. Waldo's face fell.

"Harold, for years I thought I loved you, but I was wrong. I'm sorry."

Harold looked at her with astonishment.

"You mean, no happy ending for us?" he asked weakly.

"Did you ever see *The Alamo?*" asked Juanita, and Harold shot her a hateful look.

Waldo put his arms around Gigi and kissed her. Harold watched them sadly, then walked down to his car and drove off.

Gigi turned from Waldo, her eyes locking on Juanita's.

"Waldo, could you take care of Marcie? I need to talk with my cousin."

Waldo walked over to Marcie, embraced her, then they walked hand in hand over to the steps in front of Gigi's apartment. Gigi watched the scene, smiled, then pulled Juanita behind a tall hedge.

"I have to talk to you," she said solemnly.

"I should hope so. Shoot, I'm all ears."

Gigi closed her eyes for a second and inhaled deeply. She wished she didn't have to say what she was about to say. She would have preferred to put it in a letter, but she assumed angels had no addresses.

"Juanita, I've really enjoyed the time we've spent together. It's meant a lot to me. I've changed for the better and I know some of that is because of you."

"This sounds like a Dear John letter. Get to the point. The suspense is killing me."

"I can't be the mother of Elizabeth. I've made my final decision. No, don't say anything. Not yet. Let me finish what I have to say. You see, I love Waldo. I guess I didn't realize it until tonight, but I love him very much. It's the first time in my life I've ever felt this way about anybody. I feel whole. I feel happy."

"So you feel whole and happy. What's the problem?"

"Waldo can't have children. I don't want to bother you with medical details, but I'll never be able to conceive with Waldo, so I couldn't possibly be the mother of Elizabeth. We've decided to adopt. We talked about it in the car on the way home tonight and we're going to adopt Marcie."

Juanita started to speak, but Gigi stopped her.

"I know what you're going to say. You're going to say 'No problem, I'll just whip up a little miracle and poof, you're pregnant with the Messiah.' But you see, I still can't do it. I love Waldo and Marcie. I need them. They need me. They're my family now and I want to focus all my love and energies on them."

Gigi's face softened. She looked away from Juanita and laughed lightly. "You know, I don't think anyone has ever really needed me before. Suddenly I have two people needing me." She looked back at Juanita. "I couldn't possibly be the mother of Elizabeth now. Elizabeth will need more attention and devotion than I can give her. Everything I've got inside of me is going to Marcie and Waldo and it has to be that way. I just feel in my bones it's the right thing for me and I hope you understand."

Gigi heaved a sigh of relief after she had blurted it all out. She noted that Juanita seemed to be taking it all quite calmly.

"But you are the mother of Elizabeth. You can't change that," Juanita said slowly.

"What do you mean, I'm the mother? I told you, I'm not. Whatever happened to all that talk about free will? I thought I had a choice in this matter," Gigi said angrily, struggling in midsentence to lower her voice so Marcie and Waldo wouldn't overhear. Gigi expected Juanita to give her a difficult time, but she hadn't anticipated her total obliviousness to everything she was telling her. Still, Gigi was ready to fight.

"But you made your choice. It had to be that way. You had to choose for yourself, and you're choosing to be the mother of the Daughter of God."

"Watch my lips, Juanita. I'm choosing to be the mother of Marcie," Gigi said in a low growl.

"Bingo. By George, she's finally got it," said Juanita triumphantly. Gigi looked at her with narrow, questioning eyes. The look on Juanita's face reminded Gigi of the first time they met in her bathroom that night so many months before.

"What are you saying to me?" Gigi asked softly. Juanita took Gigi's hand and held it tightly.

"Marcie is The One. She is The Daughter. She was all along. Surprised?"

Gigi paused for a moment to mull over the information.

"But what about Elizabeth?" she finally asked.

"Elizabeth, Marcie, Bernice or Matilda—those are just names. What's important is what's inside a person and inside Marcie is a Messiah."

Juanita chuckled with self-satisfaction. Gigi still looked dubious. She shook her head. "Now wait a minute. Marcie Naylor, that kid over there on the steps with the T-shirt that says 'Savage Pubes' is the Messiah?"

"Don't worry. She'll grow to her potential, with your help of course."

"Marcie Naylor? The one who curses like a sailor, who constantly cuts school, who thinks about sex all the time? She's the Messiah? She won't even pledge allegiance to the flag."

"Okay, so she needs a little grooming. She is of heaven and she is of this earth. It was intended to be that way. She's still a child, but one day, Gigi, one day she will lift the world from the darkness and hold it toward the light. She will be the love and the truth, the power and the prophet. And you, Gigi, will be her mother on earth. After all, you chose it."

Gigi stood there silently. She turned and looked at Marcie sitting on the steps, giggling with Waldo. It was hard to believe, yet everything that had happened to her lately was hard to believe. Yet she did believe.

She turned again to Juanita. "So you knew it would turn out this way all along, didn't you?"

"I had my intuitions."

"Then why didn't you inform me of those intuitions from the beginning. It would have saved me a lot of trouble."

"Free will, remember? You had to choose for yourself. Besides, I don't like to meddle."

Gigi gave her a look, but Juanita continued, her eyes bright with excitement, her hands held up, fingers fanned.

"Just think of what the future holds. The miracle of it all, constantly evolving, changing, transforming every day into something transcendent and beautiful. We have an exciting future ahead of us."

"Wait a minute. What do you mean by 'we'? Your job is over, isn't it? Waldo and Marcie and I are together. Things are pretty much set, aren't they?"

286

"Well sure, but this is hardly adios. We've just started. Don't worry kiddo, I'm going to be around a long time," Juanita said, giving Gigi a slap on the shoulder. Gigi smiled with uncertain acquiescence.

"Well, they're waiting for me," she said, moving toward her apartment.

"So, enough chitchat," Juanita replied.

"Would you like to come inside with us for a while? It's getting chilly out here."

"No thanks. The three of you probably have a lot to talk about. You go ahead. Go on, now. I'll see you tomorrow," Juanita said, and waved Gigi along. Gigi turned and walked toward Marcie and Waldo. She paused and looked over her shoulder.

"Well, good night," she said with a now radiant smile.

"Good night," Juanita answered, and blew an exaggerated kiss through the air. She watched the three of them until they went inside Gigi's apartment and closed the door. Clasping her hands behind her back, she inhaled the perfume of the night breezes.

"At last we come to the beginning," she whispered, grinning starry-eyed as she gazed out into the night.

BLOCKBUSTER FICTION FROM PINNACLE BOOKS!

THE FINAL VOYAGE OF THE S.S.N. SKATE (17-157, $3.95)
by Stephen Cassell
The "leper" of the U.S. Pacific Fleet, SSN 578 nuclear attack sub SKATE, has one final mission to perform — an impossible act of piracy that will pit the underwater deathtrap and its inexperienced crew against the combined might of the Soviet Navy's finest!

QUEENS GATE RECKONING (17-164, $3.95)
by Lewis Purdue
Only a wounded CIA operative and a defecting Soviet ballerina stand in the way of a vast consortium of treason that speeds toward the hour of mankind's ultimate reckoning! From the best-selling author of THE LINZ TESTAMENT.

FAREWELL TO RUSSIA (17-165, $4.50)
by Richard Hugo
A KGB agent must race against time to infiltrate the confines of U.S. nuclear technology after a terrifying accident threatens to unleash unmitigated devastation!

THE NICODEMUS CODE (17-133, $3.95)
by Graham N. Smith and Donna Smith
A two-thousand-year-old parchment has been unearthed, unleashing a terrifying conspiracy unlike any the world has previously known, one that threatens the life of the Pope himself, and the ultimate destruction of Christianity!

Available wherever paperbacks are sold, or order direct from the Publisher. Send cover price plus 50¢ per copy for mailing and handling to Pinnacle Books, Dept.17-263, 475 Park Avenue South, New York, N.Y. 10016. Residents of New York, New Jersey and Pennsylvania must include sales tax. DO NOT SEND CASH.